TEMPTED AND BOUND BY BETRAYAL

S. N. CHRISTENSEN

CONTENTS

AUTHOR'S NOTES

This is book one in the Tempted and Bound series. Each book may be read as a standalone. This book also coincides with the timeline of the first two books in the fALLINg series. If you intend to read that series, it is suggested you read it before reading this one.

Some content in this book may be triggering to some readers as this is a Dark Mafia Romance. Trigger Warnings include suicide, murder, violence, torture, and the use of drugs and alcohol.

Words to know:

Cazzo – Fuck

Merda – Shit

Stronzo- Asshole

Vaffanculo – Fuck you

Stai zitto- Shut up

Chapter One

LAUREN

The moment I walk through these ridiculously fancy front doors, I'm filled with dread. I step to the side, standing in a corner watching the students interact and race around to get ready for their first class. The sounds of laughter, lockers slamming, loud voices, sneakers squeaking on the floor, along with the bright lights, make me want to vomit. I close my eyes for a moment and take a few deep breaths. I can do this.

A warm hand touches my wrist and my eyes shoot open, studying who is breaking through my little personal space bubble. A girl who looks completely normal stares down at me with a smile. She has very little makeup on, which is not what I was expecting from any student attending this school. Her thick wavy dark brown hair flows over her shoulders and down to the middle of her back. Her eyes draw my attention the most, though. They are gorgeous green eyes that are cat-like. I've never seen eyes like that before.

She breaks me out of my trance by saying, "Hey, you're the new girl, Lauren, right?"

I stare at her for a moment before replying. "I am."

"I'm Ashley. I just transferred here at the beginning of the year, so I know what it's like to be the new girl. Do you know where your locker is?" she asks while pulling me out of the corner.

I shake my head no and hand her the sheet of paper I'm holding. It's the paper my father gave me this morning with all my information on it. My locker number with the combination, along with my class schedule. I never got a tour of the school. I've barely gotten a tour of our new house, which we moved into this past weekend.

She looks at the paper and gestures for me to follow her. I walk down the hall, avoiding all the students towering over me, bumping into me, and brushing past me. I'm used to being run over with my measly four foot ten, tiny frame. Being small, people tend not to see me, which means I've been mostly invisible my whole life.

"Here we are," Ashley says, pausing in front of a locker.

"Thanks," I say, while trying to put the code in.

Surprisingly, it unlocks on the first try. I unzip my book bag and place all my items in the locker. My father also gave me all the textbooks and school supplies I would need this morning. I pull out my list to see what my first class is and choose the correct book and binder for it. I wince as I slam the locker closed a little harder than I meant to.

"We have history together later and lunch. Do you want me to show you where the rest of your classes are going to be?" she asks.

"Uh, no thanks. I'm sure I can find them," I say, not wanting to inconvenience her more.

"Alright, then I'll walk you to your first, since I have to go in that direction anyway."

I nod and follow behind her again. As we walk, I notice no one tries to stop and say hi to her. Pretty much everyone I've seen has been talking with a group of friends. I know she said she was new this year too, but I wonder if she hasn't made friends yet and why. She seems nice enough, but she doesn't seem like she belongs in this school any more than I do. Maybe I can make a friend, and this school will be bearable after all.

We stop abruptly in front of a classroom door. "Here's your English class. I'll see you in a bit for history and lunch, okay?"

I nod. "Thanks."

I walk into the classroom and head toward the teacher's desk. I stand in front of the teacher who is writing something in his notebook, so I don't interrupt. Watching all the students trickle in, they take their seats. The rustling sounds of zippers, pencils hitting the desks, and books slamming down make my nerves act up again. I've always been an anxious person, and all the excess noises bother me more than it would someone normal.

I look back toward the teacher, who is still writing in his notebook. Staring at him for a little longer, I notice he looks like he's in his sixties with short, fully gray hair. Has he not noticed that I'm standing here? Should I say something? I hate these situations. I really don't want to bother him, but I need to know where my seat is.

Shifting on my feet, I try to make a little noise to get his attention. It doesn't work. I make some more drastic movements by pushing my hair back and then switching my textbook to my other arm. He still hasn't looked up. I finally get the courage to clear my throat, which I know will get his attention. Nope. That doesn't work either.

Alright, I'm going to have to just be brave. I have to speak.

I clear my throat again before saying in a low voice, "Excuse me..."

He doesn't stop writing, and I'm wondering if he hadn't heard me. I'm about to try one more time before he looks up at me, annoyed.

"Yes?" he asks.

"Um... I'm Lauren. I'm the new girl, and I was wondering where I should sit," I say as quietly as possible, but loud enough for him to hear.

He looks back down at his notebook and says, "Anywhere. We don't do assigned seats."

Fantastic. I don't even bother thanking him, considering he didn't want to give me the time of day. I look around and notice a few empty desks left around the room, but I'm not sure which one to take. Should I wait until class has started before taking a seat? I don't want to take someone's usual seat.

I continue looking around the room and notice everyone staring at me. Great. I'm going to have to just pick one because this is getting too awkward. I make my way toward the back, where there is an empty seat in between a nice-looking girl and a really good-looking boy. I think he might be saving it for his girlfriend or something, but I need to find somewhere to sit.

When I get to the desk, I look over at the girl and ask, "Is this seat taken?"

She grins and asks, "Does it look like it's taken?"

Everyone around her laughs, and I just sink into the desk. I feel my body heating up, and I know my cheeks are red. This is a great start to my first day.

"Hey, you're new here, right? Lauren?" the boy next to me asks.

How on earth does everyone know who I am? This school is a lot smaller than the one I used to attend, but it's not that small. He didn't laugh at what the girl said, so I figure I owe him a response.

"Yeah, that's me," I say while placing my stuff on the desk.

"I'm Ben. It's nice to meet you."

He holds out his hand, and I eye it for a moment before shaking it. I'm about to say something, but the bell rings and the teacher begins class. He tells everyone to pull out their copies of Romeo and Juliet. Great. That's something my father did not give me.

"Do you not have a copy?" the old man asks me. Yeah, I called him old man because he's grumpy and old. I know his type.

"No," I state.

He sighs and walks over to me with a copy, throwing it on my desk. "I expect you to have your own tomorrow."

I don't say anything because I don't feel like he deserves a response from me. I mean seriously, I'm new here, and you're going to treat me like that? I can see exactly how this is going to go.

The students read their assigned roles, and thankfully, I don't have one. I try to pay attention, but I've already read this in my last school. I enjoyed the story, but it was tragic. It's dumb to fake your own death as it is. I mean, so much could have gone wrong with that, anyway. Then the issue with communication? There had to have been a better way, so it could've ended with a happily ever after. Then again, I suppose it wouldn't be a tragedy then.

As the students continue to read, and I'm thinking about how I'm already hating it here, my mind drifts to the conversation I had with my father before moving here.

"We're moving to New York. Next weekend," my father said with no room for argument.

I tried to process what he said. I knew I would eventually have to move there, but I didn't expect it to be so soon. I especially didn't expect it to be in the middle of the school year. I stared at my father for a minute before responding. He sat behind his desk while I sat in front of him. He didn't have a fancy office, but it had everything he needed.

"Okay. Can I ask why so soon?" I asked.

My father's posture and facial features relaxed slightly. He expected a fight from me. I didn't have any fight left because I knew it was no use. It didn't matter what I wanted. My fate had been decided.

"He wants me closer for work and thought it would be beneficial for you to get to know him better," he said like he rehearsed this response.

"Okay," I said again.

I got up out of my chair and left his office before I let myself think of anything. I went down the hallway to my bedroom and locked the door behind me after I entered. I threw myself on my bed and laid there wondering how my life had turned into this.

Just a few months ago, my father told me I was getting married. I laughed so hard because I thought it was a joke. He explained to me it was a smart business move, and it would ensure that I would be taken care of for the rest of my life. He showed me a picture of the man I was supposed to marry, and he was handsome, but he was much older, like nine years.

Who arranges a marriage for their daughter? I was sixteen at the time he told me I'd marry a man named Lorenzo. Apparently, he was a very wealthy man. He gave my father a lot of money, and there would be more to come. I only met him once, and he seemed nice, but he also looked like he wanted nothing to do with the marriage arrangement. I hoped that he would have called it off by now, especially before forcing us to move to a completely different state.

A knock came on my door. I didn't respond, but Brandon, my brother, fiddled with the lock and walked in anyway. He sat on the edge of my bed and looked angry.

"What are you doing here?" I asked.

"Dad called me earlier and told me the news. I came to talk him out of it, but you can guess how that went. Are you okay?" he asked.

Brandon was an amazing big brother. He really cared for me, and he was trying to talk my father out of the whole arranged marriage. He was in college, though, so he wasn't home much. Clearly, his efforts were for nothing.

I shrugged my shoulders in response to his question.

He looked at me with pity. "We'll figure this out, okay?"

"Yeah, okay," I said back. We both knew there would be nothing we could do to change my father's mind.

I'm forced back into the present when the bell rings, signaling the end of class. Had I really been in my thoughts the entire class? I gather my stuff and head back up to the teacher's desk. I don't say a word as I toss the book on his desk and leave the room to head to my next class.

CHAPTER TWO

ROMEO

I sit impatiently in my brother's office, waiting for him to arrive. Technically, Lorenzo, or as I call him, Lo, isn't my brother by blood, but we're family. There are some days where I consider relinquishing that title, like today. The bastard asked me to meet him here twenty minutes ago for something important. Clearly, it's not that important if he's keeping me waiting.

I walk around his office studying everything like I haven't seen it a thousand times before. His dark mahogany desk sits in the middle of the square room with only one window to the right of his desk. Bookcases line the left wall, and the back wall is bare minus the outdated dark patterned wallpaper that looks like it's from the sixties.

There's not much décor in here, as it's solely for business purposes. The floor is dark tiled, almost black. One would say it's not the most pleasant to look at, but its usefulness isn't to look pretty. It's the easiest to clean up after a business meeting has gone wrong, which happens way more than we'd like.

Before I can consider leaving, he finally makes his way into the office and sits behind his desk. I walk over, sitting in the chair I was occupying for the last twenty minutes. Lo says nothing, but his face shows he's pissed about something.

He also looks tired. His dark brown eyes are droopy with dark circles under them. He clearly hasn't shaven in over a week, and his short thick black hair sticks up in all directions like he's been pulling on it.

"What do you need me to do, brother?" I ask without hesitation.

He looks me in the eye and studies me. He knows I'll do whatever he asks, especially when he's like this. Though, I'm not liking the look he's giving me. He's about to ask something that I'm not going to want to do. I would kill for him, and I have, many times, so it concerns me he thinks I may protest.

"I have a new job for you," he states.

"What do you need me to do?"

He sighs and leans back in his chair, folding his hands in his lap. "My fiancé moved to town this past weekend. I need a trustworthy guard on her."

I look at him, confused. "What happened to Tommaso?"

"He's currently six feet under," he says while rubbing his hand through his hair, making it even messier.

"What happened?" I ask, wondering who killed him.

"He ran his mouth about how pretty she is and what he'd like to do to her," he says with a disgusted look on his face.

I shake my head. Damn. Tommaso was one of the best we had, but the guy wasn't very smart when it came to running his mouth. He was put in charge of watching out for Lauren and keeping her safe. That's a position anyone would kill for as the don is putting his trust in them to keep his fiancé safe.

"You need me to find someone else?" I ask, assuming that's why he called me here.

"No," he states, but doesn't elaborate.

If that's not it, then what is it? I hope he doesn't intend to keep the poor girl locked up. It was something he considered when they first got engaged, but I talked him out of it. She's only seventeen. I don't know much about teenaged girls, but I can't imagine they would do well locked up and forced to marry someone they don't even know.

"I'm assigning the job to you," he states.

"What?" I ask, hoping that I heard him wrong.

"I can't trust anyone else with her. She's beautiful, and you're the only one I can trust to keep it in your pants. You'll keep her safe, and you'll make sure she's not a flight risk. You'll keep her in line."

"Lo... for how long?" I ask before I say something I may regret.

"Indefinitely," he says seriously.

I choke on my spit. "I can't be babysitting a teenage girl, Lo. How am I supposed to do everything else?"

"Matteo is going to take over your current duties while you fulfill this one."

I shake my head. "I'm not a babysitter. I'm your underboss."

Lo slaps a hand on his desk, making me sit up straighter. "And as my underboss, you will do everything I say. If I say you're a babysitter, then you're a babysitter!"

I take a deep breath and pause for a moment before speaking. He rarely uses rank to get what he wants. He rarely has to. This is obviously something serious for him. While I'm not wanting to babysit a teenager, if this is what he needs, then it's what I'm going to do.

"Okay," I say, letting out the breath I was holding in.

Lo relaxes back in his chair. "We're going to meet with her father and her tonight. We'll make it clear that you will go with her on all outings. You'll have access to the cameras set up inside the main areas of their house, along with the outside. You'll move into the house next door, which has already been cleared of Tommaso's stuff. When she goes to school, you'll plant yourself right outside that school and wait for her."

I nod, even though I want to argue. I want to ask if all that is necessary, but I know it is. We have too many enemies, and the arrival of Lo's fiancé might be too good of an opportunity for them to pass up. We can't risk someone going after her to get to him.

Before I can say anything else, a knock comes on the door. Lo tells whoever it is to come in, and I look to find Matteo entering the room. Matteo is a couple of years younger than Lo and is his real brother. They look exactly alike, but Matteo has a more boyish look to him. I'm Lo's age, and we all grew up together.

Their father took me in when I was younger. I was left alone on the streets, abandoned by my parents, or they were killed. I don't know, and I don't really care.

Since day one, Lo has always treated me like his actual brother. He always has my back. My battles are his, and my enemies are his enemies. I feel the same with Matteo and treat him like he's my little brother. Just as I'd do anything for Lo, I'd do anything for Matteo. I owe them everything.

"By the look on your face, I see Lorenzo has shared the news you're demoted from underboss to babysitter," Matteo says with a large grin on his stupid face.

"Shove it," I groan.

Yeah, while I love them like my brothers, I also hate them like my brothers. We all know how to get under each other's skin, and we do it a lot.

"It's alright, I'm sure it'll be an easier job than what you're used to. You can't screw this job up like you're constantly doing with your current one," Matteo continues.

Fucking asshole. He knows damn well that I'm the best at my job, even better than him. He's fucking with me, and I know it, but it doesn't stop me from firing back.

"Quite sad really that Lo can't even trust his own brother with the most important job of keeping his fiancé safe. First passed up for being underboss, and then passed up for protecting his most precious possession," I spit back.

Matteo's grin falters for a split second before returning with a laugh. He hits my shoulder before sitting down. "*Stronzo.*"

Matteo loves these pissing contests, and I don't understand why. I usually win. I used to think that he was mad Lo chose me over him to be underboss, but he really isn't. I don't think Matteo wants the responsibility, or at least he wasn't ready for it.

Lo finally speaks up, ignoring us. "Romeo, I need you to go over everything current with Matteo. Make sure he has access to everything and give him your schedule. He'll be taking over completely, starting now."

I nod and wait for Lo to continue. "I'll get your stuff immediately moved over to the house. We'll leave at 6:30 to head over there."

"Okay," I state.

Lo stands up, dismissing us. I lead Matteo to my office, where I'll spend the next few hours going over everything that he needs to know to make this a smooth transition. Alright, I might leave out a few things to mess with him.

CHAPTER THREE

LAUREN

"How was your first day at school?" my father asks at the dinner table.

I stab my food a little too hard before responding, "Fine."

"Did you make any friends?" my mother questions.

"Yeah," I say while shoving the fork full of chicken in my mouth.

I'm not one for family dinners and talking. My father is usually working, and my mother rarely seems concerned about what I do. At least, as long as I do what I'm told and don't make any trouble for them. I've lived in a household where children are meant to be seen, not heard. With that said, I try to apply that rule to every area of my life.

"Well, tell me their names." My mother acts like she's interested.

I sigh and go along with it. "Well, I met one girl named Ashley. She has lunch and history with me. There was a nice boy named Ben in my English class."

Both my father and mother put down their forks and stare at me. Did I say something wrong?

My father clears his throat. "I suggest you stick with friends that are girls."

I look at him, confused. "I'm not looking at boys like that. He was just nice to me when others weren't."

"Others weren't nice to you at school today?"

I turn toward the door where the voice came from. My father and mother scrape their chairs back while quickly standing at their entrance. Lorenzo, my fiancé, walks in with another man behind him I haven't met before.

"My apologies. I must have gotten the time wrong, but please come sit. Can we get you both a plate?" my father asks and gestures toward the empty seats at the table.

Lorenzo doesn't take his eyes off me while speaking. "No, thank you. We're early. Please continue with your dinner."

Both of my parents take their seats again. Lorenzo sits next to me and the other guy sits across from him, next to my mother. My heart races and my appetite is gone. While I can feel Lorenzo still staring at me, I can't help but study his friend.

He's handsome and looks like he might be a little younger than Lorenzo, or maybe he is the same age. He has shaggy, dark brown hair that goes past his ears just above his shoulders. It's thick and wavy. His eyes are green, almost as piercing as Ashley's. He has the perfect tan, which I can tell is his natural skin tone and not because he's been in the sun. His facial hair is neatly kept and trimmed. He's hot, and I know I shouldn't be looking at him this way with my fiancé sitting right next to me.

Pulling me from my thoughts, Lorenzo repeats, "The kids weren't nice to you today at school?"

I shake my head and sink down into my seat. "It was nothing, just typical teenager stuff."

Lorenzo stands and holds his hand out for me to take. Am I supposed to take it?

He looks at my dad and asks, "May I have a word with Lauren in private?"

"Of course," my dad responds and sticks another piece of food in his mouth.

My heart continues to race as I place my hand in his, and he helps me up. He leads me in front of him and out of the room into our living room. I follow his lead to sit on the couch right next to him, not believing my father just let him take me out of the room alone. I've only met the man once before. He intimidates me.

I stare at him, and his face is serious. I don't think I've ever seen him smile. Lorenzo is also handsome, but not as good looking as his friend in there. He has dark brown eyes which have bags under them like he's tired, but he's clean shaven. He has short thick black hair, which clearly, he styled before getting here, or his hair is just always that neat.

"Lauren, I need to know when people aren't treating you right. If there are kids at school that are bullying you or saying rude things, you need to tell me," he says seriously.

I want to roll my eyes at him. He doesn't even know me. There's no way he cares about me and how kids at school are treating me. I want to say something sarcastic to him, but I know better.

"Okay," I state.

I inwardly groan at myself, but what am I supposed to say or do? This man is going to be my husband. I can't get on his bad side. I don't know all the details about him yet, but I know he does some shady stuff. Making him angry is not a good idea.

Lorenzo leans back and says, "If anyone disrespects you, they are disrespecting me. As the don, I can't accept that. There will be consequences."

Wait, what? What is the don?

As if his friend could hear my thoughts, he walks into the room and says, "The boss... of the mafia."

My head spins his way, and I watch him sit in the chair in front of us. Mafia boss? He's joking, right? I want to laugh, but my heart is currently beating out of my chest and somehow in my throat at the same time.

"Romeo..." Lorenzo says, shaking his head.

"What? You told her what you are. She'd go do the research online," he responds, shrugging his shoulders.

I don't say anything. I have nothing to say. So, I'm about to be the wife of a mafia boss? Holy crap. What is this? What did my father get involved with? Has Lorenzo killed people before? Of course he has! Does Brandon know? Oh my God, Brandon knows! He's been so against this marriage, and it all makes sense now.

Lorenzo places his hand on my knee, which is bouncing up and down uncontrollably. "There's nothing to be afraid of. You're going to be protected and well taken care of. You'll have everything you could ever want."

I stare at him for a moment and try to will my knee to stop bouncing. When I accomplish that, I can feel my hands shaking, so I put them both under my legs and take a deep breath.

"Okay," I say with a shaky voice.

Ugh. Okay? Is that really all I can say? What is wrong with me? I need to think of something more to say than that. He's going to think I'm stupid. If so, would he choose not to marry me? No, that wouldn't work. My father said something about him not having a choice, either. Wait... Would he kill me to get out of this marriage?

I can feel myself on the verge of hyperventilating. I can't do this here in front of him. I need to get myself under control.

Taking a deep breath, I ask, "Why me?"

Maybe if I know more about why he wants to marry me, I can ensure my safety. I know he said I'd be safe, but if he decides he doesn't want me anymore, he could kill me. Stop it. Stop thinking about this right now with him right in front of me. I need to wait until I'm alone to figure this out.

"My uncle thinks it's a good business move. We need your father to stay loyal to us and only us," Lorenzo states professionally.

"Oh." I don't really know how else to respond to that.

My breath catches as I hear his friend laugh. He called him Romeo, right? Romeo sits forward in his chair as he wipes his mouth like he's wiping the smile off his face.

"Lo, come on. That was the least romantic thing I've ever heard. At least tell the girl she's beautiful," he says while staring at me.

Lorenzo glares at his friend as he stands up and holds his hand out for me to take again. I stare at it for too long because he grabs my hand, not wanting to wait any longer, and pulls me up.

"Let's go talk in your father's office," he says, pulling me with him.

My father is already in his office when we reach it. I guess he lost his appetite with Lorenzo's early appearance, too. He leads me to a seat beside my father's desk, and they both sit in front of it.

Lorenzo clears his throat. "I'm not going to take up much of your time. This is Romeo and he's going to be Lauren's new guard."

My father interrupts him. "What happened to Tommaso?"

Tommaso? Who is that?

"He's no longer with us. Romeo will live next door to ensure the safety of your daughter, and he will have access to the cameras. If she goes anywhere, he needs to be notified before she even steps foot outside the front door. He will accompany her to and from school. He will be on campus at all times."

My father just sits there and nods while I'm having another panic attack. Am I really going to have this stranger watching everything I do? Going everywhere I go? Did he say that there are cameras?

Lorenzo turns to me and continues, "This is for your safety, Lauren. I need you to take this seriously. You will not leave without contacting Romeo first. His number is already in your phone. If anything seems off, you will call him immediately. Do you understand?"

I nod and keep my mouth shut. I'm going to have a babysitter? Seriously? Or bodyguard? What is happening right now, and how is his number already in my phone?

Lorenzo pulls something out of his pocket and holds it out to me. I look at it and my eyes widen. It's a beautiful diamond ring. A huge diamond ring. Is this an engagement ring?

Once again, I must take too long to respond because Lorenzo says, "I should've given this to you the first time we met, but it wasn't ready yet."

I just continue to stare at it. Is he serious? I can't wear that thing to school. I already don't fit in, but let's throw in a freak with an engagement ring. Sure, people know that I'm engaged. I don't need to flaunt it.

"Is there something wrong with it?" Lorenzo asks, breaking me out of my thoughts once again.

"Um... No... It's beautiful," I state, but still don't take it.

"Then put it on," he says in an authoritative tone.

I continue to hesitate, but I know I need to. If I don't, it might make him mad or think that I'm ungrateful.

Just as I'm about to raise my hand to take it, Romeo clears his throat, grabbing our attention. "Since she is just starting a new school and making friends, maybe it's best if she doesn't have an engagement ring on to add to the talk about her?"

Lorenzo looks back toward me, and I just give him a shy smile with a nod. Romeo understands. While I'm not sure how I feel about this whole bodyguard thing, I'm thankful for him at this moment.

"Alright, we can hold off on the ring for now." Lorenzo stands up, kneels in front of me, and leans in with his mouth to my ear as he whispers, "But if I find you are interested in anyone else, this ring will be on your finger permanently. If anyone touches you, then I will personally cut off his hands."

I gulp and swallow a sob as he pulls away and stands up. While trying to keep my emotions in check, he shakes my father's hand and says goodbye. I don't move, and he heads out the door with Romeo following him. Romeo turns back around, giving me a pitying look. Does he know what his boss just said to me?

I turn my head toward my dad, who looks at me with concern but says nothing. There's no point telling him what was just said because he's not going to do anything about it. Lorenzo is clearly someone who isn't to be messed with. Going back on a deal is most likely a death sentence. I can't ask that of my father.

All I can do right now is head back to my room and go to sleep while I pray I wake up from this nightmare.

Chapter Four

ROMEO

It's been about a month since I've become Lauren's babysitter, and I'm already going insane. It's not because of her, no. Lauren has been great. She follows the rules and does everything that she's supposed to do. She rarely goes out, which makes it even easier for me.

I've only seen her with one friend outside of school, named Ashley. We did some digging into her and her family. Everything checked out, so Lo cleared Lauren to hang out with her if she wants to. She's only been out with her once and that was to the mall.

I agreed to keep my distance and not make myself known to any of Lauren's friends unless absolutely necessary. She wants to live as normal of a life as possible given the circumstances. I don't blame her.

She had two dates with Lo this past month, and it's the most awkward thing to watch. I honestly feel bad for her. Lo is a great guy, and he does care about her. He just doesn't know how to show it. I don't think he has ever had a real girlfriend before, so he doesn't know how to be romantic. Then again, neither have I, but I know a lot more than he does.

She just sits there and does what she's told like a good girl. So no, Lauren isn't the problem. My fucking dick is. I haven't gotten laid in months, and watching a beautiful girl 24/7 that I can't touch and not allowed to think about is pure torture. She lays around the house in shorts that I don't even think you can call shorts. She's basically just wearing underwear. Then she wears those flimsy tanks without a bra under them.

I understand why Tommaso is dead. It's impossible to keep your eyes off her, but I'm smart enough to keep my mouth shut. She is tiny, under five feet tall while I'm six-two. She's adorable and fucking hot. Her dirty blonde hair goes all the way down to the middle of her back. It's straight but has a bit of a wave to it. When she puts it in a ponytail, I can't help but imagine what it would be like to wrap it around my hand and force her against the wall.

I try not to get too close to her, but when I do, I'm drawn into her large hazel eyes. Her dark eyelashes are so long, I don't think she puts any makeup on them; they're just natural. I've caught her staring at me on multiple occasions as well, which doesn't help the situation. Knowing that there's some attraction on her end makes it even more difficult not to think about her.

She's my brother's fiancé, and I have no right to be thinking about her in that way. Besides, she's not my type. She's perfect for Lo because she does exactly what she's told. He needs someone like that. He can't have a wife that goes around disobeying his orders. Having someone that respects him is important because everyone's going to be watching. If he can't keep his wife in line, then how is he going to keep his men in line?

The cameras are up on the monitor, and movement catches my eye. I click the screen and watch Lauren come out of her room wearing those pink short shorts and matching tank top. It's basically thirty degrees outside. Why is she wearing this to bed? Is she purposefully trying to torture me?

I pull out my notebook and look through the names and phone numbers of my past hookups. There aren't many in here as I don't typically like to hook up more than once, but there are a few that were fun and on the same page as me. Amanda... Sarah... Courtney... No, why didn't I scratch that last one out? She got clingy at the end, but she was fun. I probably should scratch out Sarah, too. She was way too sweet, and I could tell she had never had a hookup before. She is gorgeous, and we had a really great time, but she's not meant for my world.

I sigh and close the book. While having a random hookup might solve my problem for a few days, I'm just not in the mood. Plus, I'd have to call Matteo to watch Lauren, and I'd rather not.

Speaking of the devil... Matteo's name appears as an incoming call on my phone screen.

I answer on the fifth ring, just to make him angry. "Yeah?"

"Hello to you too," Matteo says.

"What do you need?" I ask curtly.

"Wow, someone needs to get laid," he says.

"You're telling me," I mutter under my breath.

I don't believe in ESP, but at this point that's a huge coincidence that I was thinking about Matteo and getting laid then he calls saying that.

"I wanted to tell you about an interesting meeting that I had today," he says, pausing to wait for my response.

"Oh yeah? With who?" I ask, while taking a sip of my water.

"Miguel Martinez."

I spit out my water all over my desk and let out a deep laugh.

"*Stronzo*!" he says while I continue laughing.

He can call me an asshole all he wants, but he's done worse. I actually forgot that I set up that meeting just to mess with him. I left out a good bit of information here and there to make him have more work to do as he took over my position, but that wasn't good enough.

Speaking of hookups, I set him up with one of my old hookups, who was literally crazy. Her name is Martina, and she was fun for one night, but she didn't understand the concept of a one-night stand, which I made very clear. She stalked me and confessed her love for me. It was a wild ride, but eventually, she toned down the stalking.

"How did it go?" I ask, pretending like it was a normal meeting.

"She literally threw herself in front of my car so I couldn't leave. Then she tried to break my window so she could jump into the passenger seat," he groans.

I laugh even harder, picturing that. I almost forgot how crazy she is, almost. Now she's Matteo's problem.

"Did you hook up with her?" I ask, controlling my laughter.

"Of course not! For one, I don't take your seconds and two… she's crazy!" he finally begins to laugh over the phone.

"I thought you'd get a kick out of this one, though," I say.

"It was a good one, but now I'm going to be investigating every meeting that's on the calendar, which will make even more work for me." He sighs.

That was the point. Our relationship is exactly like an older and younger brother's relationship would be. He messes with me, and I mess with him. Except, I always have the better pranks.

"Well, I need to let security at the club know not to let Martina in. But seriously, let me know if you need a break from babysitting to go out for a night," he states.

"Thanks, but I think I'll be able to last a couple months," I say, but I'm not even convinced of that myself.

Matteo laughs. "Good luck with that. Lorenzo is going to keep you on babysitting duty until they're married."

"Wait, what?" I ask, concerned.

"You think he's going to trust Lauren with just anyone? After Tommaso, he's never going to let anyone near Lauren again that's not one of us," he says.

"Did he say this to you?" I ask, hoping he didn't keep this from me.

Matteo pauses before answering. "Nah, not in so many words, but you know it's true."

Shit. I do know it's true. I'm going to be stuck being her babysitter for over a year. What the hell am I going to do for that long? I'm crawling out of my skin just thinking about it. It's like having kids and that's something I don't particularly want. I'm responsible for keeping someone alive and if I even want to go out to the store alone, I have to get a babysitter. What has my life come to?

"You okay over there?" Matteo asks.

"Yeah, it's fine. Go have fun with Martina. I bet she's waiting outside for you right now." I laugh.

"*Vaffanculo*," Matteo spits before hanging up the phone.

I continue laughing until I look back at the screens to see Lauren laying on the couch with a book and one leg crossed over the other. Her entire thigh is bare, and you can basically see her ass. Ugh. Maybe I should've taken Matteo up on the offer to take over for a bit.

Chapter Five

LAUREN

I've been mostly staying in the past month. The only reasons I go out are when I have to go to school or go on a date with Lorenzo. I did go out once with Ashley to the mall because she insisted. After everything was said and done, I had a good time with her.

Making new friends is challenging, and honestly, I just don't have it in me. I'm almost done with high school, and I'm about to be married to a mafia boss. I just don't feel like having many friends is wise right now. Plus, I'm not into the whole partying scene which the entire school seems to be a part of. I wouldn't mind the occasional party, but every weekend is a little excessive for me.

Anyway, staying in is getting boring. I love to drown myself in books, but even that has been getting old. I really think I just need some fresh air or something. The other reason I don't go out is because it feels weird having a bodyguard with me. Romeo has been great and hasn't complained once about escorting me anywhere, but it's going to take some time getting used to. I feel like an inconvenience asking him to go out. That's also something that's hard to get used to, asking permission to leave my house.

I'm thankful that he agreed to keep his distance when we are out. I don't want anyone knowing he's there to babysit me, and I also hate small talk. If he was walking beside me, I would have to come up with something to say. It's bad enough that he drives me to and from school every day. I try to do my homework or study on those rides to avoid the awkwardness.

Despite all the reasons it's easier and less awkward to stay in, I decided it was time to go out. It's freezing outside, but at least there's no snow. I asked Romeo to take me to a park, thinking it would be nice to clear my head and enjoy nature. I walked around for a good hour, completely forgetting Romeo was following me. All of this contributed to where I currently am. Stuck in a tree.

This is why I just don't do anything. I don't do sports, I don't do after-school activities, and I certainly don't go out in public just for fun. Why did I think it was a good idea to go for a nice walk in the park for fun? I have no idea, but never again will I be going out unless I need to or am forced to.

"You okay up there?" Romeo yells up from the bottom of the tree.

"Yep!" I yell back.

No, no, I'm not okay up here. I'm stupid, so stupid. Why did I think it was a good idea to climb a tree in the first place? Oh, that's right... I was avoiding my fiancé.

I was enjoying my walk around the park when I noticed Lorenzo taking a walk as well with two other men. They were all dressed in nice, long, dark gray winter jackets and black gloves. They looked warm and like they had planned to go for said walk.

What type of mafia boss goes for a walk in the park?! And why did he have to be taking this walk on the day that I finally decided to go out? Regardless, I did what any normal person would do when they are about to run into their fiancé... I climbed a tree to avoid him.

I'm really high in this tree, but the good news is that I have a good vantage point. I can see Lorenzo and the guys he's with, and they are pretty far away. They've been sitting on a bench for about ten minutes now. So yes, that means I've been up here for over ten minutes with no way down. Unfortunately, as I climbed the tree, some of the thick branches broke off. I'm tiny, so I can't reach the other ones around me.

I try to figure out how I'm going to get down out of this tree. Of course, I'm not going to attempt getting out of it until Lorenzo leaves the park. I'm wondering if just jumping down would be the best way. I may break an arm or a leg, but that's probably better than being freezing cold stuck in a tree.

Romeo stands with his back against the tree below me, and I groan. I can't believe this is happening. He's not even offering me suggestions on how to get out of this predicament. Then again, I did tell him I was okay up here.

Another five minutes pass, and I hear Romeo stirring below. "Are you sure you're good? Can I get you anything?"

I can tell he's enjoying this. I can't see his face completely, but I can hear the humor in his voice. If I could see him, I know there would be a smirk sitting on that handsome face.

I sit back and continue to watch Lorenzo. Finally, he gets up, but as I watch, my heart races because, of course, he's heading this way. If he gets much closer, he's going to see Romeo and if he sees Romeo, then he'll know that I'm nearby. Romeo will for sure out me, and Lorenzo will know I'm hiding in a tree because of him.

"Romeo, get up here!" I whisper-shout at him.

"What?" he shouts up the tree.

"Shhh! Get up here, now!" I say a little louder.

"You need help?" he asks, and I can just hear the humor in his voice.

"For the love of... Romeo, please. Climb this tree, now!" I say much louder.

I can hear the rumble of his laughter, but he does as I say. He takes less than thirty seconds to make his way up the tree and onto the large branch I'm sitting on. The dead leaves mostly conceal us, but I feel nauseous as Lorenzo continues walking closer. I watch intently and quietly as he passes right by us and continues on. I let out a sigh of relief.

After composing myself, I look over at Romeo, who is staring at me with the biggest grin on his face. I don't think I've ever seen him smile that widely before. I can't help but roll my eyes at him. There's a spark in his eyes.

"So, may I ask why you wanted me in this tree with you?" he asks, keeping the grin on his face.

"Just thought you'd enjoy the view," I state, and shrug my shoulders.

"While the view is fantastic, I have a feeling there's another reason."

"Well, it's not to play out the song if that's what you're thinking," I state, trying to bring some humor into this and avoid the truth that I'm hiding from Lorenzo and we both know it.

"What song?" he asks.

"What do you mean, what song? Have you never heard of the song about two people sitting in a tree?" I ask.

He looks seriously perplexed. "No."

I just stare at him.

"Are you going to tell me what song?" he asks.

"If you don't know it, then no," I say.

"Okay, then we can talk about why you're really hiding in this tree." He laughs.

I groan. "Fine. The song that uses your names..." I begin to sing, "Lauren and Romeo sitting in a tree, K-I-S-S-I-N-G... You know... that song. Don't tell me you haven't heard it."

He stares at me and his eyebrows pull together. Wow, alright then.

"Look, never mind. It's a stupid elementary song. Can we go now?"

He shakes his head like he's trying to get whatever thoughts he has in there out of it. "I think the question is, are you ready to go?"

I look around to ensure that Lorenzo isn't anywhere nearby before answering, "Yes."

"Are you able to get out of this tree?" he asks.

I groan again and look up at the sky. How did I get into this situation? It's so embarrassing on so many levels. Why do I have to have a bodyguard that follows me everywhere? Now I have someone to witness every time I make a stupid mistake.

"Maybe..." I say.

He shrugs his shoulders. "Alright, well, I'll go first."

I watch as he climbs down the tree like it's super easy. He barely uses any branches at all to get down and just hugs the tree trunk to climb down, jumping the last few feet. There's no way I can do that. My arms can't fit around the thickness of this tree, and I'm so much shorter. Not to mention that I'm not that strong. I would immediately fall on my butt if I tried that.

"You coming?" Romeo yells up to me.

"Yep..." I say.

Alright, it's now or never. There's a decently thick branch a bit down from me I should be able to reach if I jump over there a little. I was hoping to get my footing and not make any quick movements, but I don't have a choice since some branches I used are now on the ground.

I lower myself from the branch I'm currently sitting on, holding on for dear life with my arms. Rocking my body back and forth, I swing a little to the thick branch below. Once I think I have enough momentum, I get the courage to let go and my right foot lands on the branch, but the other slips right off. I lose my balance and tumble through the tree branches toward the ground.

I close my eyes, waiting for the impact and pain to hit, but it never comes. Right before hitting the ground, I'm stopped by strong arms around my waist and shoulders. My feet are on the ground within seconds of Romeo catching me, and I'm caught off balance. I fall back against the tree to steady myself.

We stare at each other for a moment, and I don't know what to say. I don't know if it's because of the adrenaline wearing off or what, but I start dying of laughter and sit on the ground. Romeo has a smirk on his face.

"Thanks…" I say as my laughter subsides.

"You're welcome, but I thought you didn't need help," he reminds me.

"I didn't," I state.

We both know that's a lie. I mean, if he hadn't caught me, I would most likely have a broken arm or leg. Maybe a broken neck. But it's fine, I'm not going to admit it.

"Sure," he states.

I stand up and brush the leaves and grass off me. "I'm ready to go home."

He nods. "Too much excitement for you?"

"Something like that," I reply.

We're silent the whole walk back to the car, but the moment we get in and start driving, he asks, "So why were you hiding from Lorenzo?"

I shake my head. "I don't know."

"Really?"

I contemplate for a moment before speaking again. "Honestly, it was just my initial reaction, and I don't know why. I guess... I just don't really know him that well, and I wasn't expecting him to be there. So, I figured it was best to hide."

He doesn't respond to that. I can tell he's thinking something, but he says nothing. I want to ask what he's thinking but decide not to. Hopefully, this whole thing will be forgotten by the morning. I especially hope that Lorenzo never finds out about it. If I'm being honest, I think my reaction boils down to being scared of him.

Chapter Six

Romeo

Ever since the tree incident with Lauren, she hasn't left the house other than to go to school. She's back to staying in, and I don't blame her. I think she's embarrassed about the whole situation, but I found it fucking adorable.

The fact she had just bolted up that tree so fast when she spotted Lo was amazing. I didn't think she had it in her to climb a tree, but I guess when you're trying to escape someone, you get the strength to do what you need to. Personally, I would've hidden behind one of the nearby bushes. They were big enough to conceal both of us.

Then when she was begging me to join her in the tree because Lo was heading our way, I almost lost it. She panicked, and I could tell that she would do anything for me to hide as well. I felt bad for her, so I did what she asked.

Then she had to go on with some stupid song about kissing in a tree... What was that about? I'm hoping it was to distract from the fact that she was stuck up there and hiding from her fiancé. When I got home that day, I looked up that stupid song. It does exist, and it's ridiculous.

My phone buzzes with a text from Lauren, distracting me from my thoughts.

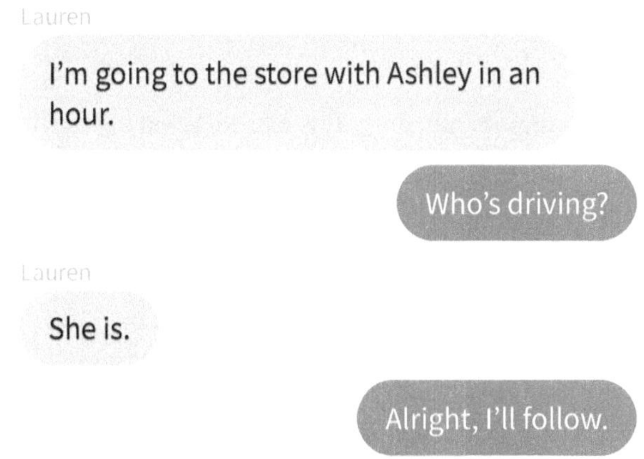

I get ready and sit in my car, waiting for Ashley to pull up in Lauren's driveway. Once Lauren jumps in, I follow behind at a safe distance. I also have Lauren's phone tracked on my GPS, just in case.

Once we enter the store, I continue to follow behind them at a distance, but I notice Lauren acting more anxious than normal. I've gotten to know her well while watching her this past month. She's typically an anxious person, but this is different. When she's with Lo, I notice that she's nervous and slightly scared to be around him. When she's in situations she doesn't want to be in, she starts to fidget. If she's sitting, her knee bounces up and down quickly.

This is different, though. She's looking over her shoulder every couple of minutes, and she's whispering to Ashley like she doesn't want anyone to hear what she's saying. I look around and don't see anyone following us, but I'll stay more alert.

As I watch them go through the store, I can feel my heart rate pick up when I realize what's happening. She wouldn't... Would she?

Ashley has quite the cart going, while Lauren has nothing in her hands. I've noticed Lauren pointing to a few items, but she never picks them up. Ashley does. Currently in Ashley's cart is a duffle bag, a whole new wardrobe, hair dye, and a bunch of other necessities. If I wasn't paying attention and Lauren wasn't so anxious, then I'd probably think that Ashley was going on a trip, but that's not what's happening here.

Lauren is going to run.

"Everything alright?" Lo answers his phone on the first ring.

"I think we have a problem, Lo," I state.

After the shopping trip, Lauren went back to her house, and Ashley went home shortly after. I pulled up all the cameras and have one open on each screen in my office. Lauren hasn't come out of her room since getting home, which makes me think that she's preparing to run. Tonight. Conveniently when both of her parents are out of town.

"What is it?" he asks, on alert.

"She's going to run," I state casually, trying not to get him worked up.

The last thing I want to do is upset him, which will make her life miserable. She's already afraid of him. I don't want him scaring her more. I wanted to take care of this myself. After getting back, I even debated telling him. I thought of every way this could play out.

I could confront her and tell her I know she's planning to run, but I don't know her well enough to know how she'd react to that. I never thought that she would attempt to run, so I'm not sure what else she's capable of. Following her and stopping her before she gets too far is another option. Then I'd let her know that I'm always watching and know everything, but again, there are too many variables.

Besides, Lo deserves to know what his fiancé is doing. Plus, I'd feel guilty keeping it from him when I've already been keeping my dirty thoughts about her from him. Regardless, it's his choice how to approach this. She's his fiancé, after all.

"When?" he asks calmly.

"I'm thinking tonight. She's preparing now."

The line is silent for a moment. He's thinking of the best course of action.

"Let her. Follow her, and let her think she escaped, but then bring her back. Scare her and keep her in line. Bring her to my place, and let me know when you're on the way," he says.

"Done," I state and hang up the phone.

I set the phone on my desk and check all the cameras. She's still in her room. As I sit and wait, I try not to think of her as a person. I can't think about how cute she is when she's walking around casually or how anxious she is when she's around Lo or in uncomfortable situations. I always want to protect her and hold her hand when she's like that, but I can't think about it. This is just another job that Lo has given me, and I need to do it.

CHAPTER SEVEN

LAUREN

It's currently 2 a.m. and I pace back and forth in my room with my heart racing out of my chest. Am I really going to do this?

I've been doing a lot of thinking this past month, and this is not the life that I want to lead. After seeing Lorenzo the night he assigned Romeo to be my bodyguard, I couldn't sleep. I kept thinking about what it means to be married to a mafia boss.

While I have no doubt that Romeo will lay his life down for me, it's still unsafe. It's unsafe for me, Lorenzo, everyone I love, and my future children. Not that I really want to have children, but it's obviously something that I'm going to have to do. I don't want to put their lives in danger. I don't want to worry about if my husband will come home at night. I don't want to live like that.

The couple of dates, if you can call them that, with Lorenzo, just didn't go well. I can tell that he's trying to get to know me, but he's not romantic at all. I don't have any fuzzy feelings for him when we spend time together. It probably doesn't help that he threatened me and to cut off the hands of any guy that dares to touch me. The scary part is that I know he would do it, so I've been keeping my distance from boys.

The near run in with him the other day also gave me the extra push to do this. The fact I felt the need to climb a tree than run into my fiancé was a big red flag to me. Who does that? I mean, we're not talking about who does that in general, but who runs away from their fiancé rather than being happy to run into them?

So, I've recruited Ashley to help me escape. She's been amazing. I've confided in her a lot without giving her too much detail. She knows that I'm set for an arranged marriage, but not with who. She also doesn't know about Romeo, and I'm doing my best to keep it that way. She has been supportive of my decision even though we've only known each other for a month.

I hate to leave my family behind, especially Brandon, but I figure eventually I will contact him again. I love my parents as they are my parents, but it's not a huge loss if I never see them again. My mom and I never really saw eye to eye. My father sold me to the devil, literally. Brandon is the only one fighting and looking out for me.

My bus leaves in a little over an hour, so I need to make my way to the station. Ashley is picking me up down the street to drive me. I wanted to make sure that Romeo would be asleep, so I texted him earlier that I would go out around seven to breakfast with Ashley. I figured that would make sure he's asleep and not watching the cameras. I'm leaving my phone with Ashley, so she can text him that I canceled breakfast and am staying in. I changed Romeo's name in my phone, so she thinks she's texting my father. I told her he wants to know every time I leave the house even though he's not home. That'll buy time in the morning, so Romeo doesn't notice I'm missing.

To be safe, I've carefully figured out the camera angles and where to go not to be noticed. There aren't any blind spots unfortunately, but if I'm quick enough, I won't be detected if Romeo is watching them. Both of my parents are out of town, so this is the best night to do it.

I take a deep breath and throw my duffle bag over my shoulder. I keep the lights off as I walk through the house and out the back door. Staying close to the walls of the house, I walk as quickly as possible. Once I make it to the sidewalk, I sprint down the street toward where Ashley's car is waiting. I throw my duffle in the backseat and jump in the passenger seat. Ashley takes off as I continuously look in the mirrors to make sure we're not being followed. We're not.

My heart rate doesn't slow until I'm about to board the bus. I hand Ashley my phone and give her a hug.

"Thank you so much for helping me, Ashley. I'll contact you when I can," I say.

She pulls away and gives me a small smile. "Don't do it too soon. I don't want them to find you. The moment you get there, dye your hair and cut it. Lie low for a while. The money will last a long time, so don't panic. The longer you stay out of sight, the better the chances they'll give up."

I nod and don't say anything back. There's nothing to say. We've planned this out perfectly and it should work. I took a good bit of money from my father, and Ashley gave me some of her savings. It should last an entire year for everything that I need. The owners of the cabin I'll be renting in Georgia accepted cash up front with no questions asked. Once things die down, I'll get a job and figure out my life from there. I'll probably move again before getting the job, just to be safe.

I take my seat on the bus and look out the window at Ashley. She waves and gives me a small smile. I hate leaving her when we just met, but I have to. I'm thankful for her and that she understands. She is the first one that I'll be contacting when I can, and then Brandon. I know that neither of them would betray me to Lorenzo. I just need to make sure enough time passes that Lorenzo gives up and moves on.

Twenty-three hours later and I've finally made it to Atlanta. That was the longest bus ride I've ever been on. Thankfully, my seatmate kept to himself. If he wasn't sleeping, then he was reading a book or listening to headphones. I tried to get some sleep, but it was hard when I kept looking over my shoulder.

I'm still looking over my shoulder, expecting to see Romeo or Lorenzo come up behind me.

I get a ride close to the cabin, which is over an hour away from the bus station. He drops me off about a mile away. I'm exhausted, and it's dark, but I figure it's best to walk the rest of the way just in case they somehow track me to this point.

After the long walk with my heavy duffle, I just want to lie in bed and crash, but I can't. Rummaging through the bag, I find the hair dye and scissors. I've been dreading this part, because I love my hair as I've worked hard to grow it out for so long, but it needs to be done.

Standing in front of the mirror, I pull all my hair to the front of my shoulders. I run my fingers through it one last time, trying not to think about what I'm about to do. Taking a deep breath, I hold the scissors in my right hand while I hold my hair with my left hand and take the first cut, about an inch above my shoulders. I close my eyes as I do it, and once the scissors stop, I open them to see the hair I'm holding in my hand.

I lift it up in front of me, looking at my beautiful long strands that are no longer attached to my head. Out of nowhere, I get angry. Rage courses through my body as I finish cutting my hair and begin the process of dying it. Angrily putting the dye in my hair, I pace around the room, getting my stuff settled as I wait for the allotted amount of time. I occasionally go to the couch and punch the pillows on it to alleviate some of the anger.

When it's finally time to wash out the dye, I do so over the sink and angrily scrub at it while screaming. I hate this. I hate that Lorenzo has made me lose everything. Now I've lost my entire life and my hair, so I have nothing. He took everything from me. He took me away from my old friends and school. Now he's taken my new life and the friend that I made in the short time I've been in New York. I hate him!

I blow dry my hair to see the hair dye did its job. My hair is completely black, and it's so short, above my shoulders. I hate it. It looks nothing like me. I suppose that's the point.

After getting over my new hairstyle and color, I decide to lie down in bed to get some sleep. I figure I can finish unpacking and get food when I wake up in a few hours. I check the cabin doors and windows to make sure they are locked before heading to bed.

A sound startles me awake. Reaching for my phone on the end table, I find nothing there. I groan as I roll over and remember that I'm not in my bed. I feel nauseous as the memories come flooding back to me at what I've done.

Leaning over, I turn the lamp on. When I go to sit back in bed, I jump and scream as I see a figure sitting in a chair in the corner. No, it's not just a figure, it's Romeo.

Frozen in place, he says with a smile, "Good morning, sunshine."

I don't respond. I want to run, but I can't.

"Did you have a good trip?" he asks, like this is nothing but a vacation.

I still don't respond.

He looks me over for a moment before saying, "I see that you've changed your hair. I don't like it."

Neither do I... Crap, I need to figure this out. I can't be caught already. I thought I was safe, and that I did it! What's going to happen if he takes me back to Lorenzo? Am I going to be locked up forever? Is he going to kill me?

"Romeo... Please don't make me go back." My voice cracks.

I swear I see his whole demeanor change for a split second, like he pities me and doesn't want to, but then it's back to his uncaring attitude.

"You know I don't have a choice," he says, standing up.

I don't think as I lunge off the bed and open the end table beside me, reaching for the gun that I placed in there before falling asleep.

I aim it at Romeo and say, "I'm not going back."

His eyes light up like he's amused. "Now, where did you get that?"

"I'm serious Romeo. I can't go back. I won't!" My hands shake, but my voice is determined.

Romeo takes a few steps toward me, and I take a step back, realizing I'm against a wall with nowhere to go. "I'm not kidding, I'll shoot!"

He laughs as he gets closer, and I don't know what to do. I want to pull the trigger, but I can't. I only hesitate for a second and he's on me, taking the gun away. He throws it on the bed and presses me against the wall with his hand gently over my throat.

My breathing becomes rapid, and I feel the tears burning in my eyes. What is he going to do to me? I just threatened to shoot him. Is he allowed to kill me?

I watch as he leans closer, his face inches from mine. My breath hitches with his close proximity. What is happening? My emotions are going haywire. I'm scared to death then all of a sudden, I'm turned on with his face inches away and his body pressing mine against the wall. Thinking about how I want him to close that extra inch to kiss me, I can't breathe. I stare at his lips and would do it myself if he wasn't holding my throat with his hand.

He leans even closer but moves his lips beside my ear. "If you're going to threaten to shoot someone, you should take the safety off."

He leans back, towering over me again, and takes his hand away from my throat. His body is still pressing against mine. I breathe a little better as the fog over my head clears, and I remember the situation that we're in.

"I can't go back, Romeo. Please don't make me go back to him," I plead.

He closes his eyes for a moment and then says, "You know I can't let you escape and have to bring you back. Don't make this difficult for either of us."

I shake my head, and a few tears slip from my eyes. If he wasn't keeping me pinned against the wall right now, I'd slide down it and fall to the floor. I can't believe I was found so quickly. I really thought I had a chance.

As if I said that aloud, he says, "You never had a chance, Lauren. He's never going to let you go. You can run as fast as you want, but he will run faster. You can go as far as you can, but he will go further. You will never escape him, Lauren. He will always find you."

I feel defeated and deflate with his words. I know he's right, and I know the type of man that Lorenzo is. After all my research, I know how powerful he is and what he's capable of. Why did I think I had a chance? I have a feeling the only way out of this marriage is death.

Chapter Eight

ROMEO

To my surprise, Lauren came without a fight. We threw her duffle bag in the trunk, and she got in the passenger seat, not saying a word. I think she understands how serious I am when I say that she will never escape. Regardless, I'm not letting my guard down around her.

When she pulled that gun out on me, I was surprised and impressed. I was disappointed when she didn't take the safety off it, though. She has clearly never used a gun before and doesn't know how to use one. That's something I'm going to have to teach her. If she's going to be the don's wife, she needs to know how to use a gun and how to kill. Fuck. Imagining her having to kill someone pulls at something inside my heart.

Speaking of pulling at something inside my heart, I never wanted to disobey Lo's orders more than in the moment she pleaded with me not to take her back. She does something to me, and I don't know what to do about it. I want nothing more than to keep her safe and give her everything she has ever wanted in the world, but I can't. She's not mine.

I look over at her in the passenger seat, as she stirs in her sleep. I'm sure she's exhausted from running and constantly looking over her shoulder. She did good, but not good enough. That's another thing I'm going to need to teach her, how to be aware of her surroundings. I'm good at staying hidden, but if you know what you're looking for, you'll find me.

Placing my hand on her shoulder, I gently shake her awake. Her eyes slowly flutter open as she looks over at me, confused.

"We're going to pull off to get some sleep in a hotel," I tell her.

"Okay," she says as she lays her head back down on the door and her eyes close again.

I can't help but smile at how cute she is. She's so tiny and curled up in her seat with her legs under her. She always seems so agreeable and like she won't argue, but I have a feeling that's not how she is under the surface. I think I'm about to find out once we get into this hotel room.

"Absolutely not. You can't be serious," she says, searching my eyes to see if I am indeed serious.

"I'm serious," I state.

She looks over toward the bed in the middle of the hotel room and then back at me. I hold back my smile as I see her cheeks turn red. She's blushing. Shit, I didn't think this through all the way. I knew that we would have to share a bed because I'll wake up if she tries to get out of it. I can't risk staying asleep and her escaping, which I know she'll try to do. I need sleep as I've been awake for two days. Regardless, I didn't think about the fact that I would literally be sleeping next to her, and my body reacts to her in ways it shouldn't react to my brother's fiancé.

"I can sleep in the chair," she counters, looking over at the uncomfortable recliner.

She heads toward the chair, but I catch her arm. I pull her back to me and don't let go. She looks down at where my hand meets her forearm and then back up at me.

"No. You have two choices here. Either you sleep next to me in this bed, or I tie you to the bed. Your choice," I state, staring into her eyes.

I watch her eyes widen for a moment, and a bunch of emotions swim through them. Anger, fear, curiosity, and... lust? I don't need to be thinking about that last one. Back in the cabin, when I had her pinned against the wall, I thought I saw her staring at my lips, begging me to kiss her. By the way she looked back there and now, she doesn't want to be feeling these things either. Or she doesn't fully understand what she's feeling.

"Bed it is. Well, I mean, sleeping in bed with you. Not being tied up to the bed and sleeping with you... Or I mean..." she rambles.

I can't help but smirk at her getting so flustered and the fact that her cheeks are red again. She's fucking adorable. She's so innocent, and I'm fairly certain she's a virgin. I can't help but imagine... No. I can't imagine these things with her. She. Is. Not. Mine.

I clear my throat. "Get in bed. We're only staying a few hours, and then we're heading back."

She nods and obeys. She lays down on the bed and pulls the covers over her. I shake my head and groan at the fact she obeys so easily. Lo has no idea how lucky he is to have someone like her.

I turn off the bedside lamp and lay beside her on top of the covers. I also leave my clothes on for multiple reasons. First, I don't trust she won't try to run. The last thing I want is to be half naked and running out of the hotel room chasing after her. Second, I don't want to make her any more uncomfortable than she already is. Third, the more clothes between us, the better.

It doesn't take long for me to drift off to sleep. It's been a while since I've slept, so I need a solid four hours to keep me going again to drive the rest of the way home.

My eyes pop open as I hear her whisper my name. "Romeo?"

I turn my head to look at her. It's dark, so I can only make out the silhouette of her body. "Yeah?"

"What is he going to do to me?" she asks so low that I can barely hear her.

Fuck. She's scared, and it's destroying me. Without thinking, I roll to my side and wrap my arm around her waist with her back pressed against my front. I don't say anything and neither does she. She doesn't pull away from my touch. In fact, it feels like she relaxes into me.

"He's not going to hurt you, Lauren. You will always be safe with him and with me. Okay?" I say, trying to sound as convincing as possible.

"Okay," she whispers back.

I hate that she's so scared of him, and I hate she doesn't trust me enough to know that I would never let anything happen to her. I don't know what's going on with me as I've become so protective of her from guarding her for one month. Holding her like this... it's wrong, yet it feels so right. I'm betraying Lo right now, and I can't find it in me to care enough to let her go and roll over.

My phone rings, waking me out of a dead sleep. I notice I'm still holding onto Lauren and reluctantly let her go as I answer the phone on the third ring.

"Yeah?" I answer.

"Everything going to plan?" Lo asks on the other end of the line.

I look at my watch to find it's been seven hours since we fell asleep. Crap, I was only supposed to sleep four hours. I never sleep seven hours straight, ever.

"Yeah, no problems here. We're about to hit the road again. I'll let you know when we're an hour out," I say.

I don't really need to let him know, considering he can track my location. I'm sure he already has, and that's why he's calling.

"You sure there have been no hiccups? She's behaving?" he asks as if she's a dog.

"None. I overslept, and she's still asleep. There's been no arguments."

The line is silent for a few moments before he says, "Alright, keep me updated."

The line disconnects, and I throw my phone on the end table. Sitting up with my feet on the floor, I rub my hand through my hair. I know he doesn't suspect anything, but I feel guilty. I slept all night with Lauren in the same bed while I held her, and I liked it. More than liked it. I haven't slept that comfortably in a long time.

Lauren stirs and sits up. She looks over at me with puffy, red eyes. Has she been crying all night, and I didn't notice?

"Can I take a shower before we go?" she asks.

I nod, and she throws the covers off before heading into the bathroom. The shower turns on, so I get myself dressed and ready for the drive back. I'd love to take a shower too, but I can't trust that she wouldn't run while I was in there.

While I'm waiting for her to finish, I decide to go through her duffle to see what she has packed. She's clearly smart, and I can't underestimate her. I've been trying to figure out if her obedience is really her personality or if it's all a ploy. She was so well behaved before trying to run away. With how smart she is, she could have been pretending to have us let our guard down. If that was the case, though, I'm confused about why she's coming back so willingly. Is she trying to plot another escape on the way back? What lengths will she go to, to not have to return to Lo?

I pull out everything inside of her duffle, piece by piece. The contents are mainly the new clothes she bought, along with feminine products, makeup, and other necessities. As I continue pulling items out, I find a knife wrapped in a shirt. It's a small pocketknife, and it looks brand new. I pocket it and continue my search. Unzipping the inside pocket, I find some pepper spray. I pocket that as well and tip the bag upside down to ensure I removed everything.

So, it looks like she was prepared for a fight. She brought a gun, which I took before we left the cabin, a knife, and some pepper spray. She came prepared, but I have a feeling she doesn't know how to use any of it. It makes me wonder if she was going to use it on the way back home. Regardless, it's good to know that she is willing to do whatever it takes to survive.

I hear the shower turn off, so I quickly throw all the items inside the bag, making it look like I haven't gone through it. I sit on the edge of the bed and wait for her to leave the bathroom.

Too many minutes go by without her coming out, and I wonder if something is wrong, so I head toward the bathroom door.

I knock. "Is everything okay in there?"

There's silence for a moment before I hear her say, "Um... yeah. I just... I forgot to bring my clothes in here, so I'm only in a towel. Could you... look away?"

I smile, thinking about her standing on the other side of this door in just a towel, embarrassed. "Yeah, sure. I'm not looking."

I turn around to face the wall as she comes out of the bathroom. It takes everything in me not to look her way. She's so innocent, or at least she acts it. After finding the knife and pepper spray in her bag, it makes me wonder if it really is just an act. Did she purposefully go into the bathroom without her clothes so she would have to come out to get them? Was she planning on making me look away so she could get what she needed, use it on me, and run? As much as I don't want to believe that's the case, I need to keep my guard up around her. I haven't survived this long in our world by underestimating people.

"Get what you need?" I ask as she's taking a while rummaging through her bag.

"Yeah, I'll get changed in the bathroom," she says as she walks by me and closes the bathroom door again.

She didn't mention anything about the missing pepper spray or knife, so either she didn't notice it missing or she knows that I have them. I have a feeling it's the latter.

CHAPTER NINE

LAUREN

I'm about to throw up. I know I'm going to throw up all over Romeo's car. I'm not even going to make it to Lorenzo's house before being murdered. Romeo is going to murder me for getting vomit all over his pristine car. I'm going to throw up.

I have no idea where Lorenzo lives, but I know we can't be far now. We've made it back to New York City and since then I've been feeling nauseous. I know Romeo told me that Lorenzo isn't going to kill me, but he could do much worse things than kill me. I have nothing to get out of this situation anymore.

Romeo took the gun that I had, but clearly, I didn't know how to use it anyway. I don't even know how to take the safety off the gun. After the shower, I went to get the knife and pepper spray to keep on me after getting dressed, but he must have taken it out while I was in the shower. He didn't say anything about it, and I wasn't going to say anything either.

Romeo has done nothing to hurt me. In fact, he's done the opposite. This past month, he has done everything to keep me safe and respect my wishes. He has always kept his distance so I could live a normal life. Well, as normal as I possibly can. He never questioned when I told him I wanted to go out, he just followed.

Then there was also last night... I have never felt safer and more comforted than when I was sleeping in his arms. It was so wrong, but it felt so right. What would Lorenzo do if he found out about last night? Would he kill Romeo? Would he cut off his hands because he touched me? Obviously, nothing happened between us, and it probably meant nothing to Romeo like it did to me. I bet he did it so I couldn't escape. If I had moved his arm off me, then he would've woken up. Regardless, he could've just tied me up to the bed, but he didn't.

I'm pulled from my thoughts when we pull up to a gate with a guard in it. Romeo rolls his window down and nods as the gate opens for us. This must be where Lorenzo lives. I guess it will be where I live whenever we get married. Or maybe he's going to keep me in a dungeon. We can't see the house yet, but I'm pretty sure it's probably a scary-looking castle with a dungeon that he keeps prisoners and murders people in.

As we drive down the gravel driveway, the house peeks through the trees. The closer we get, I see I was wrong about the scary-looking castle. It's just an enormous mansion that looks like it's over a hundred years old. It's well kept, so it's not creepy looking. I'm still not convinced there isn't a dungeon inside.

Romeo pulls up right to the front door and parks the car. He turns it off, gets out, rounds the car, and opens my door. I don't move.

"Come on, we don't want to keep him waiting any longer," Romeo says, while holding the door wide open for me.

I stare at him and can't bring myself to move. If I go in there, I have a feeling I won't be coming out. What do I do now? I don't have any weapons, and this place is completely guarded. Why did I let him take me this far? Why didn't I open the door and jump out when I had the chance?

I feel myself shaking, and the bile reaches my throat. What is wrong with me? Why am I always so scared and anxious? I want to be strong like all the main characters in the books that I read. They wouldn't be sitting here shaking right now, about to throw up all over the place. They would fight to the end.

Romeo leans over into the car. "Lauren... You will be safe, I promise."

I let out a breath and am comforted by his words. I know I'll be safe with him, but I'm not so sure how Lorenzo is going to react. I ran away from my fiancé... from a mafia boss! There's no way he's going to let that go.

"Drag her out and carry her in if you have to," Lorenzo's voice reaches us from the front door.

My eyes widen as I stare at him. His arms are crossed, and he stands in front of the open door to the mansion. His voice is authoritative and calm. I don't know why, but it's scarier than if he was yelling.

Romeo gives me a pitying look. "Please don't make me do that."

As much as I don't want to disobey Lorenzo, I don't want to just walk into his house and offer myself to him to give whatever punishment he deems appropriate for running away. What about my parents? Do they know? Did he tell them I ran away and what he was going to do to me? If so, would they even care or try to help me?

"Romeo," Lorenzo states, and it's a command.

Romeo grabs my arm to pull me out, but now I don't know what to do, so I resist. I pull back so he can't get me out of the car. I don't know my end game here, but I can't let him bring me inside. I can't.

"Lauren, please. Don't fight me," he pleads with me again.

I want to trust him; I do. I want to do what he says, but I just can't. I start sobbing and shaking worse, kicking at him as he continues to pull me out. My attempts to evade him are pointless. He's so much bigger and stronger than me. I'm so small that he easily lifts me up, even as I'm kicking and screaming at him. He pulls me from the car and throws me over his shoulder.

"Please..." I beg. "Please don't do this."

He doesn't say anything and continues to carry me up the steps and into the house. There's nothing I can do. There's no way I can overpower these men. I knew I couldn't trust Romeo. He's not here for me, he's here for Lorenzo. He's going to do whatever he asks him to do. Will he be the one to lock me up?

Romeo drops me on the couch, and I quickly sit up, trying to stand. I want to run, but it's useless. Romeo is kneeling in front of me with his arm on my legs like he's telling me there's no use running.

All I can do is wait for whatever's going to happen. My heart is racing as I watch Lorenzo pull up a chair directly in front of me and sit in it. He nods to Romeo, who releases me and stands leaning against the wall.

I turn my focus back on Lorenzo, who is staring at me, not saying a word. He looks so calm.

His hand reaches out toward my face, and I flinch. He pauses for a second with a scowl, but then continues to move his hand closer. He wipes underneath one of my eyes and then the other. He's... wiping away my tears?

"Lauren... I'm not going to hurt you. I need you to know that I will never hurt you. Ever. No matter what. Do you understand?" he asks in a serious voice.

His words should be comforting, but they're not. How can a man like him promise such a thing? I know he has hurt people before. He hurts people now. I just nod anyway, because what else can I do?

"Are you hurt?" he asks, like he really is concerned.

I shake my head no.

"Why did you run away?"

I don't answer. He knows why I ran away. Does he really need an explanation?

"Answer me," he demands in his cool tone.

"I... I'm scared," I say.

"Of me?"

I nod and shrug my shoulders.

"You never have to fear me. Have I done something to scare you?" he asks, as if he doesn't know.

Once again, I don't respond. I look at the floor. I have the urge to look over at Romeo for comfort and protection, but I know he won't provide me with either of those.

"What have I done to make you scared of me?" he asks.

Somehow, I have the courage to speak. "You threatened to cut off the hands of anyone who touched me."

Lorenzo sits back in his chair as he studies me before replying. "Is there someone touching you?"

My eyes widen as I think about Romeo and quickly say, "No!"

"Are you sure?"

"No, there's no one. I'm not interested in anyone. I just... You would really cut off their hands? Have you done that before?" I ask.

He smirks. "You know that I'm not a good man, Lauren. I don't think we've gotten off on the right foot. I would never harm you. You are safe with me. I do not harm women or children, ever. As for men, I do when they deserve it. Don't you think that someone touching my fiancé deserves that?"

I stare at the man before me and see someone who believes everything he just said. He has odd morals. He won't harm women or children, yet he'll literally cut off someone's hands because they touched his fiancé, and he finds nothing wrong with it. This is the man I'm supposed to marry?

"Do you believe the same if it were reversed? If a woman touched you, then I have every right to cut off her hands?" I ask, closely watching his reaction.

He leans back in his chair and smiles. "Ah, so is that what this is about? Are you worried that I'm not going to be faithful to you?"

Honestly, that never crossed my mind. Not that it wouldn't be a concern, just that my main concern has been the fact that he hurts people and everything about my situation is dangerous. Would I care if he was unfaithful to me? I guess I would be upset knowing that the man forcing me to marry him was sleeping with other women. I nod in answer to his question.

"I'm going to be honest with you because I never want to lie to my wife. I have recently been with others before you came to the city. Now that you're here and we're officially to be married, no one else will touch me as no one will touch you. So, tell me, has there been anyone else?" he asks as if it wouldn't matter, but I know better.

I don't know if he thinks that I'm stupid or that I would just fall for it because he's being honest and nice, but I'm not.

"No. There has never been anyone. No one has ever touched me," I say.

He seems happy with that answer. "And there's no one that you want to touch you?"

My heart skips a beat as I take a quick glance at Romeo and then back toward Lorenzo. Crap. Lorenzo saw that. I know he did. Yeah, I wanted Romeo to touch me. I enjoyed his touch, wanted him to kiss me, but I can't let Lorenzo know.

"No, and if there was, then your friend would know and tell you," I nod toward Romeo again, hoping that covers why I looked over toward Romeo when he asked that question.

"You're right, Romeo knows everything and in return, so do I. I'm only going to say this once. You are my fiancé, and you will do as I say. You will not try to run away again. This is your only free pass and act of rebellion against this marriage. If this happens again, I will find you, and you will be locked in this house with no contact with your friends or family until I think you have learned your lesson. Do you understand?" Lorenzo asks seriously with his face just inches from mine.

I nod. "Yes."

He scoots his chair back and stands up. "You'll be staying here for the night. Elena will bring you up to your room. You can rest, and she will take you for a tour of the house later. I expect to see you tonight for dinner."

"Thank you," I say.

I silently beat myself up for saying thank you. Really? Thank you for what? For not killing me? For telling me what I'm going to do with the rest of my day and life? For forcing me to marry you? Yeah, I'll never be like the heroines in the books I read.

Chapter Ten

ROMEO

I sit in the chair across from Lo by the fireplace in his office. We both sip our scotches in silence. We're waiting for the other to start the conversation. He wants to say something about Lauren, and so do I.

"I thought you said she was obeying," he states.

"She was. I had no problems until we pulled up to the house. She got scared," I say with no emotion in my voice.

She was scared, and I literally saw her shaking as we pulled up, and it broke my heart. I also hate how Lo forced me to pick her up and carry her inside. I don't want to be the bad guy with her.

"Why is she so scared?" he asks, like he wants my advice.

"Lo, you're a scary man, and you literally threatened to cut off someone's hands the second time you saw her. You keep threatening to take away her freedom every time you see her. She's 17. I don't have a teenager, but I'm pretty sure that's when they really rebel and want nothing but freedom," I say, hoping he's listening.

"*Merda*. Romeo… She's 17. What am I doing engaged to a 17-year-old? I don't know what to do. Uncle told me I need to be strict with her and let her know she can't get away with anything. I don't want her scared of me, but I can't have her running off or messing around with other guys. You know how that'd look," he says, taking a gulp of his drink this time.

I nod. Yeah, I know how that would look. Everyone knows that she's his fiancé. She needs to show him respect and listen to him, otherwise it'll look bad. If he can't control his fiancé, then his men are going to be all over that. Not to mention his enemies.

"I don't think that approach is going to work with her. She wants to please others, and I don't think you're going to have a problem with her obeying you. She's just scared. Get to know her more and what she likes. Show her something about you that's not… scary," I say with my stomach feeling sour.

Why do I feel like this when telling him how to win over his fiancé? I'm not going to dig into this feeling right now, or ever.

"What about me isn't scary?" he asks.

I stare at him, and we're both silent as we think. After a few moments, we burst into laughter.

"No idea, brother. That's something you're going to have to figure out on your own," I say.

Lo shakes his head as his laughter fades. "Thanks. So, everything is going okay with watching her? There's nothing I should be concerned about? No one at school she's hanging out with?"

I shake my head. "No. She hangs out with Ashley and that's about it. I've seen her talking occasionally to some boys, but she mostly looks uncomfortable and avoids them while still being friendly. I think you terrified her with the cutting off hands thing."

He shakes his head. "I didn't think it would affect her so much. I just didn't want her messing around with someone else."

"Do you like her?" I ask, watching his expression.

He swirls his drink in his hand. "She's beautiful. She seems kind and like she'll make a good wife."

"But?" I ask.

"But I don't know her. She's 17. I feel like she's still a child, and yet everyone wants me to marry her and have kids with her. It feels... wrong," he says while looking up at the ceiling.

"I think you need to get to know her better. You met her when she was 16. She's about to be 18 and she's not a child anymore. She's smart and funny. I think once you spend more time with her, you'll view her differently," I say and then sigh.

Lo stares at me, studying me before speaking. "Are there any feelings there I should be concerned about?"

My heart skips a beat. "What?"

"Are you starting to have feelings for her?" he asks seriously.

"No, of course not. I'm just trying to help you see her differently," I say, trying to keep my cool.

I'm anything but cool at this moment. My heart is racing, and I feel like I'm sweating in 100-degree weather. What is wrong with me? I feel guilty when there's nothing to feel guilty about. Okay, I've had some thoughts about her, but I would never act on them. Lo's my brother. I'd never do that to him.

He nods. "Just making sure. You'd come to me if so, right? We'd figure something else out. You know you wouldn't be immune to what I'd have to do if you touched her. It would be worse for you. If you ran away, I'd have to find you, and you know I would."

"I'd expect nothing less," I say, while taking a sip of my drink.

Fuck, he knows. I know he knows. Somehow, he knows my thoughts, and this is his warning to me. I know he'd have to kill me. Would he actually do it, though? I'd like to think he wouldn't, but I wouldn't blame him if he did. I need to figure this out because I can't put him in that position.

This is the most awkward dinner I've ever had. Lo invited me to eat with Lauren and him to take the pressure off. Matteo was supposed to join us as well, but he's running late. Nico, our cousin, has been out of the country for months now. Nico and I aren't the best of friends, but right now I'd love to see his face. I'd love to see anything but this shit show going down in front of me.

After a whole five minutes of silence, Lo finally speaks. "So, tell me about your classes at school. What is your favorite?"

I watch as Lauren pushes the food around her plate. It doesn't look like she has taken more than two bites since dinner was served. She's taking a bit to respond, and I can tell that she's thinking of the best answer. It's a simple question, but she never speaks without thinking over her words.

"English," she states.

"What do you like about it?" Lo asks, trying to get her to elaborate.

She shrugs her shoulders. "I enjoy reading and living in another world. I like to put myself in the character's shoes."

"What's the most recent book you've read?" he asks.

She grins. "Romeo and Juliet."

"And you enjoyed it?"

"Sure. It was a good story. Tragic, but it was written well. I think it would be nice to have a love like that." She sighs.

I somehow choke on the water I'm drinking, and Lo glares at me. I clear my throat and try to contain my cough and continue shoving food into my mouth. Lo shifts uncomfortably, and I can see the smirk on Lauren's face, even though she's trying to hide it.

The front door slams and startles us all. Matteo noisily enters the dining room and takes the seat beside me. He fixes some food on his plate while apologizing for being late again.

Matteo shoves food in his mouth before saying, "So this must be the famous Lauren."

He holds out his hand for her to shake, and she stares at it for a moment before putting her hand in his. "I'm Matteo. Lorenzo's brother. I've heard a lot about you," he says.

Lauren scoffs. "I'm sure you've heard great things."

Matteo laughs. "Indeed. Lorenzo has failed to mention how beautiful you are. No wonder Tommaso was killed..." he looks over at me, "I hope you won't repeat his mistake."

Lauren drops her fork, and it makes a loud clanging noise on her plate. She looks pale.

"What do you mean, he was killed?" Lauren asks in a whisper.

"Matteo!" Lo says sternly.

"Whoops. And that's my cue," he says, grabbing his plate and leaving the room.

Lauren looks over at Lo, waiting for him to answer her question. It's silent for so long that I don't think he's going to answer. I'm not answering for him.

Lo clears his throat. "Tommaso made some comments that should have never been said. He wasn't trustworthy with keeping you safe anymore."

"So, you killed him," Lauren states rather than asking.

Lo nods.

I can see the gears turning in her head, but she doesn't say anything. Here I thought that dinner couldn't get any more awkward. Thanks Matteo.

CHAPTER ELEVEN

LAUREN

Lorenzo let me go home the next morning after I promised not to run away again. He has no stipulations on what I can and can't do, other than the obvious. I should be thankful, but it's hard to be.

Of course, my parents found out about my runaway attempt, so they are watching me like a hawk. Well, my mother is. My father is rarely home. She's mad at me for being so stupid. Her words, not mine. Though, I can agree with that. I should've planned my escape out better before attempting it, but I panicked.

I'm not sure what I'm going to do in the future. Right now, I feel defeated and like I need to accept my fate. I'm getting married to a mafia boss who kills people and does other illegal stuff that I have no idea about. I've thought of asking, but what's the point? It would just make me feel even worse being caught up in the middle of these illegal activities.

"Are you and Lorenzo doing anything for Valentine's Day tonight?" Ashley asks as she closes her locker.

"You're funny," I respond.

"Really? Has he even mentioned it? No flowers? Nothing?" she asks.

"Nope."

"Wow," she says under her breath.

"It's an arranged marriage, Ashley. It's not like he's the romantic type, anyway. He can get whatever he wants, when he wants," I say, but something sinks in my gut.

Lorenzo is handsome, but I'm not into him. It does hurt to think that I'll never have a true love and get to experience what it's like. It would be nice to have someone actually care about me, not because they have to, but because they love me. Getting flowers or even just a message that I'm on his mind.

I walk her to the door, but stay inside the school until she leaves, like always. I don't know why I don't want her to know about Romeo, but I don't. She thinks either my parents pick me up from school or that Lorenzo sends a driver. She has offered to take me home, but it's a good distance from her house, so I'm not going to do that to her.

I make my way out the door to find a group of girls standing on the stairs by the entrance. I have a class with a couple of them, and they are all the typical schoolgirls that go here. This is a rich school, and everyone who is here comes from money. Lorenzo insisted I go here, and because of that, he is paying for it.

"Oh, hey Lauren," one girl, Nina, says as she stops me.

I don't respond and just stare at her.

"Is your fiancé picking you up at school today with some romantic plans tonight?" she asks in a sarcastic tone.

I ignore her and continue walking, when another girl grabs my arm. I look back to see who it is, but I don't know her. She must be one of Nina's groupies.

"It's rude to ignore someone when they ask you a question," she says in her fake friendly voice.

I yank my arm out of her grasp. "It's rude to touch someone without their permission."

"Oh, so she can speak!" another girl that I don't know says.

What is happening right now? I've been mostly keeping to myself with Ashley. Why are they trying to start something with me when they don't even know me? I try to step around her, but the others step in my way. My nerves act up, and my heart races.

I don't comprehend the door opening behind me until a gentle hand lands on the small of my back.

"There you are. I need your help. If you ladies will excuse us," the male voice says from behind me as he pushes me past the girls and down the stairs.

He guides me around the corner near some trees before I realize it's Ben from my English class. I'm still shaking from the encounter. When I notice he has his hands on my shoulders, I take a step away. I don't want him to be caught touching me.

"Hey, don't let them bother you. They're just jealous," Ben says.

I give a small laugh. "Jealous? What is it they have to be jealous about?"

Ben lifts his eyebrow. "You're joking, right? Not only are you the new girl, but you're beautiful and smart. And, while I don't agree with them, they think you're lucky to land a rich fiancé and be set for life."

I look back and forth between his eyes to realize he's serious. That was really sweet of him to say all of that, but I can't help but laugh. It's probably the adrenaline wearing off, but I find it funny anyone would be jealous of my situation.

Ben smiles at me as his expression softens. He's cute too. He has short blond hair and piercing blue eyes. I've noticed that he's one of the most popular boys in the school, but he doesn't act like it. He's been nothing but nice to me. I still sit next to him in English where he shares his notes and knows what to say to make me feel better. He makes me wish I wasn't engaged because I would love to date someone like him. I've never dated anyone before.

"I appreciate your help, but I have to go. I owe you one," I say while patting his arm. I want to hug him, but I know better.

"You don't owe me anything. Seriously, just forget about them. They mean nothing," he says, calling after me.

I wave at him and head to Romeo's car, but realize it's empty the closer I get. I turn around to see Romeo following behind me. Crap, he must have seen everything that just happened with those girls and Ben. Did he see Ben touch me? Is he going to tell Lorenzo?

I open the passenger door and get in. Romeo slides into the driver's seat a few seconds later and starts the car. My heart is racing, not knowing what he's thinking. Should I say something to him? I don't want him to have the wrong impression of what happened and tell Lorenzo something.

"What happened?" Romeo asks, pulling me out of my thoughts.

"Nothing," I say too quickly.

He glances over at me and then back to the road. "Didn't look like nothing. You were upset."

I place my elbow on the door and rest my forehead on my hand. I close my eyes for a moment and take a deep breath. Lorenzo said he wanted to know when people weren't being nice. I should at least tell him about that because I don't want him to think I'm keeping secrets.

"They were just being typical mean girls. They were being sarcastic about my engagement and it being Valentine's Day. Nothing I can't handle," I say.

Romeo taps his finger on the steering wheel. "With the help of Benjamin Crawford?"

My head snaps in his direction as my hand falls to my lap. "How do you know Ben?"

"I know everyone in your life," he states.

"Ben was just being nice helping me. He's in my English class. He knows I'm engaged," I add quickly.

Romeo nods and keeps his eyes on the road. He doesn't say anything else, and I don't know if that means he believes me or not. He keeps the brief interactions we have professional, so I haven't figured him out yet. If this is going to be my life, I need to get to know the people in it more and the things they are involved in.

"What do you do for Lorenzo?" I spit out before I can chicken out.

He scratches his chin. "I'm his underboss."

"What is that? Like second in command?" I ask.

"Exactly," he states.

I think for a few moments. If that's the case, then what is he doing being my bodyguard? Wouldn't he have better things to do? Like threaten and kill people for Lorenzo?

"Why are you here with me? Don't you have better things to do?" I ask, studying him before he responds.

He glances at me for a moment and then back to the road again. "I have a lot of things that I should do, but Matteo has taken over while I'm watching you. Lorenzo doesn't trust anyone with you, so he assigned me to the role."

"I'm sure you were so happy about it," I say sarcastically.

He laughs. A genuine laugh, which I don't hear often. "I wasn't when he first told me about it, no."

"And now?" I ask.

"Now... I know why he doesn't trust anyone else to guard you, and thankfully, you make the job easy. At least, when you're not trying to run away," he says with a smirk.

"Why doesn't he trust anyone else to guard me?"

He's silent again for a moment, thinking over his response. Is it something I'm not going to like? Maybe I shouldn't have asked that.

"You're beautiful Lauren. I don't think many could resist the temptation, especially when they watch you 24/7."

I can feel myself blush. Did he really just say that? I've been called beautiful before, but I've never felt this way from someone saying it. Like when Ben said it, it felt nice, like coming from a friend, but when Romeo says it... I don't know how to explain how it feels, but it feels good.

"That was a kind compliment, but I doubt there's any temptation there. Boys don't pay attention to me like that." I fidget with the zipper on my jacket.

"Trust me... there is," Romeo says under his breath.

My breath hitches at his words, and I have nothing to respond with. Did he just mean what I think he meant? No, there's no way that I'm a temptation to him. He's freaking hot. The man could have a model for a girlfriend. Heck, he probably has had many models at the same time. There's no way he looks at me like that.

But what if he did? Sometimes I look at him like that. I've thought about what it would feel like to run my hands through his thick, long hair. To see what's under that shirt because when he's wearing short sleeves, you can see his muscles. To know what it feels like to kiss those thick lips of his. Ugh, it's so wrong to be thinking about another man when I'm engaged. And why do I feel this way about him? He's just as bad as Lorenzo, if not worse. Speaking of Lorenzo, are they related?

"Are you and Lorenzo related?" I ask, wanting to know everything all of a sudden.

"By blood, no. We are family, though. I consider him and Matteo my brothers," he says.

"Do you have any family? Other than Lorenzo's?" I keep the questions going.

"No. I don't know who my parents are and don't care to. Lo's father took me in when I was younger, and he treated me like his son. So as far as I'm concerned, they are my family."

It's weird thinking how these people who do horrible things can actually be... good. As much as I don't want to, maybe it's time I get to know Lorenzo a little better. Get to know his family better. First, though, I need to get to know my family better. I'm going to talk with my father and understand his involvement in everything going on here.

"Have you killed anyone before?" I ask, needing to hear it for myself.

"You already know that answer," he says.

"How many?" I ask, my voice shaking.

I know he has killed people. I know Lorenzo has killed people. To actually hear him say it, though, it's different. I don't know if I want to know the answer to my question, but I need to.

"I don't know. Too many," he states.

"You don't keep track?"

He sighs. "No, Lauren. I don't keep track. I don't particularly like killing people, but I don't have a choice. Everyone who dies at my hands deserves it. Trust me, the world is better off without them."

That doesn't make me feel better. "How do you do it? How do you kill someone knowing that there's someone being left behind that loves them?"

Romeo grips the steering wheel hard and clenches his jaw. Maybe I pushed him too far. I shouldn't have asked that. He doesn't answer my question, and we drive the rest of the way in silence.

CHAPTER TWELVE

LAUREN

The rest of Valentine's Day went exactly how I imagined. Radio silence from Lorenzo. He didn't even text me to acknowledge the day existed. I get it, he's busy and probably doesn't believe in Valentine's Day, but would it hurt to text your fiancé that you're thinking about her?

It's been two weeks since then, and I still haven't heard anything from him. I've been tempted to text him, but what would that accomplish? If he wants a relationship with me, then he's going to have to work at it. Maybe it would be best if we didn't speak. Maybe we could just live our lives happily and separately. My stomach sinks at the prospect of that. I don't want a loveless marriage.

A knock sounds on my bedroom door. "Come in!" I answer.

The door opens, and my father is on the other side. He's dressed nice, ready for work. Sometimes when I look in the mirror, I see him. We look so similar, or we did. I kept my black hair for now, but I'll probably dye it back soon. I don't know why I decided to keep it because I hate it.

"Ready?" he asks.

"Yeah, let's go," I say as I grab my purse from my desk and head out the door.

I officially decided I need to know everything about the life that I'm about to be thrown into and that starts with getting to know my family. I know my father is a scientist, but not much more than that.

We talked, and he agreed I should know if I want to. He explained to me that someone recruited him to work at a lab when he graduated from college. He thought it was great because it paid so well, but he didn't know that what he would do was illegal. By the time he found out, there was no going back. One thing led to another, and he ended up working for Lorenzo's family.

Apparently, he was approached by some others trying to take him for themselves. Lorenzo's uncle insisted a union between his nephew and me would ensure that they both get what they need. My family would be well taken care of financially, and I would be too. He promised me he tried to deny the request at first, but doing so made him seem disloyal. He didn't need to say what happens to those they don't think are loyal.

We arrive at a building that looks like a warehouse, which is not at all what I expected. In fact, there are a lot of people working inside and it looks legit. I suppose that's the goal. We get on the elevator and head down, which I didn't know you could do. Clearly, this is like a secret basement.

When the elevator stops, we step off and there are three guards with guns standing on opposite sides of the room in front of us. We walk up to the closest one and my father nods at him. The guard buzzes the door open as we enter. I don't know why, but I hold my breath and don't release it until we're through the door. My heart is racing.

When we enter the lab, the place is enormous. It's bright and everything is white, including the tile on the floor along with the walls and ceiling. There are glass looking cubicles in rows along the room. In the middle, there's a large desk with a couple of computer monitors on it. There's no one else here.

"This is where I work. Each cubicle has its own password protected code. The glass is also bulletproof. There's no way anyone is getting into these without the code," he says while bringing me closer to one.

"What if someone hacks your computer for them?" I ask.

"They can try all they want, but they won't find them on any computer. The codes are all in here," he says, pointing to his head.

"What if you're killed?" I ask.

I wince at what I just asked. The more appropriate way to ask would've been what if you died, but we all know that killed is more probable in this line of work.

"They are all written down and only one person knows where they are. I don't even know who has them or where," he says as he enters the code in one.

The door opens with a click and a swooshing noise. We step in, and he brings me closer to some vials.

"What are these?" I ask.

"These are some test drugs for a truth serum. It's not perfected yet, but it's getting there," he says while typing something on the small computer inside.

I look around and notice that every cubicle has a computer in it. This place is ridiculously fancy and secure. I can see why though if they are creating drugs like truth serums. It makes me wonder though.

"How do you test them?" I ask.

My father looks at me with a concerned face. Oh, no. That's all I need to know.

"Got it," I say.

I walk out of the cubicle and look around. There must be at least twenty-five cubicles, if not more. I wonder if this is the only floor of the lab. Where are all the workers? My dad can't be the only one that works here, right?

I stand in front of one that catches my attention. I look inside to find eight vials filled and under a little glass cube in the middle of it. The liquid inside looks blue. My father walks up behind me.

"What's that one?" I ask.

"Ah, that's one I've been perfecting for a while now. It's finally complete." He enters a code and leads me inside.

He lifts the glass cube and pulls out one vial, holding it out above me to see. "If someone takes this guy, their body will appear dead. It works so well that even technology can't detect the person is alive. Their skin will be cold, and they will look dead, but they're not."

I look at him oddly. "Why would anyone want to do that?"

"To fake their own death or someone else's, of course. Trust me, it can come in handy with criminals, especially those who have the law after them," he states, putting the vial back.

That makes sense. If they can pretend they're dead, then they can disappear, and the police will stop looking for them.

"It's risky though," he says while picking up a vial beside it that has green liquid in it. "You have to inject this one within twelve hours to revive the person. If you don't, then they really die. You'd be trusting whoever has it to do their job properly by getting your body to a safe place and then injecting it in time."

That's a big risk to take. You would have to be willing to die if you took that. It amazes me that my father created these. I knew he was smart, but this is next level. I can see why Lorenzo wants to ensure he stays loyal to him.

We leave that one and enter another across the room. This vial is clear, like most of the other ones.

"What do these do?" I ask as my father heads to the computer.

"This is a basic sedative. It will stay in their system for up to 24 hours, depending on how much is given," he says without looking back at me as he types.

Interesting. I'm curious about what every one of these drugs does, but I don't want to push my father or annoy him. We go through a few more, but I don't ask questions until we reach another one that catches my attention. The liquid is pink.

"What is this one? A love potion?" I chuckle.

"Good guess," he says.

"Wait, really?" I ask, not believing that's what it is.

He laughs. "Let's just say it'll make pretty much anyone look appealing if taken."

"So, would they fall for everyone or just the first person they see?" I ask.

"It probably has a couple of years before it's perfected, but the end result is that the attraction will be to only one person," he answers and continues to type on the computer.

We step outside the cubicle, and he locks it, just like he did with all the others. "So, is that all that's inside this lab? Drugs you're creating like these?"

"No. Well, this floor, yes. We have another floor dedicated to the usual drugs that you get on the streets. I mostly work up here, though," he explains.

"How much do you get paid?" I ask curiously.

"Let's just say that if I was allowed to retire today, I would have enough money to support you and Brandon without either of you working a day in your life," he smiles.

That's insane. I understand how he got roped up in all this with the promise of money, but I'm still not over the fact he sold me to Lorenzo. I know he didn't know this would happen when he took the job, but it still doesn't make it any better.

My father continued showing me around his lab and the one below. While what he is doing is illegal, it was cool seeing what he does. He needs to stay to finish up some work, so Romeo is driving me home.

"Have you been in that lab before?" I ask Romeo as he drives us home.

"Yeah, I have to make visits now and then to ensure everything is running smoothly," he says.

"I suppose that's Matteo's job now?"

"I suppose it is," he replies coolly.

I have a feeling that he's still not pleased about being my bodyguard. He doesn't say anything about it or act that way, but who would want this job? He seems to take it seriously, though. He never lets me leave the house without him, and he's always carrying multiple weapons at any given time.

He also seems to care about me on some level. Last week, he spent some time teaching me about gun safety and how to use one. He spent more than enough time on how to take the safety off a gun. I think he was doing it to make fun of me, but he did it so professionally that I'll never know for sure.

The more time we spend together, the more I want to know about him. As much as I don't want to, I consider him a friend. I feel safe with him, and I feel I can trust him. I may have also had a dream or two or ten about him. Dreams that should be about Lorenzo, not him.

We're ten minutes from home, and I really don't want to go back to the house to do nothing. I could call Ashley to hang out with her again, but I just don't want to leave Romeo's side yet.

"Can we go somewhere else?" I break the silence, asking.

"Where?" he asks.

I shrug my shoulders. "I don't care. Just somewhere quiet. I don't want to go home right now."

He doesn't respond, but I notice him take a different turn than the one that leads us home. I don't question where we're going because I literally just told him I didn't care where we went. Looking out the window, I try to recognize the roads we're on, but I don't. I don't think I've ever been to this area before. It seems like we're heading into the middle of nowhere.

After another ten minutes, he pulls the car into a dirt parking lot. There's nothing around for miles, just trees and what looks like a hiking trail. Are we going on a hike? I wouldn't mind, but I don't think I'm dressed for that. It's cold, and I don't have the right shoes. I guess we'll see how this plays out.

Romeo gets out of the car, rounds it, and opens my door. "Come on."

I step out and stay by his side as I follow him down the walking trail. It's currently 38 degrees, which isn't horrible, but it's still cold. Thankfully, I dressed warmly and have on my heavy winter coat. I forgot my gloves at home, though.

We don't walk far before he veers off the path and leads me through some thick trees. My heart rate picks up when I consider what we might do out here. Is he leading me somewhere to murder me? No, of course not. He's my bodyguard. Why would he murder me?

I continue looking around as we pass through the trees, and I get hit with a branch every now and then. Okay, he might not be leading me out here to murder me, but has he come out here before to bury a body? This looks like an area where someone could easily bury a body and get away with it.

I look toward the ground in the distance to see if there might be any signs that the ground has been dug up. If someone recently buried a body, there would be signs, right? Like there would be a pile of dirt. There are a lot of leaves though, but I feel like the leaves would be disturbed, unless when burying the body he was smart enough to put leaves back over the hole.

Before I know what's happening, my foot gets caught on something, and I'm falling to the ground. I feel an arm wrap around my waist and yank me back to my feet, but my back hits something hard. When I catch my breath, I realize my back is steadied against a tree and Romeo's body is pressing on the front of mine. I'm pinned between him and the tree.

He's so much taller than me, but he's hunched over with his face only inches from mine and one hand is on my hip. His other is flat on the tree as he leans closer to me. I stare into his green eyes, which are currently narrowed and dark. I'm not breathing again as I study his expression, which is unreadable.

Staring at his thick parted lips, I once again want to close the space between us. Butterflies flutter in my stomach the longer we stand here together. I'm tempted to make the dreams I've been having at night a reality.

Screw it, what's the worst that could happen? I lean forward to close the gap, but Romeo clears his throat and takes a step back. My heart sinks as he retreats.

"Are you alright?" he asks, letting his hand drop from my waist.

"Fine," I state.

He nods and steps back further to continue our walk to wherever we're going. I take a deep breath and shake my head. What the hell was I thinking? Was I really about to kiss him? That would probably be the worst mistake of my life. I'm engaged to Lorenzo! He's about to be basically my brother-in-law! What was I thinking?!

I continue to beat myself up for the rest of the walk until we reach a small cabin. Romeo takes out a key from his pocket and unlocks the door. He pushes it open, and we both enter.

"Where are we?" I ask as I step through the doorway.

"This is a place I like to go when I need some time to think," he states.

Wow. He took me to his special place? Why would he do that?

He walks in further and turns on a lantern. He then proceeds to the fireplace and begins lighting the firewood inside. I look around and notice that it's just as small inside as it looks outside.

It's just one large room. There's what looks like a twin-sized bed on the wall to the right and a small end table. A loveseat sits in front of the fireplace with a brown furry rug on the floor. There's a small kitchen area with a little table, but it doesn't look like there's a fridge or stove or anything. I'm assuming there's no electricity or running water in this place.

When he finishes lighting the fire, the whole cabin lights up. It wasn't really dark to begin with since it's still daytime, but it's now easier to see. I can't help but eye the blanket on the couch, as it's chilly here. Would he mind if I made myself comfortable there?

"Take a seat," he says, gesturing toward the sofa.

He doesn't have to tell me twice. I sit down and grab the blanket off the back of the couch, curling up with it. It's soft and warm. Add the warmth of the fire and crackling sounds it's making, and I could easily fall asleep. Staring at the fire, deep in thought, Romeo moves around the cabin. I don't know why he brought me here, but I'm thankful because it's exactly what I asked for, quiet.

CHAPTER THIRTEEN

ROMEO

I lean against the wall of the cabin as I stare at Lauren sitting on the couch, curled up under a blanket. I rub my face with my hands as I try to think, why the fuck did I bring her here? This is my safe space. It's somewhere I come when I need to get away from everything and everyone. Lo is the only one that knows about it, and that's for safety reasons. Well, now Lauren knows too.

The way she asked if we could go somewhere in the car told me she needed an escape. When she said she didn't care where, this was the first place that came to my mind. She didn't seem like she wanted to be around other people or out in the open. She needed a safe space where no one knew where she was. I could feel it. So that's why I didn't hesitate to drive here.

Then there was the moment in the woods when she almost fell on her face. After catching her and pushing her against the tree, I almost lost it. I did lose it. I was about to kiss her, or worse. I wanted to take her up against that tree. Thankfully, I came to my senses when she leaned in to kiss me. It doesn't help knowing that she feels something between us too. I can't stop thinking about her. I see her every damn day during my waking hours and every damn night while I sleep. She's everywhere and the only thing I can think about.

My job is simple. I'm supposed to protect her. She's Lo's fiancé. There were never supposed to be feelings for her. I was never supposed to have feelings for any woman, ever. I've had my fun with women, but I've felt nothing for any of them. Women complicate things in our world, that's something all of us agree on. Lo, Matteo, Nico, and I have always said we would never fall in love and let a woman complicate what we have, and so far, we haven't.

Even though Lo is getting married, we all know he would rather not. It's an arranged marriage to ensure we keep what we have, which is Lauren's father. He definitely doesn't have feelings for her. Hell, he hardly ever talks to her. The idiot didn't even say a word to her on Valentine's Day. I was about to call him to give him some advice on that, so Lauren didn't feel like shit, but I was selfish. I didn't want him to do anything for her. Honestly, I don't know how he couldn't fall in love with her because she's perfect.

As I continue to stare at her, I can feel the tension in the room. She's been watching the fire to avoid looking at me. Taking a deep breath, I grab an axe from the cabinet. I can't stay here any longer. I need some fresh air.

"I'm going to get us some more firewood. I'll be right back," I say as I open the front door.

She says nothing, but I see her nod as she continues to stare at the fire. What I wouldn't give to know what she is thinking right now. No. I don't need to know what she's thinking. I need to get her out of my thoughts.

Rounding the cabin, I begin chopping wood. I already have a large pile against the house that can be used, but I need to take my energy out with this axe. I need to get my mind off her.

After about ten minutes of chopping wood, my phone rings.

"Yeah?" I answer on the second ring without looking at the caller-ID.

"How's everything going?" Lo asks.

"Good," I state, straightening at his voice.

There's a long silence on his end. What did he call for?

"Where are you?" he asks.

Seriously? We haven't talked in a while, and this is the time he has to be checking in on me? I mean, I text him every day with an update, but that's about it.

"I'm at the cabin," I state.

"I know. What are you doing there?"

Of course he knows, and I bet he knows Lauren is here, too. I'm sure he looked at both of our locations. There's no use lying to him. There's nothing going on between Lauren and me, so there's nothing of concern.

"Lauren didn't want to go home. She seemed like she just needed some... space," I say.

"Why?"

I laugh involuntarily and quickly state, "I think she just needs some time to figure things out. She's been asking a lot of questions about you and what we do. She just visited the lab with her father and is finding out what he does for a living. It's a lot to take in."

"What type of questions is she asking?" he asks.

"Things like what my role is and what we do. She wanted to know about our family and relationship. How many people we've killed, you know, the typical stuff," I state casually.

Lo laughs. "So, it sounds like she's curious. Why doesn't she ask me?"

I think for a moment about the best way to answer this. "I think you intimidate her, and she doesn't think you care about her."

"I told her I care. Why would she think that?"

I shake my head, knowing he can't see it. "Lo, actions speak louder than words. You haven't spoken to her in weeks. You didn't even say hi on Valentine's Day..."

Lo interrupts, "I don't do Valentine's Day."

"Yeah, I know, but she doesn't."

He's silent again before saying, "*Cazzo*. Why is this so hard? Was she upset about it? Why didn't you tell me?"

I sigh. "She didn't seem upset, but we don't talk much or share feelings. I do my job to drive her around, watch her, protect her, and answer questions about how many bodies we bury. I'm not her therapist."

"Thanks Romeo," Lo says sarcastically.

"Anytime brother. Anything else I can do for you?" I ask.

"No... Just let me know when she makes it home," he says and hangs up the phone.

Well, goodbye to you too, brother. I shove the phone back in my pocket and pick up where I left off chopping the wood and clearing my head.

I walk back into the cabin with some firewood to find Lauren sleeping on the couch. She's curled up on one side, so I decide to sit on the other side after checking to make sure everything is secure. No one has ever found this place before, but you can never be too safe. Especially if someone was following us without my noticing.

I sit on the couch and go through some emails on my phone. I only get a chance to respond to one from Matteo before she stirs beside me.

"Why did you bring me here?" she asks sleepily.

I think for a moment before answering. "I figured you just needed someplace away from everyone to think."

"Well, it's not away from everyone since you're here," she says.

"Would you prefer I wasn't here?" I ask, trying to hide the tightness in my chest that the comment just made.

She sits up and scoots closer to me, putting her hand on my leg. "No, I want you here."

I stiffen at her words, and I hold my breath. I'm trying not to think about how her hand currently feels on my leg and her close proximity to me. We can't do this. Lo trusts me with her, and she's his. It doesn't help that she's so beautiful and smart. Plus, she obeys so well that I can't help but wonder what that would look like in the bedroom.

I clear my throat and ignore everything I'm feeling. "We can stay as long as you want or if you're ready, we can go get dinner and head home."

She removes her hand from my leg and sits up straighter. "I'd like to stay for a bit if that's okay."

I nod and slouch back onto the couch, staring into the fire. She places her back against the armrest and brings her knees up to her chest so she's facing me. Angling my body toward hers, I can tell she wants to talk. I'm not much of a talker, and I don't do emotions, but something is different with her. I could sit and talk to her all day, or more so, listen to her.

"I want to know more about your world, about what you and Lorenzo do," she says, looking at me intently.

Sighing, I say, "I'm not sure that's something I should tell you. You need to talk to him for those answers."

"Why?" she asks.

"I don't know how much I should tell you or how much you should know," I state.

Honestly, I don't think Lo would hold back any information from her. He might hold back the gory details, but I don't think he'll have a problem with her knowing. She needs to be having this conversation with him, not me. As much as I want to talk with her, I know I shouldn't. Neither of us needs to feed into whatever feelings we have for each other.

"I don't want to talk to him. I want to talk to you," she says.

Well shit. That's not helping. This was a mistake. What was I thinking, bringing her to this cabin and being alone with her? Clearly, I wasn't thinking. I need to stop my stupidity and start pushing her to spend more time with Lo.

"Lauren... I can't," I say.

She stands up quickly and folds the blanket back over the couch. "Sorry, you're right. I'm ready to go."

I stand. "Are you sure?"

She nods without looking at me. "Yeah. We need to go. You can just bring me home."

I don't understand the sudden shift, but it's for the best. After putting out the fire, I grab both of our jackets by the front door. I hand her jacket to her and shrug on my own, holding the door open for her to exit first. As we leave the cabin, I prepare to leave all feelings for her here.

Chapter Fourteen

LAUREN

The rest of my junior year and most of the summer vacation flew by uneventfully. None of the girls bothered me again, and I'm assuming that's Lorenzo's doing. Ashley and I kept to ourselves, though occasionally we hung out with Ben at school. He is super sweet, but I did my best to keep my distance there. Ashley has a crush on him, even though he had a girlfriend which I had no idea about. Unfortunately, she just broke up with him at the end of the year, and I could tell his heart was broken. He's a sweet guy. I don't know why anyone would break up with him.

Regardless, staying to myself is the best course of action. Lorenzo and I have been on many more dates, and I'm really trying with him. He answered all the questions I had about his business and what he does. The honesty was refreshing, but the answers not so much.

From what I could understand, they basically run New York. They have so many police and government officials in their pockets, it's not even funny. They own clubs and restaurants to make all the money they earn look legit. They aren't the only ones that want to run the city, though. Apparently, there are quite a few others that they consider enemies that would be happy for Lorenzo to be dead, and by proxy, me.

Regardless, I've come to terms with there being nothing I can do about this arranged marriage. Lorenzo doesn't seem to mind that I want to keep to myself. Like I said, we've been on more dates, but there is nothing romantic about them. He has bought me flowers, books, and other random things the past few months, but nothing that really means anything. I feel like he's just going through the motions because he thinks it'll make me happy.

He doesn't know my favorite color or what type of pet I would want in the future. He doesn't know what television shows I watch or who I talk to when I'm upset about something. He doesn't know my favorite store or restaurant. He doesn't really know me, but I can tell you who does. Romeo.

Romeo knows everything about me, and he knows how to make me feel better when I'm down, which is often. He's been keeping his distance from me and trying to push me toward Lorenzo. I know he tells Lorenzo when to bring my favorite flowers or to send a new book from a series that I love that just came out. He doesn't think I notice him watching me, but I do. It's tragic really. We both have feelings for each other, and yet there is nothing we can do about it other than try to ignore them, which is getting harder by the day.

"Got them," Ashley says, walking into my bedroom with a box in her hand.

"Finally," I state, getting settled on my bed with her doing the same.

She opens the box and pulls out two joints. Her brother, Dillon, is home for the summer, so he usually has a rather large stash of them when he is. She convinced him to let her have a few. He's an amazing brother and always looking out for her. He always wants to make sure she's safe, but he finally gave in on letting us have these.

She lights the first one, handing it to me. I place it to my lips and suck in, inhaling the smoke. When I exhale, I go to hand it to her, but she has already lit another. I guess we're having our own tonight.

"We're going out tomorrow," Ashley says.

"We are?" I ask.

She knows I don't like to go out. My parents have been a little more in my business since my runaway attempt, and it's just easier to stay in. Ashley and I hang out sometimes, but it's usually at my house. It's just easier to avoid having Romeo out, too. I feel like the more he's around, the better chance Ashley may catch him. I don't know why, but I still don't want anyone to know about him.

"Everly invited us to go to the mall and hang out with her," she says while pulling out a bottle of vodka from nowhere.

"Where the heck did you get that?" I ask, laughing.

She smirks. "I stole it from my parents."

She pulls out two shot glasses from her bag and pours the vodka. I guess we're going to have drugs and alcohol tonight. Honestly, I'm down for it. It's summer, and what do I have to lose?

"Anyway, you're good to come tomorrow?" she asks, changing the topic back to going out with Everly.

"I don't know..." I say.

"Do you not like her?" she asks.

I met Everly at a party that Ashley's brother threw a few weeks ago. She seems nice enough and down to earth. She's completely rich, which isn't unexpected for someone that will attend our school. Apparently, she moved from Boston and is living with the Crawfords, which is Ben's family. During the party, she was dating Ben's best friend, Jake. I had a class with him last year and he's funny, but he's a player. He sleeps around. I'm pretty sure they broke up once Everly caught him flirting with another girl at the party. She left crying, so I didn't get much of a chance to interact with her.

"She seems nice," I say because there really isn't anything about her I didn't like.

"She is. We had coffee the other day. I think it would be good for her to have friends before school starts, since she's new," she says, knowing exactly what to say to get me to say yes.

"Alright, alright, fine. I'll go."

Ashley does a little squeal and hugs me. I laugh because she's clearly already high. We take a shot of the vodka, knowing full well we don't need it, but I know it'll make a fun night.

It is not making for a fun night. Ashley started feeling sick after her fourth shot and went to bed. I only had three shots and one joint. Thankfully, I'm not feeling sick, but I'm feeling really antsy and in my head.

My parents aren't home right now, and I'm pretty sure my brother is staying over at some random girl's house tonight. Brandon came home for the summer hoping to convince my parents again not to marry me off. Spoiler alert, it hasn't worked.

I don't want to wake Ashley, so I'm currently pacing around the living room. My heart is racing, and I feel like I'm going to crawl out of my skin. Maybe mixing alcohol and drugs wasn't the best idea.

I force myself to sit on the couch, hoping that will help. I rub my face and groan. Ugh. I can't stop thinking about Romeo. He has been so distant lately, but I know he's feeding Lorenzo all this information about me. He notices the small stuff, and it's killing me because I know he cares about me.

I keep thinking about the time he brought me to his cabin, and we almost kissed against that tree. Something changed that day between us. I think we both realized that we had feelings for each other, but knew we couldn't act on them. I've been doing my best to not think about him too, but he makes it impossible.

He's so ridiculously hot with that stupid long hair of his and those eyes. I can't get those green eyes out of my head.

Sometimes when we're out, which isn't too often, he gives me gentle touches. I get up off the couch and start pacing again with my hands behind my back. I think about when he places his hand on my lower back to lead me somewhere. When he leans over me to grab something or when he opens the car door for me. One time I caught him absentmindedly holding his hand out for me to take, but he quickly pulled it away.

I don't know what to do. I know it's wrong to want Lorenzo's brother, but I do. Is there a way I can convince him to let me marry Romeo instead? I know they aren't really family, but it's close enough, right? Why does it have to be Lorenzo that I marry? I need to do something because I'm going crazy.

My phone buzzes on the coffee table, and it makes me jump. I look down to find a text from Romeo.

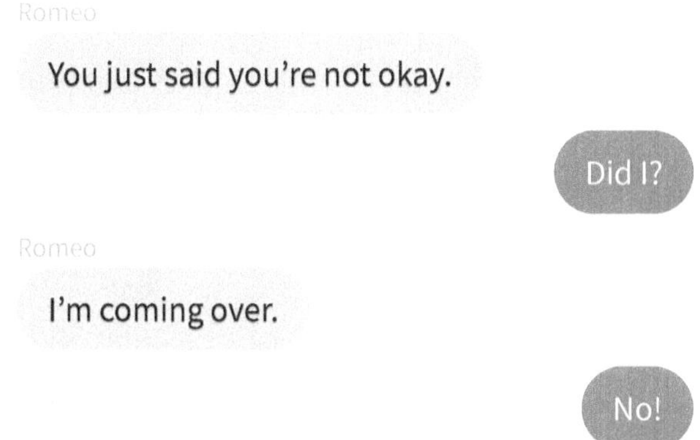

There's no response. Crap! He can't come over when Ashley is here! I know she's asleep in my room, but she could wake up any minute and find us together. I don't want to explain to her about Romeo being my bodyguard and then how I'm in love with him and not Lorenzo. Oh my God! Did I just say I'm in love with him? I can't be in love with him. I barely know him!

Before I can think about that further, Romeo walks into the room in a t-shirt and sweatpants. I've never seen him not wearing jeans and some sort of polo shirt. Ugh, what is he trying to do to me?

He comes over and places his hands on my shoulders. "What's wrong?"

I can feel myself shaking below his hands. I only respond by shaking my head.

He looks back and forth between my eyes, studying me for a moment. "Have you been doing drugs?"

I swear I see a smirk tug at his lips, but he has concern in his eyes, too. There aren't any cameras in my bedroom, so I know I could lie if I wanted to. I mean, I don't think the lie would do me any good. Clearly, he figured it out just by looking at me. I'm a mess, and I know it.

"Yeah," I say nonchalantly.

"What did you take?" he asks.

"It was just some weed and three shots of vodka."

He sighs. "You mixed alcohol and drugs? Why?"

I shrug my shoulders.

"What's going on Lauren?" he asks, concerned.

Why did I do it? Why did Ashley? I don't know. I just feel like I have nothing to lose at this point in my life. I'm getting freaking married soon, and I don't have control over who it is to or when. Drugs are probably the only thing that's going to get me through this future that has been laid out for me. Thankfully, Lorenzo seems to be in the business of dealing with drugs. So, it shouldn't be a problem for me to get them.

"Lauren," he says, bringing me back to his question.

"I don't know, Romeo. I don't know. I just... I don't want to marry Lorenzo. I don't want this life. I want my life back," I say.

He looks at me with pity in his eyes. He doesn't say anything as he leads me back to the couch and keeps his hand on my shoulder as we sit. Oddly, I don't feel as antsy anymore and don't need to pace the room. I'm comfortable here with him.

"Drugs are not the way to do it, Lauren. Don't use them as an escape. It doesn't work," he says like he's had experience.

"Why do I have to marry him?" I ask, but it's not really a question I intend for him to answer.

"You know why Lauren," he says.

"I mean... why him? If it's just an alliance to form with your family, why can't it be someone else in your family?" I ask, trying not to indicate that I mean him.

"Because Lorenzo's the don and single. He's going to have to be the one to get married. He needs heirs. It's all about appearances. It's stupid, but it is what it is," he says.

"But what if I'm in love with someone else? Say... his brother. Would that mean nothing?" I ask, grasping at straws.

Romeo's breath hitches as he looks in my eyes. "Are you in love with someone else?"

I hesitate before responding, which I know is a mistake. "It's just a what if scenario."

Romeo takes his hand away from my shoulder and rubs it through his hair. "No, Lauren. It doesn't matter if you're in love with his brother or if his brother loved you back. Don't say things like that anymore, okay? It would get someone killed and you most likely locked up. Just... try to love him."

Wait, what does that mean? He said if his brother loved you back. Does that mean? No, definitely not. He's just playing into my what if scenario. He's right though. I can't be talking like this. I'm lucky it's Romeo because he won't do anything about this or tell Lorenzo.

"You're right, I'm sorry. I just... I don't know. I shouldn't have drunk so much," I say, trying to stand up.

Stumbling forward, Romeo catches me. I'm inches from his face... again! I want nothing more than to lean the extra few inches to close the gap, but I know I shouldn't. Even in my drunken high state, I know better. It would be a mistake.

He clears his throat and pushes back further. "Drink a glass of water and head to bed, Lauren. You'll feel better in the morning."

I know I'm blushing, and I nod. "Okay. Yeah. Ashley and I are going to the mall tomorrow with Everly. Her security guards are going to pick us up. Is that okay?"

He turns around and heads toward the doorway. "Yeah, that's fine. I'll follow behind discreetly."

I don't say anything as I walk away toward the kitchen to get some water. I grab a glass for Ashley too for when she wakes up. After heading upstairs, I lay back down in bed next to Ashley, trying to forget about Romeo and everything for just one night.

Chapter Fifteen

Romeo

I follow behind the SUV that Everly's security team is driving. I'm trying to be as discreet as possible because I know Lauren doesn't want anyone to know about me. I still don't understand why, especially now that she has a friend with her own security. She would understand more than anyone, but if it's what Lauren wants, then I'm going to respect her wishes as much as I can.

I almost lost it last night when I was talking with Lauren. I know she was wasted, but when she brought up loving Lo's brother, I wanted to throw her down on the couch and take her right there. Who am I kidding? I haven't almost lost it... I have lost it. All my hard work the past few months has been thrown out the window by three little words. She fucking loves me.

Why does she love me? I've been so careful to make sure she doesn't know I'm the one behind Lo's thoughtful gifts and date plans. It's been hard watching him give her everything that I want to and taking her out to places I would love to take her.

I never thought I could be jealous before, but here I am. I'm jealous of my fucking brother and his fiancé. I want her to be mine, and yet, she's his and there's nothing that will ever change that.

She's clearly been feeling the same way and has been trying to think of ways around her marriage with Lo. She was obviously thinking about seeing if there was a way to marry me instead. A year ago, I would've laughed at getting married, but last night... Fuck. When I got back to the house, I couldn't stop thinking about it. I couldn't stop thinking about what it would be like to marry Lauren. To have her as mine.

This is a problem, but I'm in too deep now. If I were smart, I would go tell Lo that I'm having feelings for Lauren, and he would replace me with Matteo or Nico. Fucking Nico. There's no way I can have him watching over her. I'd rather die than allow that. And Matteo... Damn it, he wouldn't do anything, but I can't let him watch her. He's just not mature enough, and I wouldn't trust her life with him. Hell, I wouldn't trust her life with anyone. I don't even trust Lo with her at this point. I need to be the one to protect her.

We pull up to the mall, and I follow them inside at a distance. I watch Everly's two guards closely, Barry and Declan. Neither of them has appeared to notice me yet, which is not a good thing. I've been keeping my distance, but anyone with training should've noticed me by now. We'll see what happens when we get inside.

I had Matteo run some background information on these guys. On paper, they seem to be the best of the best. I needed to know what I was up against in case they thought me to be a threat. Apparently, Everly has a few more guards on rotation as well. Honestly, with who her father has gotten involved with in the past, it's not a bad idea. It may seem excessive, but it's smart.

That's another thing we were concerned about with Lauren becoming friends with Everly. Everly's father and boss aren't working with us, which automatically makes them a threat. Thankfully, who they are working with aren't necessarily rivals of ours at the moment, but still.

The girls head into a dress shop while Declan and Barry have a quick chat at the entrance of the store. Barry heads inside while Declan stands watch at the entrance. I notice his hand sliding to his gun as I get closer. Ah, so he has noticed me.

As much as I want to hold my own gun, it would be considered a threat, and that's not my intention here. We need to get through these formalities so we can stay out of each other's way. I walk up slowly beside him and don't make eye contact as I step to his side. His body tenses, waiting for me to make the first move.

"I'm here to watch Lauren. It has nothing to do with Everly," I say.

"Elaborate," he grunts.

"Lauren is marrying my brother, Lorenzo. I'm on duty to keep her safe," I state.

He glances at me and then back toward where the girls are looking at dresses. "You're Matteo?"

"No. Romeo. Not brothers by blood, but they're my brothers, nonetheless."

"Yeah, I know. Alright, so there won't be any problems between us," he states because there's no need to question that.

"None, but Lauren doesn't want anyone to know about me, and I intend to keep it that way."

"Noted," he states.

I nod and walk off to put some distance between us, but not too far so that I won't be able to see her. You would think that with two more guards, I'd be a little more relaxed, but I'm not. I'm on higher alert. There are many people that would want Lauren dead, but probably two times that amount that would want to hurt Everly. Lauren could easily be caught in the crossfire. I'm not a fan of this friendship, but I'm not going to tell her who she can and can't hang out with. Her future is already decided for her. She doesn't need someone telling her who can be in her life.

The girls finish their dress shopping and decide to head to a restaurant. As I follow, I notice two familiar boys walking up to them. Benajmin Crawford and Jacob Hale. Both attend the same high school. I've made it my business to know almost everyone in that high school, but these two are on top of that list since Benjamin, or as she calls him, Ben, spent a little time with her last year.

Jacob is his best friend, and he also had a class with Lauren. I never saw them outside of school together, so I don't think they really became friends. I wonder if she knew they would be here today. As I walk a little closer, I can safely say that she didn't. She looks uncomfortable. Lo terrified her when it came to talking to and hanging around other boys. He made it clear what would happen if anyone touched her.

They all head inside, and I grab a table a few down from theirs. Lauren hasn't said a word and looks like she's going to be sick. Is she really that uncomfortable hanging around with them or is it something else?

She excuses herself from the table and heads toward the bathroom. I quickly follow her to see that she veers left to go out the back door. I catch it before it closes and come up behind her. She turns like she knew I would be there, following her.

"I didn't know they would be here. None of us did. It was a coincidence," she blurts.

I walk closer to her, and she backs up toward the wall of the restaurant. "What are you so scared of?"

Her eyes widen as she notices our close proximity. I have no idea what I'm doing, but I can't seem to stop myself.

"I... I just don't want them to get hurt. I'm trying to stay away from all boys, so Lorenzo doesn't get the wrong idea," she says with her voice low.

I continue to step forward until her back is against the wall. She looks so fucking cute when she's nervous. I don't know what's wrong with me, but what she said last night really got to me. Does she really fucking love me?

"So, what about me? I'm a boy. Are you afraid he's going to hurt me?" I ask.

Her eyes widen again as I lean even closer. "Why... why would he hurt you? You're my bodyguard. There's nothing between us."

She says it with such conviction. If I didn't know differently, I would believe her. But I know. I know how she feels about me. She knows how I feel about her.

"Nothing?" I ask, with my lips just above hers.

"Nothing," she states.

"Are you sure?" I ask.

My lips barely brush over hers, and both of our breaths hitch. We're staring into each other's eyes, waiting to see who's going to break first. It's not going to be me. It can't fucking be me.

It's not me. She breaks the last centimeter between us and smashes her lips into mine. She grabs the back of my head and pulls my lips against hers even harder. I place my hand on her hip and my other arm is still above her head on the wall, helping me keep my balance.

She moans in my mouth, and I lose all control. I grab her ass and lift her off the ground as her legs wrap around my waist and her back steadies against the wall. My erection is digging into her, and she grinds against me. Fuck. I want nothing more than to rip off her clothes and screw her right here.

With one hand still in my hair, the other pushes my shirt up as she runs her hand over my abs. She moans in appreciation as we continue to make out, and I fight every urge that I have to rip off her shirt. A car backfires in the distance. We quickly part, and I set her down on her feet, backing away from her. We stare at each other for a moment as I rub my hand through my hair and down my face. Fuck.

I say nothing as I walk away toward the corner of the building. Hearing the back door open, I glance back to see her friend, Everly, coming out and Lauren heading in her direction. I continue to round the building to remain unnoticed and head back inside through the front entrance to find Lauren sitting back with her friends.

I watch as they laugh and enjoy their slices of cheesecake. Lauren is barely concentrating on her friends, and I can tell she's thinking about what just happened in the back of this building. She glances at me every now and then with her cheeks blushing. Fuck. What did I just do?

Chapter Sixteen

Lauren

What did I just do?! Did I really just make out with Romeo? My bodyguard, who is entrusted to keep me safe for my fiancé, Lorenzo? Oh my God, I just made out with someone who isn't my fiancé. I just had my first kiss with someone who isn't my fiancé! What did I do?!

Ashley and Everly wanted to go to a bookstore after eating, and I gladly agreed. There's no way that I can face Romeo right now. I don't know what we are supposed to do now. Is he going as crazy as I am?

As we walk through the bookstore, I grab a random book and sit in the corner with some comfortable chairs. I need a moment to compose myself. I curl up on the chair and pretend to read while I have a mini panic attack.

Okay, it's not as bad as it seems. I mean, I kissed Romeo, but we can pretend it didn't happen, right? Clearly, I have feelings for him, but I'm sure he barely has any for me. I'm the one that kissed him, not the other way around. Though he had me pressed up against that wall and placed his lips right above mine, like he was begging me to do it. Like he knew he couldn't be the one to initiate it and wanted me to so badly.

No, I can't think like that. We're going to have to pretend none of this happened... right? I mean, he made it clear that there is no way out of this marriage with Lorenzo. Even if there was, he wouldn't want me like that. It's probably just one of those things where guys like to chase what's off-limits to them, and I'm the most off-limits Romeo can get. Not only do I have a fiancé, but I'm engaged to his brother, the don. You can't get any more off-limits than that.

"What on earth are you reading?" Ashley asks, plucking the book out of my hands.

"What?" I ask innocently.

I can't answer her question because I have no idea what I'm reading. I didn't even look at the title. I literally just grabbed a book and sat down so I could have my mini freak out alone.

"I didn't think you were into erotica," she states, looking at me with her eyebrows raised.

I cough. Seriously? I grab the book back from her and read the description. Oh my God. I picked up a book about bondage and crap. Wow! I couldn't have picked up a non-fiction book or something boring?

"Well... I figured I need to do some research for when I'm married to Lorenzo," I state, like I really mean it.

"Is… is he into this stuff? Wait, don't tell me. I don't want to know this. Alright, I'll buy you this one," she says, adding it to her basket of books.

"What? No! I don't need that book," I say, getting off the chair and trying to reach for it.

"Nope, consider it one of my wedding presents. Everly's ready to go, come on," she says as she heads toward the register.

There's no use fighting her. At least the book will fit in my purse, so no one will see me with it and the cover isn't telling for what it is. Then again, if it was, then I wouldn't have picked it up in the first place.

After this eventful day, Everly's security team drives us back home, and Ashley leaves my house shortly after gathering her stuff. I decide to take a quick shower to clear my mind. Romeo hasn't texted me or said anything yet about what happened, so maybe he's just going to pretend it didn't. We can do that, right? Pretend it never happened?

No, no, we can't. I couldn't stop thinking about that kiss the entire time I was in the shower. I could feel the tension building between my legs, and I needed to stop thinking about it because I wanted to do a lot more with Romeo than kiss him.

I've read some books that describe in a little detail what happens between the sheets, and I've seen it in movies too, of course, but I've never watched porn or anything. I haven't had "the talk" with my mother, so all my knowledge comes from my old friends, health class, and the few internet searches I've done.

I lay in bed with just my white robe on because I'm too lazy to change into pajamas. Out of curiosity, I grab the book that Ashley bought me. She asked if Lorenzo was into that stuff, and now it got me curious. What if he was into this type of stuff? What is this type of stuff, anyway?

I flip through the pages to find a random sex scene. My eyes widen at what I'm reading. Do... do people really do this?! I continue to read as the scene unfolds. The girl has her wrists tied up to the headboard and her ankles are bound by a... bar? She continues to move around on the bed which widens the bar, keeping her legs further apart. The man climbs on top of her and begins licking all the way down her breasts, stomach, and gets to her... Okay, wow.

I find myself opening my robe and moving my hand down my own body, in the path the guy in the book is taking. I've never touched myself before, but after Romeo's kiss, there's an ache that I just can't get rid of. Maybe if I...

The door to my bedroom flies open and it closes as I sit up quickly, closing my robe. Romeo stands in the doorway, staring at me. His mouth is open, and he narrows his eyes at me.

"What are you doing?!" I squeak out, throwing the book to the side and holding my robe closed.

"I... We need to talk," he says, clearing his throat.

"You can't just barge in here like that!" I say, panicking. What did he see when he opened the door?

"I didn't have a choice. No one's home right now, and I only had a moment with the camera glitch so no one would see me come in. I can't keep erasing footage or someone's bound to notice," he says.

He made the camera glitch so he could come in here to talk to me?

"If you wanted to talk, why didn't you just call me?" I ask.

"What we say and text on the phone can be tracked. No one can know about what happened with us," he states seriously, walking closer to me.

He stares at the book on my bed and picks it up. He reads the back and places it down, cocking an eyebrow. "This is the type of thing you like?"

"No!" I say too quickly.

He laughs.

"I... Ashley bought it for me. I just..." I can't finish what I want to say. I don't even know what to say.

"Just doing some research? I get it," he says, sitting on the bed next to me. Too close to me.

We're both silent for a few moments, staring at each other. I have no idea what I'm supposed to say to him. He's the one that came in here to talk to me. I know we should say we need to pretend it never happened and forget about it, but the way my body is reacting with him so close is making it impossible. What I want to say is please kiss me again and touch me. Risk everything for me.

He clears his throat, and I know my face is saying everything that I'm thinking. "Lauren... What happened at the restaurant..." he begins.

I interrupt, "Can never happen again, got it."

"Right..." he whispers, staring at me.

I don't have any experience with guys, but the way he's looking at me right now is not the way someone should look at someone they are trying to stay away from. I should really kick him out of my room, but I can't. My body aches for him so badly, there's no way I'm going to forget about him.

Before I know what I'm doing, I let the top of my robe fall over my shoulder. My left breast is peeking out, but not fully. He watches the robe fall intently, and his throat bobs. He wants this just as much as I do.

I let it fall just a little more, completely exposing my breast. I don't know where this confidence came from, but the way he's looking at me gives me the confidence I need to continue.

"Fuck, Lauren," he hisses and looks away, but doesn't move.

"What if... What if we give in just this once?" I ask seductively.

He mutters something under his breath that I can't understand. I take my robe completely off and scoot closer to him. He looks at me for only a second before he pushes me back onto the bed and crawls on top of me.

His face is inches from mine. "You don't know what you're doing to me. We shouldn't be doing this, Lauren."

He's looking at me like he wants me to tell him to get off. Like he wants me to tell him to stop, that I don't want this, but I do. I can't. I wrap my arms around his neck and pull him in for another kiss. This time, it's so much more than at the restaurant.

We're both moaning into each other's mouths as our tongues clash. I know I've never kissed anyone before, but I can't imagine that it gets any better than this.

He pulls away from me and begins kissing down my neck and to my breasts. When he reaches one, he swirls his tongue around my nipple and sucks it into his mouth. He repeats on the other side, and I arch my back, moaning. The tension low in my belly has increased, and I need it to be relieved now.

He kisses down my stomach, over my belly button, and makes it all the way to where no one has ever touched me before. I want him to touch me there, so bad.

"Is this what you want? You want me to touch you? To relieve the ache you have for me?" he asks as he stares into my eyes.

"Yes... Romeo, please," I breathe out.

He smirks and buries his head between my legs. His tongue licks and he sucks. I've never felt anything like it before. He rubs his finger in circles over the most sensitive spot I have. That tension builds and builds until I can't take it anymore. I release a loud moan as the tension finally releases, and I crash back down to reality. God, that was so good.

He crawls back up my body, still fully clothed, and brushes my hair back. "Does that feel better?"

"Yes..." I say breathlessly.

"Good. Maybe now we can talk without that need getting in the way," he says while rolling off me and throwing my robe back at me.

I can feel my cheeks heat at what we had just done and what he said. He knew how much I wanted him. That's embarrassing... right?

"What about you?" I ask, seeing his erection through his pants.

He shifts himself to cover it. "I'm fine."

I bite the inside of my cheek. He's clearly not fine. He gave me my first orgasm. I can't let him go like that. I need to return the favor. I want to return the favor.

Standing up with my robe still off, I place my hands on his chest.

"Lauren, what are you doing?" he asks, but knows exactly what I'm doing.

"I think you need a release too, so we can talk, of course," I state seductively.

He groans as I unzip his pants with my right hand and keep my left on his chest. He doesn't protest, so I continue and pull his pants completely down. I rub my hand down his stomach and over his huge erection. I have never touched or seen a man before. Is this how big they all are? How would that even fit inside me?

I stroke him, and he pulls me in for a kiss, moaning against my mouth. I stroke him harder and faster as his kisses become more eager. He cups my breast and then pushes me down on the bed. I crawl backward into the middle, and he straddles on top of me, above my stomach.

"Baby, you make me lose my mind," he says while stroking himself above me.

I try to take over, but he grabs my wrist with his free hand and then the other, both fitting perfectly in one of his hands. He holds them over my head, locking them in place with his. He continues to stroke himself until he's about to lose it.

"I'm going to cum all over you, so you never forget you're mine," he growls.

Spurts of cum shoot out all over my chest and stomach as he curses and moans, making me need him all over again. I feel like this should be gross, but it's the hottest thing I've ever seen.

After he catches his breath, he rolls off me and heads into the bathroom without a word. He comes back out with a towel and begins cleaning me up. Neither of us say anything. I need a moment after what just happened, so I excuse myself to the bathroom to continue washing up and to think, which clearly, I wasn't doing twenty minutes ago.

CHAPTER SEVENTEEN

ROMEO

F uck. Fuck. Fuck! What the fuck did I just do?! It was bad enough when I kissed Lauren behind the restaurant earlier, but now I just ate her out and came all over her, claiming her as mine. I'm not thinking straight. My dick is doing the thinking for me, and Lo specifically said he trusted me to keep it in my pants. FUCK!

I pull my pants back on and zip them up. Pacing around the room, I drag my hand through my hair and pull it out like that's going to erase everything that just happened. I can't believe that just happened.

After an eternity, Lauren finally comes out of her bathroom, fully clothed. Thank fuck. She sits on the edge of her bed and stares at me. I'm leaning against the wall with my arms crossed, demanding my body to stay put. Clearly, I can't think when I'm near her.

"I'm so sorry," she whispers and looks down at the floor.

Damn it. I can't help myself. I close the distance between us and kneel on the floor in front of her. She's so short that I'm basically the same height as her sitting on the bed. I lift her face with my hands to look at me. She has tears in her eyes. Fuck.

"Lauren... You have nothing to apologize for," I state in a calm voice.

"I... I just seduced my bodyguard. Lorenzo's brother. I have everything to be sorry for!" she yells.

Her outburst startles me for a moment until I realize what this is about.

"Nothing is going to happen to me, Lauren. This wasn't your fault. I'm just as much at fault," I say, pleading with my eyes for her to understand.

She shakes her head. "No, this is on me. I literally threw myself at you."

I laugh because I can tell she thinks I wouldn't have wanted her otherwise. She doesn't know how many times I've thought about taking her and claiming her as mine. I've spent the last six months trying to keep my hands off her, and it's impossible.

"Lauren... You're so fucking perfect. I don't know where to begin. I've wanted you for so long, and I couldn't hold back anymore. I'm the one that needs to be sorry. That never should've happened. I never should've given in. And I had no right to claim you," I say, but the words burn in my throat.

I've betrayed my brother, but at this moment I couldn't care less. The guilt for that will come later, but right now, I just want to ease her pain.

"I don't know what I'd do if he ever hurt you," she says, finally looking me in the eye.

I was supposed to be leaning against the wall, but screw that. Lifting her up, I cradle her in my lap on the bed.

I kiss the top of her forehead. "He won't hurt me. We'll figure this out, okay?"

She nods, but the tears keep coming.

"Lauren... We'll keep our distance as much as we can, and we'll keep this our secret. No one has to know. Like you said, it was just one time. We can do that, right?" I ask, knowing full well what torture this is going to be for me.

"Yeah... Of course... You're right," she says, wiping the tears from her eyes.

My heart is literally breaking for her. Rolling her to my side, I continue to hold her on the bed as she drifts off to sleep. I, on the other hand, lay here hating myself. I've never felt this way before about a woman. The need to protect her and make her mine. What the hell is wrong with me? She's so off-limits it's not even funny.

My brother trusted me with her. He chose me because he trusted me, and I just broke that trust. I'm no better than Tommaso and deserve to be put six feet under. My loyalty has always been to my family, especially Lo. He's my brother, my don. How could I betray him like this? Sadly, that's not even my biggest issue right now. My biggest issue is the fact that knowing I've betrayed him, I still can't find it in me to leave her alone.

I stand outside my brother's front door, trying to get the courage to walk in. Security at the front gate let me through with a nod, as always, not knowing that I just betrayed my brother. I might as well have put a knife in his back. Taking a deep breath, I push the door open. I know that he's here, most likely in his office. He and Matteo have been busy picking up the slack, while I've been fucking around with his fiancé behind his back.

Shit. What was I thinking? I can't be here right now. I'm not in the right state of mind for this. He's going to take one look at me and put a bullet in my head. He'll know. Of course he'll know.

"Romeo, what a surprise," he says, walking down the stairs to greet me in the foyer.

He must have seen me come in on the camera. Great, he saw my hesitation coming in and knows something is wrong. My heart is racing as if I just ran the entire way here. I might as well have.

"I wanted to talk to you," I state super guiltily. Jesus, what am I doing?

He cocks his eyebrow. "Alright, let's head to the office. Who is watching Lauren?"

After I left Lauren sleeping alone in her bed, I immediately called Matteo to come over. He's sitting in my house monitoring things to make sure she's safe. If Lo would've put Matteo on babysitting duty, none of this would've happened.

"Matteo is," I say.

We walk into his office, and I sit in the chair next to the fireplace. He pours us a scotch and sits in front of me, just like we've done a hundred times before. This time, I take the drink and down it in a few gulps. I'm acting guilty as hell, and I don't know how to stop.

Lo laughs. "Alright, just spit it out, Romeo."

I place the glass on the table beside me. "What's your plan with Lauren? Have you figured out who you're going to have watching over her?"

He sighs. "Is that what this is about? It's only been six months, and you're wanting to call it quits already?"

I shake my head. "I just need to know what the game plan is."

Lo snaps. "I don't know, Romeo. Right now, you're the only one I trust with her. Uncle is breathing down my neck and apparently, we're moving up the wedding to Christmas."

I sit up straighter. "This Christmas?"

"Yes, this Christmas. As in a few months from now," he growls.

Shit. This is a good thing though, right? She'll marry him, and we'll have no choice but to ignore whatever is between us. I won't be babysitting her anymore because she'll mostly be here, and there's security everywhere. When she goes out, I'm sure Lo will either be with her or she'll have a new guard by then. This is good.

"That's good. So, I'll be able to get back to my old role in a few months to pick up the slack," I state more to myself than him.

He laughs again. "I suppose you're right. Matteo isn't you. I need you back."

I smirk. "Then why don't you let him continue babysitting her, and I'll come back now."

He shakes his head. "No. I love my brother, but I don't trust him the way I do you."

His words stab me in the heart. Damn it. He has no idea what I've done and how much I've betrayed him. He can never know.

"I don't either," I say under my breath.

I don't trust Matteo. I know he wouldn't do anything like I just did, but I don't trust that he would lie down his life to protect her. I would. I'd fucking die for her in a heartbeat. Something sinks in my stomach. Is this how our story is going to end? How ironic. We were just talking about Romeo and Juliet as a tragedy.

"What else is on your mind?" he asks, knowing me too well.

"Nothing. I just want to come back. I miss how things used to be," I say.

"You're being too sentimental, Romeo. What's going on?" he asks.

I shake my head and look away from him for a moment. I knew I couldn't keep my mouth shut. I should've just ended it there. I kill people for a living. Why is it so hard to lie to my brother?

"Nah, I just didn't realize how much I missed seeing your ugly face and beating people up," I joke.

Lo laughs and stands, patting me on the shoulder. "I miss you too, brother. Not much longer, I promise. Things will go back to normal."

Will they though? He's going to be married and have Lauren to take care of. I won't be seeing her every second of the day like I am now, but I'll still see her around. Will my feelings for her eventually fade? Will hers? Or will we forever be giving each other glances across the room, wishing things were different? Wishing we could be together. Yeah, I know the answer to my earlier question. Our future is depressing. Our story was never meant to have a happily ever after.

CHAPTER EIGHTEEN

LAUREN

Christmas... Christmas... Christmas! I'm marrying Lorenzo on Christmas Day! Who the heck planned that one? It wasn't me, that's for sure. Oh, and it's not just the fact it's on Christmas Day. It's the fact that it's a few months away! I'm still in high school! What are my parents thinking?!

Romeo snuck into my room again the next day after we... did whatever you want to call it. This time, he glued himself to my wall while I glued myself to the door of my bathroom. We were acting like opposite ends of magnets pushing each other away. It probably would've been comical to watch, but for us, it wasn't. We both could feel the tension and the pull toward each other, but we didn't have a choice. We had to ignore it.

He told me he went to see Lorenzo and shared the new wedding date with me. I wanted to laugh and cry at the same time, but surprisingly, I did neither. Ultimately, it was a quick conversation. We boiled it down to lust and being in close proximity to each other for over half a year. We agreed it would never happen again, and we would both take it to our graves. Fine by me.

Now Lorenzo is in my face all the time. He wants to go on a date every Saturday and texts me every day. It's what I wanted, right? He's showing interest in me and wants to get to know me, but I know better. He's doing it because he has to. I'm not sure why, but I'm angry all the time. Like, all the time. Is it just part of those hormones for teenaged girls, or is it because I'm finally realizing my fate since it's now right in front of me?

Regardless of the reason, I've started pushing everyone around me away. I've been slowly ignoring Ashley's messages and invites out, which has been difficult. She's not giving up on me. I've been claiming my parents are cracking down on me and keeping me inside, though it's my doing. I already pushed away my old friends from my old life, so I can do it again. I've learned it's just easier if you forget about them. My old friends had no problem letting me go, though. Ashley is persistent.

My door flings open and my mother walks in. "Romeo is here..." my mother pauses to look at me and continues, "Lauren! What on earth are you wearing? Go put on a pretty dress... And would it kill you to wear some makeup?"

I roll my eyes at my mom, and she continues to yell. "Don't you roll your eyes at me! Lorenzo is waiting for you at the restaurant for your date. Now go make yourself look presentable, and I'll stall for you."

"You realize you can't tell me what to do anymore, right? You're marrying me off to a freaking mobster," I spit back at her.

I can see the anger rise in her face. Good. She stomps over and slaps me on the face. Hard. Bitch.

"While you're living under my roof, you will do as I say. Now go put on your little black dress and put on some makeup," she demands, heading toward the door.

"Screw you!" I yell back at her while holding my cheek.

Damn, that burns. Speaking of burning, I can feel the tears welling up in my eyes. I don't want to cry because of her. I'm sick of crying because of everyone else. The anger continues to rise in my chest, and I rummage through my closet, choosing any dress other than the black one she told me to put on. I also ignore her advice about makeup. Why do I need to look good when I have no choice but to marry Lorenzo? He's stuck with me, so he gets what he gets.

I walk downstairs with my anger still bubbling at the surface. I'm doing my best to keep it in, but I don't know how much longer I'll be able to hold it for. Hopefully, at least until I get back from my date with Lorenzo. Maybe I'll punch a hole in the wall as a parting gift to my mother.

I walk past Romeo, and he stops me by placing his hand on my arm. "What happened to your cheek?"

I don't know how, but I completely forgot my mother slapped me. I suppose it would leave a mark.

"Nothing, let's go," I state, trying to continue walking, but he doesn't let me.

"What happened?" he asks again, but this time through gritted teeth.

"I pissed my mother off, so she slapped me," I say.

He turns around to face my mother, who is standing in the doorway to the kitchen. He stalks over toward her and her eyes grow wide. My anger turns into fear as to what's about to happen.

He towers over her and stops right in front of her. His voice is low but menacing. "You will never lay a hand on Lauren again. She is... Lorenzo's. No one hurts her without consequences. This is your one and only warning."

He turns his back on her, and I can see the anger on his face. My heart can't help but tighten at what he just said and did for me. I know he said it's because I'm Lorenzo's, but could it be that he does really care about me? He doesn't say a word the entire drive to the restaurant, and I know it's for the best.

Romeo made my anger fade when he confronted my mother about hitting me, but my anger has done nothing but rise during this entire meal. Usually, my dates with Lorenzo consist of just the two of us. Today it consists of him, Matteo, Romeo, and

Nico. I've heard about Nico from Romeo, but this is the first time meeting him.

He looks similar to Lorenzo, but his eyes are much darker, and his jawline is sharper. He scares me only because he doesn't seem like a mobster at all. He's funny and charming. I feel like he could sneak up on you and kill you in an instant before you realize what's happening. I shiver thinking about that.

They continue mostly talking to each other, and I keep to myself. Romeo used to include me, but he doesn't anymore. Either he's working hard to pretend there's nothing between us, or he's over it. Like whatever we did got me out of his system. It's probably for the best if that's the case, even though my heart believes otherwise.

"So, I've been thinking about how things are going to go once we're married," Lorenzo starts, capturing my attention. "You'll live with me, and my security at the house will keep you safe. I'm working on finding you a guard, but until then, I want you to stay home and not leave the house unless it's with me or one of these men here."

I know my mouth is hanging open. Is he serious? Does he expect me to just stay inside and do nothing once we're married?

"What about school?" I ask.

He shakes his head. "There's no need for you to continue once you're my wife. You will never have to work a day in your life."

"What?" I ask, completely shocked.

"You'll be taken care of with everything you need. The best thing for you to do is stay home and stay safe. You will take care of things around the house and raise our kids."

I laugh. I don't mean to laugh, but a laugh escapes me, anyway. He can't be serious. Does he really think that I'm going to give up my entire life to be his wife and a stay-at-home mom? Was this what it was going to be the whole time?

"You're joking. I'm not allowed to get my high school diploma? You want me to stay home and play house with you? I was planning on going to college..."

He interrupts me. "That's out of the question."

I stand up with my heart racing. I've never had an outburst like this before, but I can't sit here and let him tell me what my life is going to be like. He can force me to marry him, but he can't force me to give up my entire life.

"No," I say and walk off toward the door.

He catches my arm and spins me to face him. I try to pull my arm away, but he grips it tighter, and I wince at the pain. I glance over toward Romeo, who is sitting with his hands on the table with gritted teeth. He's not going to say or do anything about this.

Lorenzo pulls me closer and whispers in my ear, "You will do as I say. You will be my wife and my wife is obedient. Do not make a fool of me in front of my family."

He pulls back a little but doesn't let go of my arm. My anger quickly turns to fear when I see how angry he is with me. Is this how it's going to be? We have an argument, and he demands me to obey? What happens if I don't? I don't know if I have it in me to find out at the moment.

His grip relaxes on my arm as he says, "Come sit back down, we're almost finished."

I do as he says because what is my alternative? I don't want to know what would happen if I were to disobey him. He promised me he would never hurt me, but can I believe him? I rub the arm where he grabbed me. That sure felt like it hurt.

I sit at the table in silence as everyone finishes their food. I don't take another bite of mine. Instead, I sit and will the tears that are threatening to fall to stay put, at least until I'm in the privacy of my home. I don't want to give him the satisfaction of knowing how much he can affect me.

CHAPTER NINETEEN

ROMEO

Fuck. I've been doing so good keeping my feelings at bay when it comes to Lauren, until today. First, she comes down the stairs with a red mark on her cheek. She said it was nothing, but I knew otherwise. She was hit, and I needed to know who did it to her.

When I found out it was her mother, I almost lost it. I've never hit a woman before, but it took everything I had to keep my hands to myself. When I was threatening her, I almost slipped up. I almost said Lauren was mine and she better not touch her ever again, but Lauren's not mine. I quickly fixed my mistake and said Lorenzo.

Then fucking Lo! I know he's had a shitty week. He's been calling me for advice on how to deal with our rivals all week and he needs me, but I'm not there. That gives him no right to lay a hand on Lauren. She's angry and has every right to be. I wouldn't take kindly to someone telling me I'm basically going to be a prisoner for the rest of my life. I told him this was how she would react, but he didn't listen.

When she tried to walk away, I knew it was coming. Lo can't be seen as weak in front of anyone, including his family. No one walks away from the don, especially his future wife. I could tell by her face how hard he was gripping her. It took everything in me to stay seated. She was scared. She glanced over at me like she wanted me to help her, and it tore me up to sit there doing nothing, but I had no choice. If I did something, then that's it. Lo would know, and I'd be killed. Lauren would be stuck here alone in this shitty world, with no one having her back. I don't know how much longer I can go on like this.

Lauren is currently back at her house, and I want nothing more than to be there with her. Thinking about her laying there, crying by herself is torture. I know we said we were going to forget about everything that happened between us, but these feelings aren't going away.

Lo sits in the chair across from the couch I'm sitting on. He came over to hang out after I dropped Lauren off at home. He looks like a mess, and I'm always the one he goes to for advice and to make him feel better. The shitty part is, it's not Lo who I'm wanting to make feel better. That's a problem, and I don't know what to do about it.

"I don't know what to do with Lauren. I thought spending more time with her and texting her almost every day would make her warm up to me," Lo says while taking a sip of his drink.

Shrugging my shoulders, I don't say anything.

"Has something happened? Have you noticed anything? She just seems angry with me all the time, and I don't know what I did," he says, defeated.

I sigh. "I don't think you did anything. Reality is hitting her that she's getting married and what that entails. You also just threw a huge curve ball at her. She was thinking she'd graduate high school with her friends and go to college. Now she's supposed to be stuck at home forever raising kids."

Lo stares at me for a moment. "She will have everything she could ever want. Who wouldn't want that life?"

Does he really believe that? Yeah, I could see some women wanting a life like that. A life where they don't have to work and can just sit around spending Lo's money. They really wouldn't even have to raise their own kids or cook if they didn't want to. He could hire a nanny and housekeeper. It sounds like a good life, in theory.

"But she won't have whatever she wants, which is freedom and going to school," I state.

Lo groans. "I need you to help me, Romeo. What do I do? I can't have an angry wife and someone who disobeys. I can't have her run away again. Do you think she'd try that again?"

I chuckle. "Lo, she's so afraid of you she's not going to do anything to piss you off again. You should see her around other boys. She looks so uncomfortable and avoids them because she doesn't want you to get the wrong idea. She's not even going to homecoming and is avoiding her friends."

Lo sets down his drink. "Is she really that afraid of me? I don't want to isolate her or keep her from her friends."

"Yeah, she is," I state seriously.

"Fuck. She's not happy, is she?" he asks, and he truly looks concerned for her.

"No, she's not."

"Is she depressed?" he asks.

"I'm not a psychiatrist, Lo. I don't know, but her being isolated and her mood swings might indicate that," I say.

"You don't think... She wouldn't take her life, would she?"

My heart stops for a moment. I've never considered that. She hasn't been herself lately and hasn't been hanging out with her friends much. She rarely comes out of her room or leaves the house other than to go to school. Would she consider doing that?

"I don't know..." I whisper, looking at my lap instead of at him.

"I want you to watch her closely. Keep closer tabs on what she's doing, who she's seeing, read her text messages, everything. Sleep in her fucking room if needed," he says.

I nod, as I will the panic to subside. I don't know what I'd do if Lauren killed herself. She's not mine, but damn it, I can't stop my feelings for her.

"Keep me updated. Make sure she goes to homecoming, and get her to buy whatever dress she wants," he says while standing up and heading toward the door.

"Okay, but I think you need to talk to her about it. It should come from you, so she knows you want her to go."

"Yeah, okay," he says.

"Hey, Lo…" I stop him before he leaves the house.

"Yeah?" He turns back to face me.

"I know you're busy, but… Maybe you should try to find more time to spend with her. If you're so worried about her that you'd want me staying in the same room as her… Maybe it should be you doing that," I force out.

I really wanted to just do what he said and use it as an opportunity to spend more time with Lauren. Having an excuse to stay in her room is exactly what I wanted, but it's not what I need. I've betrayed Lo enough. I'm not betraying him more. I can't do that to him.

"I'll try to spend more time with her, but I don't have time to babysit her. You know that. There's too much going on right now. If you think it gets too bad, I'll lock her in my home," he says as he finally leaves the house.

Yeah, locking her up is not going to happen. It'll make everything worse for her. I'll just have to ensure she's okay, mentally and physically. There's only a few more months left. I got this.

I don't got this. It's only been a week since Lo and I had that talk, and I'm going insane again. Lauren won't do anything except go to school, which just started the other week. I don't know how she interacts with her friends inside the school, but she doesn't interact much outside.

I've been keeping tabs on her texts and Everly has been texting her a lot, trying to get to know her more while Ashley keeps sending random messages. Lauren barely responds. I have noticed her hanging out with Benjamin a little more right after school and even during lunch. I'm not sure what that's about, but I won't lie that it's making me jealous.

Speaking of jealous, Lauren is on another date with Lo tonight. Lo told me I'm not needed, so they are by themselves. I'd say it's been nice having a few hours to myself without worrying about her, but that's all I'm fucking doing is worrying about her.

I've been sitting here wondering what she's doing with him. Is she kissing him? Is she having a good time? Is she miserable? Is she wishing it were me? Either way, it's none of my concern. I keep reminding myself of that. If I were smart, I would've taken this time to hit a bar and find a willing chick to get laid tonight. The thought of doing that repulses me.

A car door slams next door, bringing me back to reality from my thoughts. I peek outside the window to see Lauren walking up to the front of the house, with Lo following her. My heart races as I'm pulling up the front door camera feed while my mind is telling me to stop. I don't stop. I turn the volume up and watch their interaction.

"Lauren... I want you to be happy," he states.

"Right, because..." she starts, but she doesn't finish.

Lo sighs and places his hand on her shoulder. She flinches. "Lauren... I wish there was another way, but there isn't. I'm forced as much as you, you know that."

She scoffs. "Aren't you the don? How can someone force you to do anything?"

He removes his hand from her and rubs it down his face. "There are things I have to do for the family. Just because I am who I am, doesn't mean I get to do whatever I want. If it were safe for you, I'd let you go to college and be what you want to be. We've talked about this. It's just not safe. You, being my wife, places a target on your back. I'd rather you be safe and hate me than be dead."

"I'd rather be dead..." she whispers, but it was loud enough for the cameras to pick it up.

Fuck. Was Lo right? My heart pounds harder in my chest at her words. She can't be suicidal. Something switches inside me at that thought. I won't let her.

She turns to enter the house, but Lo grabs her arm. "Lauren... You don't mean that... Do you?"

She turns back to him with a straight face. "Of course not. I'm not suicidal."

Lo relaxes beside her a little. "Lauren..."

That's when I see the shine on her face. I zoom in and see the tears falling from her eyes down her cheeks. By looking at her expression, she doesn't even look like she's crying. Lo pulls her close to him and envelops her in a hug. She puts her face against his chest, and they stand there like that for a few moments, not saying anything. I want to look away, but I can't. Apparently, I need this torture. I need to see that he can comfort her. That she's going to be okay with him.

She pulls back, but Lo keeps his arms around her and says softly, "Come stay with me. We're getting married in a few months, so let's spend whatever time we can together. I'm not locking you in. You can come and go as you please with Romeo still watching out for you."

I groan as my heart tightens in my chest. I close my eyes, hold my breath, and wait for her reply. She needs to say yes. She needs to build a connection with Lo, but I want so badly for her to say no. Please say no.

"No... I... I just can't yet. I'm not ready to leave home," she says and my whole body relaxes into my chair.

Lo nods, gives her a hug, and kisses her on her forehead. "If you need anything, text me."

She nods and enters the house. Lo stands outside her front door with his hands in his pockets. He stares at it for a few moments before looking toward my house and walking this way. Crap.

I close the camera on the computer and sit back on the couch, waiting for the knock on the door. When it comes, I slowly walk to the front door and open it for him. I look at his face and he looks... defeated?

"Hey," he says.

"Hey," I reply.

There's a silence between us as he stands in the doorway. "Want to talk about it?"

He stares at me and shakes his head. "I just... I need my friend tonight."

Fuck. There's only been a few times he's come to me to just hang out like this. I step aside, letting him enter as I close the door behind him. "I'll get the scotch."

Chapter Twenty

LAUREN

I lay in bed staring at the ceiling, not wanting to get up today... or any day. I feel like I'm just going through the motions until I'm married off to Lorenzo. What's the point? I'm not going to go back to school after the Christmas break or do anything with my life.

The date with Lorenzo went okay, I guess. He was trying his best to be nice and romantic. He bought me flowers, opened the car door for me, pulled out my chair at the table, and held my hand as we walked. I tensed up at his physical contact. I'm not sure if it's because he hurt my arm that time or what, but I didn't want it. I tried to want it, but I couldn't.

I felt... guilty? Yeah, definitely guilty. He's my fiancé, and I should want those things with him. I should be thankful he's trying and wanting them with me. But... I couldn't stop thinking about Romeo. I wanted it to be Romeo, and that made me feel even more guilty.

I don't get those butterflies in my stomach with Lorenzo like when Romeo is around. All I have to do is look at Romeo and my whole body heats up. I've been trying to convince myself he doesn't feel the same way, but I know that's a lie. I see the way he looks at me when he thinks I'm not looking. He's been purposefully keeping his distance and keeping our conversations short when we're forced together in a car. I can feel the tension between us, and I know it's not just me.

My phone buzzes with a text message.

Ashley

> Time for dress shopping. Pick me up in an hour?

I stare at the message and try to ignore it until Everly's comes through a moment later.

Everly

> YES! Lauren?

I sit up and debate for a moment. Should I? The other day we all got high at Ashley's house, and I told them that my parents aren't allowing me to do much this year because I'm supposed to be serious about Lorenzo. They didn't really say that, but I wanted an excuse to keep them at a distance. What's the point of having fun and having friends when I'm about to give them all up?

Then again, last night Lorenzo was very clear with me. He wants me to go to homecoming and spend more time with my friends. He clearly cares about me a little, but is it enough? I shake my head. I can either sit here and think about my depressing life and what's coming, or I can go out and keep my mind off it while Ashley and Everly entertain me.

It's also nice to have someone to talk to occasionally. When we went to Ashley's house the other day, I was asking Everly about her and Declan on the drive over. Declan is good looking, which Ashley likes to point out every time we're with Everly. I was curious if maybe this crush on Romeo that I have is just that, a crush because he's around all the time. I asked how she keeps her hands off him, but she said she didn't have any feelings like that for him, plus he was older, and it'd be weird. Which would be right? Romeo is definitely older than Declan though, which made that comment a little worse. I do wonder if Everly wasn't in love with James, if she might see Declan differently. I was tempted to ask, but didn't want them inquiring why I'm asking so many questions.

I'm allowed.

Everly

See you guys soon!

I quickly get ready and text Romeo that we're going. Declan and Barry, Everly's security team, are driving us to the mall, so Romeo will follow behind and keep his distance, as always.

When we get to the dress shop, Ashley wants to be funny and have us try on hideous dresses. Everly's face when Ashley hands her the one she picks out is priceless. I let her choose Ashley's to get payback, and Ashley chooses mine. We all try them on and laugh together, taking a selfie.

It feels good to genuinely laugh and have fun with my friends. I'm trying hard to stay present during these moments and not think about anything else. If I don't, then I just get too depressed. Lorenzo seemed concerned I might take my life, which never crossed my mind until that moment outside my front door. If I stay in the darkness too long, I can see the possibility of those thoughts making an appearance. I need to push that deep down and keep these moments going to bury it there.

We all find beautiful dresses to wear to homecoming. I want nothing more than to get a sexy dress like Ashley, but I know better. It's bad to think that I want Romeo staring at me all night in something like that, but I can't do it. I don't want to attract attention from other boys, so I keep it modest. It's a flowy pink dress. I hate pink, but it looks good on me.

Ashley's dress is a green, tight-fitting dress that goes down to her knees. Of course, it's sparkly, which suits her perfectly. Everly's is also sparkly, but dark blue. Her dress is also tight and shows off her body, like Ashley's. It looks like the night sky with the stars. Everly looks so pretty in it. Right now, the hint of red in her brown hair is accentuated and those hazel eyes glow. I wish I was as gorgeous as she is.

On the way out of the mall, Everly spots a store that she wants to stop in. It's a lingerie store. She mentioned she's going to be surprising James at his apartment for his birthday, so I suppose she wants to get something sexy for him. I hesitate before going in until I spot Romeo staring at me. My breath catches at the intensity of that stare. I turn away and head into the store with newfound courage.

Ashley jokes and finds some crazy lingerie sets that look like something straight out of a porno film or what would be worn in the book I was reading. Yeah, I read that whole book... We're not going to talk about how I felt about it.

Everly looks even more uncomfortable in this store than I am. She keeps looking over her shoulder at Declan, who is acting like this is nothing out of the ordinary. I suppose it would be awkward having your security team follow you into the store. It should be awkward. For me, it's not. My heart races at an idea. What would Romeo think or do if I were to purchase a couple of these?

Everly has just checked out her purchase, and I've made my decision. "I'm going to hit the bathroom real fast. I'll meet you guys outside."

They both nod, keep talking, and walk out of the store. I pretend to head to the bathroom, but at the last minute, I go to the section where I saw some lacy bra and panty sets. If you can call those panties. Most of them have just a little string down the butt.

I quickly grab three colors of each bra and matching panties, glancing out the front door to make sure Everly and Ashley aren't in eyesight. They're not, so I throw them at the cashier and open my wallet.

I have enough money in the bank account my father opened for me, but Lorenzo gave me his credit card to buy my homecoming dress. My heart races as I think about using Lorenzo's card to buy these. The fact that I'm standing here, thinking about wearing these for Romeo and paying with my fiancé's credit card... it's wrong, but I do it anyway. I stick them in my homecoming dress bag, so no one knows that I've bought them.

Four-hundred and fifty dollars later and a grin on my face, I stare at Romeo as I walk by him toward my friends. Romeo's jaw is tight, and his stare has intensified. His hands are balled in his pockets, and I can feel the heat coming off him. He's affected by what he just watched me purchase, which makes me question things more. Is he angry, thinking that I'm going to be wearing these for Lorenzo? Is he picturing me in them? Does he still want me?

I try hard to concentrate on what Ashley and Everly are talking about on the car ride home, but it's difficult. All I can think about is having Romeo see me in this lingerie. I don't know what my goal is, and I'm going back and forth between beating myself up for thinking about it and trying to figure out how I can get him to see me in it.

My brain keeps saying stop thinking about Romeo, you're marrying Lorenzo, but my heart and other body parts are saying, you're not married yet, so screw it. I feel guilty thinking that way, especially since Lorenzo said he is being faithful to me. Then again, I've already done things I shouldn't have with Romeo, so what does it hurt to do more? Or at least torture him a little.

I love the way he looks at me. Lorenzo never looks at me like that, and I don't think he ever will. I've come to terms that my feelings will never go away for Romeo. Now I just need to figure out what I'm going to do with that. Am I going to go behind Lorenzo's back and screw his best friend, or brother, as he calls him? Or am I going to live in a passionless marriage for the rest of my life and just dream about what it'd be like to be with Romeo until the day I die?

I'm not sure, but my impulsiveness hits me the moment I walk in the door and my mother wants me to try on the dress I bought for her to see. When I get up to my room, I hide the bras and panties I bought under my pillow, except for one pair. I put them on and place my homecoming dress over them. I know there aren't cameras in my room, so Romeo can't see me here, but there are in the hallway outside my room.

I head downstairs to the kitchen where my mother is. Spinning around, I show off my flowy dress and surprisingly, she smiles and tells me how beautiful I am. Not that the dress is beautiful, but that I'm beautiful. My mother and I have never really gotten along, so that comment means a lot to me. Especially since I don't have much makeup on, which she always scolds me about.

She continues what she's doing in the kitchen as I head up the stairs. Before I reach my bedroom door, I pause. When I put on my dress, I decided I was going to do this. I want to. I need to. Before I lose my courage, I stare directly at the camera outside my room. I check behind me one more time to make sure my mother isn't coming up the stairs, and she's not.

Slowly unzipping my dress, I let it fall to the floor. I step out of it gracefully and continue staring at the camera. Turning my back to it, I bend over even more slowly to pick it up. I don't look at the camera again as I walk to my bedroom and close the door with a smile on my face. I can't believe I actually did that. There's a possibility he wasn't watching, but there's even more of a possibility that he was.

CHAPTER TWENTY-ONE

ROMEO

I nearly die, choking on my water as I watch Lauren on the camera. My dick instantly stands to attention as I watch her stare into the camera and drop her dress to the floor. She knows that I'm watching. She wants me to watch.

When she turns around and bends over to pick up her dress, I nearly lose it. She's wearing one of the lingerie sets that she bought today at the mall. It's a thong, and it doesn't cover her ass at all. I'm staring at her bare ass with her basically naked in front of the camera, with her staring into it moments before. It takes everything in me not to grab my dick and rub one off.

As she walks back into her bedroom, I wish I had a camera in there. What was she doing right now? Was she excited thinking about the possibility that I was watching her? Is she just going to get dressed and move on with her day? Or... is she going to lie on her bed and make herself come, the way I wish I could do for her right now?

I groan and shake my head, trying to get all those thoughts out. Why is she doing this to me? I thought we agreed to keep that as a onetime thing. I thought she was over me and trying with Lo. When I saw her make that purchase at the mall, I couldn't help but hope she was making it for me, but then I saw her using Lo's card. It excited me even more but gave me mixed feelings. I didn't know if she was buying them for me, or if it was for him. The jealousy was taking over, but the thought of the possibility that it was for me made it impossible to keep it together. I know she saw the look I gave her. Clearly, she liked it.

I rewind the camera and watch her again. I hoped maybe I imagined her looking into the camera. That she was just taking the dress off, completely forgetting the camera was there. Obviously, that's not the case. She wanted me to see. She wants me. Now what the fuck do I do with this knowledge?

It has taken everything in me to avoid sneaking into Lauren's room these past couple of weeks. I rewound and watched that damn footage of her stripping in front of the camera for me more times than I'd like to admit. I've jacked off to it even more times. It's a fucking problem.

The other fucking problem is that she's been purposefully giving me looks into the cameras, baiting me. She even lets her shirts or sweaters "slip" down her arm, revealing her bra straps, which I know are the straps of the lingerie sets she bought. I've been good these weeks. I've kept my distance and keep it professional as I'm driving her places. She never pushes me, especially in person, but she has no problem pushing me on camera.

Lo took her out tonight, despite her objections. She wanted to go with her friends to the homecoming football game. I think she's been panicking with the little time she has left with them. Lo can't do tomorrow, which is her homecoming dance anyway, so he insisted it must be tonight.

So once again, I'm left at home with nothing to do. I didn't even think about hitting a bar and a woman tonight. There's no way I could. She's the only woman that I want and yes, she's officially a woman now. Her 18th birthday was at the beginning of September. I wanted nothing more than to celebrate it with her, but I didn't. In fact, she surprisingly didn't celebrate it at all. Not even with her family. I don't know if that was her request or if they just don't fucking care about her. Lo got her a gift, of course, but that's about as far as her birthday went.

I hear a car door slam, which is the telltale sign they arrived home. Her parents aren't home this weekend, so she'll be entering an empty house. What is she going to do all night in there, alone? I shake my head to stop thinking about it as I pull up the camera out front.

Lo is standing with her there again, just like every night they go on a date. They both look relaxed, like this was a decent date. Jealousy creeps up, but I shove it back down. It doesn't matter; I know how much she wants me. She's been making that clear for the past couple of weeks.

Lo says goodnight and rubs his hand down her arm. I hold my breath as I watch her stand on her toes to lean up to him. No, she's not going to... she wouldn't initiate a kiss between them.

Lo leans down to meet her halfway as their lips meet. Fuck. I look away from the camera, not being able to watch. The jealousy and anger are rising. I lean my elbow on the desk with my hand over my mouth. Peeking back at the camera, I see them parting. I try to even my breaths as I think about how it was just a goodnight kiss. Surely, she didn't want it. She initiated it because she's trying with him.

After they part, she grabs his hand, and I can't stop watching as she steps closer to him.

"Come inside?" she asks seductively.

I want to throw up. Is she really asking Lo inside to do what I think she's asking? She can't be. She doesn't want him. Or maybe she does now, after their date? What did they do on that date? What did he say to make her want him like that?

Lo steps forward and kisses her on the forehead before saying, "Not tonight. It's not a good idea."

I sigh with relief. Thank you, Lo, for being a gentleman at this moment. I can't help but laugh, though. Would I have been? No, no, I wouldn't have, and she's not even mine.

"Why not? You're my fiancé, and we're getting married soon. Do you think that could change?" she asks.

I'm not sure what she's thinking. Did I see a little hope on her face that it might change, and they won't be married? Or was it hope that he'll see reason and go inside to screw her tonight? I get up and pace back and forth behind my chair.

Lo shakes his head. "No, it's not going to change. I know this was arranged, but I want our wedding night to be special. I want your first time to be special."

She nods and leans into him, giving him a hug before she opens the door and enters inside. Lo looks over toward my house, and I can't. I hope to God he doesn't come over tonight because there's no way I can talk to him right now. I have too many emotions going on inside me I need to work out.

Thankfully, Lo gets in his car and drives off. I round my chair and sit down, watching the cameras again. She heads to the kitchen and starts making herself some tea. I debate back and forth what the fuck to do. I want to go over there so bad to confront her and make it clear she's mine, but that's not true. She's not mine. I've established this with myself five thousand times now.

I should head into my home gym and burn off some of this steam. I should hit the punching bag fifty times, pretending it's Lo's face. Why do I have such hatred for him at this moment? It's not his fault. I love my brother, and I hate feeling like this about him. I would never know Lauren if it weren't for him being engaged to her. I continue to debate back and forth about what to do. The urge to go to her is strong, but I don't know what I'll do once I'm in her house and in her bedroom. It would be a mistake to confront her, especially right now with how I'm feeling.

CHAPTER TWENTY-TWO

LAUREN

I'm in the kitchen on the verge of tears as I make tea. I'm not a huge fan of tea, but I need something right now and coffee is not the way to go this late at night. The date with Lorenzo went fine. He's definitely trying, but I just don't feel anything for him like I want to, and I really want to.

Clearly, whatever was going on with Romeo was all in my mind. He's over us and had his fun with me. He's been completely ignoring me and when he has no choice but to interact with me, he's professional. I know I've been trying to push his buttons and show him I'm still interested, but he's made it clear he's not.

So, it's time that I move on. Either I can be stuck living with this stupid crush on him for the rest of my life, or I can start trying to love my fiancé. I'm still not a fan of what Lorenzo does for a living and about being stuck at home for the rest of my life, but something has got to give.

I kissed Lorenzo tonight... I kissed him goodnight and invited him inside, knowing that it could lead to something more. I was shocked when he denied my request. I was fully prepared to follow through, even though I didn't want to. A part of me hoped Romeo was watching and maybe this would finally get to him.

I walk upstairs with my tea and open my bedroom door. It's dark inside. Turning on the light, I close it behind me and turn back around. I jump, almost dropping my tea on the floor, and place my hand over my heart, catching my breath. Romeo sits on top of my bed, cross-legged, staring at me.

"You scared me!" I exclaim.

"Have a good date?" he asks casually.

"What are you doing here?" I ask, trying to read his expression.

He looks bored, but I see something deeper in his eyes. Is he mad? He stands up and stalks toward me. Grabbing the tea from my hand, he places it on the desk beside me. He continues to advance, making me step back for each step he takes forward. Eventually, I'm pressed against the wall, and he's directly in front of me.

He places his hand on the wall, with his arm above my head, as he leans forward. "What game are you playing?"

"What?" I barely get the word out.

He squints his eyes at me as he leans even closer. My breath catches as his facial expression changes. Yeah, he's definitely pissed.

"You've been teasing me for weeks with glances at the camera and taking your clothes off, showing me the sexy lingerie you bought. Then tonight you invite my brother inside after a date to fuck you?" He pauses and places the palm of his hand on my cheek, stroking it with his thumb.

"I…" I begin to say, but I don't know how to continue.

"You what, Lauren? Tell me, do you want my brother now? Did you have such a great date that you're in love with him, and you've completely forgotten about me?" he asks.

My anger rises, and I've found my words. "Seriously, Romeo?! You have some nerve. I've made it clear that I want you, and you've made it clear that you want nothing to do with me. You haven't said a thing about what I've been doing. You don't want me and that's fine, but don't expect me to sit around longing for you for the rest of my life. I'm trying to make the best of a crappy situation," I yell at him.

Unexpectedly, his mouth crashes on mine. He grabs my face between his hands and kisses me harder than I've ever been kissed before. He kisses me with so much passion that I can barely contain myself. My anger quickly fades and now all I want is him. All of him.

He pulls back and groans. "Lauren…" he pauses to run his hand through his hair and take another step back. "Fuck! Lauren, I want you so fucking bad it literally hurts. You have no idea how much I want you, but I know you're not mine to take. Seeing you tonight with Lo… I… I lost control. I'm sorry."

He's retreating inside himself again. I can see it. I can see how much this is tearing him apart, and if I know what's best for both of us, it's to let him walk out of this room. He needs to walk out of this room, and I need to stop teasing him. There's no happily ever after in our story. Am I ready to dive headfirst into this tragedy?

I need to let him go. I need to. "Romeo... I..."

I don't know what to say or at least, I can't say it. I'm not ready to let him go. He makes me feel safe. He makes me feel loved. He makes me... feel.

"I'm going to go," he says, while grabbing the handle of my door.

My heart rate picks up again, and I panic. I can't let him go, not yet. If I do, it's the end for sure. It needs to be the end, but I'm not ready for it. I grab his arm and pull him back to me. He doesn't fight me as he lets the handle go, and I bury my body into his.

"Lauren..." he says as he wraps me up tight into a hug.

I stay wrapped up in him as I speak into his chest. I have more confidence when I'm not looking at him. "I can't lose you, Romeo. I love you. I think about you day and night. It hurts so much knowing that I can't be with you. I don't know what to do."

I hear him curse as he hugs me tighter. "This isn't good for either of us, Lauren."

"I know..." I whisper.

He just continues holding me, and I never want him to let go. I don't understand this connection that we've built over the short time we've known each other. These past few months, it has gotten stronger the more we try to push each other away.

I finally pull away from him, looking in his eyes. "Are you sure there's nothing we can do? There's no way to be together? Unless that's not what you want."

He shakes his head. "I want that. Fuck Lauren, I can't think of anyone but you. It's been so hard watching you with Lo and being so close to you, but not being able to touch you. I would do anything, but there's nothing."

I nod and pull completely away. I know he means it, and he's probably right. There's nothing we can do, but knowing that he feels the same way, I don't think I can live like this anymore. There's no way I can marry Lorenzo and have these feelings for Romeo. It would be torture. I'm going to figure this out. I have to.

With our confessions out of the way and nothing that we can do about them, Romeo leaves my room. I watch him close my door, and I abandon my tea on the desk to fall onto my bed and sigh. I stare at the ceiling for a few moments and then back over toward my tea. It's cold by now. I look away but quickly bring my gaze back to my desk as my eyes roam over something. My copy of Romeo and Juliet sits on the desk staring at me as I stare back at it, with my heart racing and an idea forming in my head.

Ashley, Everly, and I are getting ready for homecoming at Everly's house. Romeo drove me here, and it was almost worse than what it had been. For the past couple of weeks, I've been thinking that he didn't like me anymore. I continued to flirt with him through the cameras anyway, but his disinterest showed me he didn't care. Last night was my last-ditch effort. If he didn't show up the way he did, I was going to do my best to forget about him.

After his confession last night, things are different. He may act the same to stay away from me, but I know better now. Which is probably worse. I have an idea that I want to run by him, but I need to make sure he is one hundred percent in before I do.

Ashley took a photo of Everly and sent it to James without her knowing. James' text comes back immediately, and she's basically swooning at his response. She's pretending to be mad at Ashley for sending it, but clearly, she's not.

"You're so lucky to have someone like James who looks at you and finds you so attractive..." I say to Everly.

Ashley and Everly exchange looks before she says, "Lauren, you look hot. Does Lorenzo never compliment how you look?"

I shake my head. "No, not really. He always just looks at me and quickly looks away. It's like he just sees me as a child or something."

It's true. Replaying last night, I feel like he probably still sees me as a kid and that's why he didn't want to do anything. I think that's why he's waiting until marriage. I'm not complaining because I don't know what I would've done had we done something last night. I wasn't thinking clearly. I just really wanted to get under Romeo's skin if he did like me, and if he didn't, then I wanted to get over him. That was not the best solution, and I feel dumb for doing it. Thankfully, Lorenzo didn't take me up on my offer.

Ashley scoffs. "Well, you are basically a child to him. He should be happy he gets someone as hot as you for his wife."

I can feel myself blush, and it's not because I'm thinking about Lorenzo. I'm now thinking about Romeo and the way he makes me feel. He makes me feel hot, and he's clearly attracted to me.

"Do you ever text him?" Everly asks.

I take a moment to switch my mind back to what or who we are talking about. Lorenzo, right.

I nod. "Yeah, not often, but mainly when we're making plans for our dates. I'm pretty sure he's not into this arranged marriage any more than I am."

Technically, we text almost every day, but there's not usually anything substantial in the texts. Everly looks like she's contemplating something, and she pities me. I don't want her pity.

"Well, let's send him a picture of you as well and see what he says," Everly says, taking my phone from on top of her desk.

I gasp. Wait, what? No. I'm not sending a picture of myself all dressed up like this to Lorenzo. Especially after last night. He's going to think I'm flirting with him. While I probably should be, I can't. I have to think of a reason not to, quick.

"No! That'd be... unprofessional? I don't know. It wouldn't be right," I say, wanting to face palm myself for the stupid excuse of why not to.

Everly and Ashley both laugh. Everly asks, "Really? Unprofessional? I know this is like an arranged business marriage thing but come on. You two are going to be married. He should see what he's marrying."

I sigh, knowing she's not going to give this up. "Okay, fine."

I pose in front of the camera with a small smile, wanting to get this over with. My heart races as she texts the photo to Lorenzo. I don't know if I want to know what his response is. Will he even respond? My phone buzzes with his reply almost immediately.

Lorenzo

Lauren, you look beautiful. Be careful tonight.

"See! He said you look beautiful. Maybe he won't be the worst husband," Ashley says.

I don't know why, but that sets off my anger again. They have no idea what it's like to be forced to marry someone you don't love while you have feelings for someone else. Not that they know about Romeo, but still. They know about how everything is going to be with Lorenzo once we're married, minus me not being able to come back to high school. I haven't shared that bit of information yet. Ugh, thinking about that is making me feel even angrier.

"Then you marry him, Ashley. He's not a good man, and he's so closed off. He doesn't want me anymore than I want him. You can have him and live happily ever after throwing away all your dreams to become his wife and a mother to his kids," I yell at her.

I stomp off into the bathroom, slamming the door closed, needing to get myself together. She didn't deserve that, but I couldn't help myself. I don't want my friends to try to convince me that marrying Lorenzo isn't the worst thing in the world. They should be on my side and know how much it sucks. I take a deep breath and try to remember tonight is supposed to be fun and just about us girls.

CHAPTER TWENTY-THREE

LAUREN

The limo arrives at Everly's house, and we all go outside to head to the dance. I've never ridden in a limo before, so this is kind of exciting. I made a quick apology to Ashley on the way out the door, and she waved me off like everything was forgotten. I appreciate her not making a big deal of it or being mad at me.

The school has been completely transformed for this one night. I can't recall the exact theme, but it was some rich, extravagant person's theme. There are real chandeliers hanging from the ceiling, which I can't even imagine how much that cost. There are some tables scattered around the auditorium by the walls that have gold vases filled with roses. The roses are beautiful. A red carpet leads into the auditorium, making you feel you're really walking the red carpet. At the end, there are flashing lights from the cameras taking pictures.

Ashley, Everly, and I take our turn for the pictures. We pose nicely for the first one, but we quickly become silly. I can't help but laugh and giggle with them as we make silly faces and then do the Charlie's Angels pose for one of them.

After we finish with the pictures, we head to the dance floor. There are a lot of slow songs, which aren't great for a friend's homecoming, but when there's a fast song, we all act silly dancing. I'm having a really great time with my friends. I don't know if it's because I know that our time together will end soon, but I'm going to go with it. I actually feel... happy. Which is a rare emotion for me.

Ashley and Everly wanted to spend the night together, but I told them that my parents didn't want me to. It was a lie, one that I'm kind of regretting now. I can't take it back though.

After another slow song comes on, we step to the side. I watch Everly stare off into space, and I know what's bothering her. I feel for her.

"You're missing James," I state.

Everly sighs. "Yeah, I am. The long distance is hard. I wish we still lived in the same house, so I can go to his room to see him whenever I want."

I nod, but don't reply. I love this about Everly. She knows that I'm upset about my arranged marriage, but she still talks to me about her feelings. Some people may think that she's being selfish, but I don't think so. I think she feels comfortable talking to me, and she doesn't want to worry about stepping on eggshells around me. No one likes it when people do that. At least, I don't.

Everly's friend and ex-boyfriend, Jake, comes up to our group and begins talking to her. He's asking her to dance with him, but she seems hesitant. I'm not sure if it's because she's with James or just the fact she doesn't want to leave us. Either way, Ashley and I encourage her to go. Jake seems like a good friend, and I don't think he'll try anything with her.

He's also one of Ben's best friends. Jake has the reputation of being a playboy around the school. I can see it. He's gorgeous. He has hazel eyes, like Everly's, and shaggy dark brown hair that goes past his ears. He's clean shaven and very fit. All of Everly's male friends are fit and honestly good-looking. I don't think she could really go wrong with any of them. I have seen James, though, who looks nothing like his brother, Ben. James has dirty blonde hair and green eyes. While he's handsome, I think Ben is more my type with his blonde hair and blue eyes. Wait, why am I thinking about my type? I don't have a type. I can't have a type. Besides, wouldn't my type look something like the guy standing in the corner of the room watching my every move? My heart skips a beat as our eyes connect. Yeah, that's my type right there.

I've been staring off in his direction for too long. I didn't even notice anyone coming up and stealing Ashley's attention. She's currently talking to one of Jake's friends, which I can't remember his name. I'm sure she has a class with him, but I don't.

Ben sneaks up beside me and startles me. "Geeze, you came out of nowhere."

He laughs. "Sorry. Just wanted to say hi. Enjoying the dance?"

I smile. "Yeah, actually. I'm having a really good time with my friends. What about you? You brought a date, right?"

He nods. "Yeah, I did. She's okay, but she seems more interested in her friends than me."

I look over in the direction he's staring in and sure enough, there are a few girls sitting around at a table together, talking and laughing. If Ben was my date, I would not be just sitting around with my friends.

I peek over at Everly and can't help but smile. She's having a blast with Jake. They danced to a slow song and now they're having fun with the fast ones. They're both dancing like crazy people, just like the three of us did earlier. As the song's ending, I watch him spin her around and push her out into the crowd. No, not the crowd, into James.

"Did you know he was coming?" I ask Ben.

Ben nods. "Yeah, it was hard keeping it from Everly, but I figured this would be a nice surprise."

It's a fast song, so Ashley and I head a little further onto the dance floor and start dancing. The guy she was talking to follows her in, and Ben is close by me. As we dance, we catch Everly's gaze and give her a thumbs up. We figure she needs the assurance to ditch us so she can spend the rest of the night with James.

The next song is a slow dance, in which Ashley goes off to dance with Jake's friend. She looks like she's really enjoying spending time with him, so I wouldn't be surprised if they did become boyfriend and girlfriend.

"Would you like to dance with me?" Ben asks, holding out his hand.

I smile and go to take it, but my smile quickly fades when I remember the reality of my situation. I've been so careful not to be around boys so Lorenzo wouldn't hurt them. For a split second, I somehow forgot about this fact. This dance made me forget about my reality for a couple of hours.

I shake my head. "I'm not sure that's a good idea. I'd love to, but..."

Ben doesn't drop his hand as he says, "It's just one dance. I know you're engaged, but I feel like you deserve one dance."

I look over toward the table that his girlfriend is sitting at, and she's not even looking this way. Maybe if I dance with him, she'll get jealous. It would be nice to dance to one slow song. Romeo knows how I feel about him, and he knows Ben isn't a threat.

"Alright, sure," I say as I put my hand in his.

He leads me further out onto the dance floor, and we begin slow dancing. As much as I'd love to dance closer, I'm keeping a healthy distance between our bodies. I don't want any misinterpretation between anyone here.

The silence drags on between us, and I'm regretting my decision. What if somehow this gets back to Lorenzo? What if one of these students works for him and gives him the wrong impression about Ben? What if he asks Romeo and he tells him, but Lorenzo still thinks of him as a threat? My heart races at my stupidity.

"I had a squirrel in my room this afternoon," Ben blurts out.

"What?" I ask, snapping out of my mini panic attack.

He clears his throat. "Sorry, you looked like you were in your head, so I wanted to break the silence."

I smile again at him because somehow, he always knows what to say and do. We only talk during class, sometimes at lunch, and occasionally right after school. He is sweet to me, and I'm not sure why. I'm pretty sure he doesn't like me more than a friend because he has made it clear he knows I'm engaged. He's just so... nice.

"So, you didn't have a squirrel in your room?" I ask.

"Oh, no, I did. Everly had to help me get it out," he states like it was no big deal.

I laugh. "Um, why was there a squirrel in your bedroom?"

He shakes his head. "It's a dumb story. You don't want to know."

"Actually, yeah, I do," I state.

He sighs. "If you insist... Really, it was dumb. I had my window open, and there's a tree that's close to it. I heard some type of screeching sound, which sounded like a wounded animal, so I popped my head out to see. I noticed the squirrel trapped between branches, so I leaned out to help it get unstuck. Well, once I freed it, it jumped on me and ran up my arm and into my bedroom. I chased that thing around for a while but couldn't get it, so I asked Everly to help."

I let go of Ben for a moment while dancing to laugh harder than I've laughed in a long time. I can just picture the squirrel running over him and around his room as he chases it.

"So, how did you get it out of your room?" I finally catch enough air to ask the question.

"I gave Everly a box to catch it in and, surprisingly, it worked. She opened the window as I threw it back out onto the tree," he states.

"Wait, I thought the window was already open?" I ask, trying to picture the hilarious event.

He gives a sheepish smile. "It was until I closed it before leaving the room. I don't know why I did, but I just wanted to make sure it didn't jump out the window and miss the tree or something."

Alright, if I wasn't in love with Romeo and in a crazy situation, I would be falling in love with this boy. I glance back over at his girlfriend's table to see that they are now all watching us. She probably heard me laughing. I pull myself closer to Ben, leaning my head on his chest as we finish slow dancing. I want to make her jealous, so she can see what she's missing. Then again, maybe it's best if she doesn't, because clearly Ben deserves better.

After the song, Ben heads off to hang out with Jake, and I look for Ashley. She's still dancing with the same guy, so I'm pretty sure she's done for the night. I look around for Romeo and spot him in a different corner of the room than he was standing in earlier. I walk toward him and lean against the wall beside him, but not too close.

"Did you have a good dance with Benjamin?" Romeo asks in a cold voice.

I feel my heart jump into my throat. Ugh, I didn't even consider how the last part of that dance would look to him. I'm so stupid.

"Ben is a nice guy. He's a good friend and his girlfriend was being stupid. I was trying to get her to be jealous and realize she's missing out," I state.

I'm not sure that explanation really helped the situation. Okay, I really am stupid. I look around the dance floor to find Ben still talking with Jake and a couple of other guys now. I don't know why, but I half expected to find Lorenzo murdering him in the middle of the dance floor.

"Is that so?" he asks.

Crap. I need to defuse this situation fast. "I'm ready to go. Will you drive me home?"

"Are you sure you don't want Benjamin to?" His voice is icy again.

"Nope," I state.

I don't want to get into this with him here, and I really don't want to stay any longer when he could do something to Ben. Why am I so stupid? I was having too good of a time and pretending that my reality didn't exist. Well, my reality is dangerous for those around me, and I need to remember that.

Romeo doesn't move, so I look around to make sure no one is watching before I move in front of him, touching his chest. "Please, Romeo. Take me home."

His eyes soften at my request. "Let's go."

I nod and lead the way with him keeping his distance behind me. I stop for a quick second next to Ashley to let her know that I'm leaving. She gives me a hug, and I head out the door. I would've said goodbye to Everly, but she seems busy with James. I'm pretty sure she's about to head out with him shortly, too.

Right as I get in the car with Romeo, my phone buzzes. I glance down at it, seeing a call from Lorenzo. My heart stops as I stare at it. Lorenzo rarely calls me.

"Hello?" I answer, trying to keep my voice even.

"Good evening, Lauren. I wanted to see how the dance went," he states in a casual tone.

Is he really just calling me to see how the dance went? Does he already know about Ben? Should I go back in there and warn him? Okay, stop. Don't panic. Lorenzo knows nothing, but it might be best if I tell him before someone else does.

"I did, thank you," I state, not knowing how to bring up the dance with Ben.

"I'm glad. Sorry I couldn't take you," he states.

I give a small laugh. "That's okay. I think it would've been awkward for you to attend a high school dance…"

He chuckles. Chuckles! I don't think I've ever heard him do that before. Has he been drinking? This is all so unlike him.

"Well, I just wanted to make sure you had a good time tonight. I won't keep you. Is Romeo bringing you home?" he asks.

"Yes, he's driving me home right now," I state.

"Good. Well, I hope you have a good night, Lauren," he says.

I close my eyes and take a deep breath. "Wait," I state.

"Yes?" he asks.

"I... I need to tell you something," I say and feel like I'm about to throw up.

"What is it?"

"I... I danced with someone. One time. I danced with a friend who is a boy one time. He had a girlfriend there, but she wasn't paying attention to him. Anyway, he asked me to dance, and I meant to deny him, but he was being sweet and trying to make me feel better. He's a good friend of Everly's. I swear it was nothing, and we kept a respectable distance and...."

I would've kept rambling if Lorenzo didn't interrupt me with a... laugh?

"Lauren, it's okay. I can tell by the way you're rambling that it wasn't anything more than a fun dance with a friend, right?" he asks at the end, just for clarification.

I spit out quickly, "Yes! Right! I promise, that's all it was."

"Alright, well, I appreciate you being honest with me about it."

I close my eyes again as I take a few deep breaths to get my breathing back under control. "So, you're... not going to hurt him?"

"Did he touch you inappropriately?" he asks seriously.

"No," I state.

"Then no, I won't hurt him."

"You aren't going to ask me who it was?" I ask.

"I think I can guess," he states.

Really? How would he be able to guess? "Who?"

"Benjamin Crawford," he states.

I glance over at Romeo and glare at him as he continues to look straight ahead, staring at the road. Did he somehow already tell him?

"Romeo already told you, didn't he?" I ask.

"Actually, no. I just know Benjamin is a friend of yours. Also, I know his father, so don't worry. He is safe. Unless, of course, he touches you inappropriately..." he states as a warning.

"No! No, he wouldn't do that," I quickly state.

"Alright. Well, you have a good night, Lauren," he says.

"Good night... Lorenzo," I say as the phone call ends.

I look over toward Romeo, who has a smirk on his face. "What are you smirking about?"

"Nothing," he states.

I shake my head. Yeah, that was one of the most terrifying interactions I've ever had with Lorenzo. He was forgiving this time, but I will make sure there isn't a next time. I'm going to be more careful because I don't know what I'd do if someone got hurt because of me.

CHAPTER TWENTY-FOUR

ROMEO

I walk Lauren to her front door before heading to my house. I wanted nothing more than to walk her inside and have my way with her tonight. She was gorgeous in her homecoming dress with her hair and makeup all done. It didn't help that I kept replaying the video footage of her taking off that same dress and showing off the lingerie set she bought.

So, lust is not the only strong emotion that I was feeling tonight. I hate to admit it, but my jealousy has gotten out of control. When I saw Lauren dance with Benjamin, I wanted to go over there and rip his head off. I know he is just her friend, and that dance meant nothing, but it killed me watching them. Why? Because it wasn't me. What I wouldn't have given to be the one dancing with Lauren tonight. I think I need to beat up the punching bag a bit.

I walk through my front door to find Matteo sitting in the chair facing the door. I mentally scold myself for not checking or paying attention enough to realize he had come in. Not saying a word to him, I quickly pull up my phone cameras to ensure that Lauren is alright. I flip through each one to find nothing out of the ordinary, and she's already in her bedroom.

"What's up?" I ask Matteo.

He leans his head on his hand, with his elbow on the arm of the chair. "Lorenzo asked me to babysit Lauren for a few hours so you could have some fun."

"Fun?" I ask.

He smirks. "Remember how we thought one of ours was betraying us and giving intel to the Irish?"

My smile fades. "Yes."

"Well, we caught him, and now a message needs to be sent. Lorenzo thought you'd like to do the honor. Plus, we need some information," he states.

My heart races thinking about going back to my old job for a moment. I've never particularly enjoyed torturing and killing men, but there were some that truly deserved it. Most of the time, it's just a necessary evil. It must be my lucky day because now I can take it out on someone and not just my punching bag.

"Where is he? The usual?" I ask.

"Yep. Have fun, bro," he says.

I grab my bag and head out the door. I don't like leaving Matteo in charge of Lauren, but I'm looking forward to taking care of this. After getting in my car, I pull up my phone to text Lauren.

Matteo will be on watch tonight.

Lauren

Where are you going?

To take care of some business.

Lauren

Be safe.

Always.

I can't help but smile like a teenager at her texts. She cares about me and wants me to be safe. I don't usually text her when I'm switching off with Matteo, which isn't often, but I figured with how she's been lately, it would be a good idea. I don't want her thinking that I'm watching the cameras, and she does something sexy or embarrassing.

I call Lo on the drive over.

"Romeo," he answers.

"Thanks for the break, Lo," I state.

He chuckles. "It's been a while. I thought you'd like to get in on the action. I'll meet you there shortly."

"Just like the good old days. See you soon," I state, hanging up the phone.

I pull up to the warehouse and check my surroundings. This is our territory with a good amount of guards, but you never know, especially when keeping a prisoner. Though this is our traitor, betraying us to the Irish. It's doubtful the Irish would come to save him. He's better off dead to them at this point.

I grab my bag and walk through the front entrance of the warehouse. I nod to our men as I pass by toward the elevator. One lets me on without a word, and I push the button for the lowest level, entering my passcode on the hidden panel. Few know about the lowest floor and what goes on down there. If the police ever decide to raid our warehouse, which they are all in our pocket, so they wouldn't, but if they did, then they'd never find it.

The elevator doors slide open, and two of our guys are standing outside the door where we keep our prisoners to interrogate them. They both grin as I walk up.

"Nice to see you Romeo, it's been a while," the guard on the right, Mikey, says.

I grin back. "Too long," I state.

He opens the door for me, and I walk into the darkness. I flip the light switch on and study the prisoner chained to the chair in front of me. It looks like someone already had some fun with him as his right eye is swollen shut, and there's dried blood on the side of his face and forehead. I walk up closer and kneel in front of him, studying him. I haven't seen him before.

"What's your name?" I ask.

He looks up at me and doesn't answer. He has red hair, which makes me think he might be Irish. If so, how did he end up one of ours?

Plopping my bag on the floor, I walk toward the table with our tools used for extracting information, along with extracting other things. I pick up a simple knife and head back toward him, scooting a chair to sit in front of him.

I play with the knife. "Don't make me start already. It's such a simple request. Name," I demand.

"Adrian," he grits out.

"Good," I state.

That's not an Irish name, and he doesn't have an accent. I doubt he's Irish. Wonder what he's doing mixed up with them.

"Hello, Adrian. I'm Romeo," I state.

"I know," he says through clenched teeth.

My grin widens. "Then you must know how this works. You've betrayed us, so you're a dead man, regardless. We can either make this quick or painfully slow. The choice is yours."

"Fuck you," he spits in my face.

I wipe the spit as I rise from my chair and punch him in the jaw. His head snaps back, and he groans. I have a feeling it's not going to take much to get the information I need out of him.

"I'll give you one more chance. Hard way or easy way?" I ask.

He doesn't respond, so I take the knife and slam it into his left hand. He screams like a baby as I leave it there. I wait for his cries to subside before yanking it back out, creating more pain and blood oozing from his hand.

Once he stops crying, I ask again, "Still the hard way?"

"What do you want to know?" he sobs out.

"Why'd you betray us?"

"Anthony is my cousin. I didn't have a choice," he continues, crying.

Geeze, this guy is a wimp.

"Interesting. So, you were planted here then?" I ask, wondering how we missed the connection.

"No. I didn't know until he approached me a few months back. I tried to stay loyal, but he said he'd kill me if I didn't get him the information he wanted."

I laugh. "You must've known you were a dead man if you betrayed us. Pity. You know we protect our own. Had you come to us, we would've provided you protection."

It's not a lie. We care for our own. We protect our men and their families. Sometimes it's even extended to their friends. All they have to do is ask.

He shakes his head.

"Regardless, keep going. What information did you provide him?" I ask, while wiping the knife on my pants to clean it off.

He watches my every move. "I don't know. It wasn't a lot. I don't know much."

I point the knife at him, and he flinches. "Try again."

He whines. "Seriously, it wasn't much. I mostly told him about drug deals and drops. Recently, he wanted me to get some information on the don's fiancé."

My heart skips a beat. I know our enemies are going to want to know everything about her, but hearing it is different. This is why she's being protected 24/7. She has a giant target on her back, all because she's tied to Lo.

"What information did you provide?" I ask through clenched teeth.

"Just her name and what she looks like. I didn't know anything else about her. I just found out where she lives and that she still attends school, but I didn't get that information to him yet," he says while squeezing his eyes closed.

Standing from my chair, I place the knife over his right hand. "I suggest you rethink that and tell me the truth. What information does he know about her?"

His breathing becomes rapid as he wiggles in his chair, trying to get free. "I swear, man. I swear, nothing. Just her name and what she looks like. I didn't give him anything else, I swear."

I'm about to drive the knife through his other hand when I hear the door open behind me. Lo strides in and stops a few feet away. I sigh, letting the knife drop to my side while stepping away to meet with Lo.

"What have you found out so far?" he asks, looking him over.

"Not much. His name is Adrian, and he's Anthony's cousin. Anthony approached him a few months back saying he needs to be a mole, or he's dead," I state.

Lo sighs. "Idiot. Do they never learn? We would've protected him."

I laugh. "Yeah, that's what I said. He gave him some intel on our drugs and drops. Anthony is curious about your fiancé."

This grabs his attention. "Is that so?"

I nod. "He claims he only gave him a name and what she looks like. He hasn't passed on where she lives or her school yet."

"Think there's concern here?" Lo asks.

I shrug. "Not sure what he would plan on doing. Lauren is cause for a war, so he'd be stupid to do anything."

"*Stronzo* is an idiot like his grandfather and father. He'll be the boss in no time with how they're being killed off. We need to keep an eye on the Irish. I don't like them, but I'm not ready to create an enemy out of them... yet," Lo states as he glares at Adrian.

I nod my head toward the prisoner. "What do you want to do with him?"

Lo grins and rolls up his white dress shirt sleeves. "Let's have some fun before killing him."

I smirk and hand the knife over to him, following his lead.

Chapter Twenty-Five

LAUREN

I'm not sure what happened the night of homecoming, but once Romeo returned from whatever he was doing, he was different.

Not only did he have a change of clothes on, but his entire demeanor was different. He snuck into my bedroom in the middle of the night and woke me up, but not on purpose. He was sitting in the chair beside my bed, watching me sleep. I could feel his presence, which woke me up almost instantly.

He explained to me he needed to make sure that I was okay. That we would be a little more cautious when we go out, and he doesn't want me to stray too far from him. Obviously, that scared me because that means there's a threat. He promised me there wasn't, but what else could it be? He sensed how I was feeling, so he held me in bed until I fell back asleep. That took a while, and it wasn't because I was scared anymore. It was from his proximity and how comforted I was with him holding me.

It's hard to imagine that in a few short months, it'll be Lorenzo's arms wrapped around me in bed. Or at least, it should be. I'm struggling to come to terms with getting married and living a life with him. Before it was just that I didn't want to, but I still imagined it because I had no choice. Now... I'm not so sure.

Romeo and I still haven't talked about what happened the other night when he kissed me. I think he still believes there's nothing we can do about our feelings because there's no way out. He doesn't know what I know, though. I need to find some time to talk to him privately. I thought about it when he was holding me the other night, but it didn't feel like the right time. He seemed off and distracted.

So once again, I find myself going on a date with Lorenzo, and not the man that I love. I refused this date at first, but Lorenzo insisted we go. Why? Because he's trying. He's a freaking mafia boss, and he's trying to woo me or some crap. If I had a therapist, she'd be asking me why I'm so angry at that. Then we'd dig deeper into those feelings and talk about them.

So, let's do this. Since I wanted to become a therapist myself, which clearly, I won't be able to do anymore since I'm not allowed out of the house. Let's play this game. I'm angry with Lorenzo. Why? Well... He's forcing me to marry him and taking away all my freedoms. Great, we knew that, but why the extra anger that's been rising?

He makes me mad when he texts me. He makes me mad when he takes me on a date. He makes me mad when he's nice to me.

His face makes me mad. So why is it, besides that I'm being forced into a marriage with him, that I'm so angry at him?

Because he's a freaking mob boss who is trying to get to know me and make me feel special. Lorenzo was supposed to be some bad guy that murders people and keeps me prisoner. He wasn't supposed to be trying to be nice to me. He shouldn't want to even talk to me. Shouldn't we just be living our separate lives while occasionally trying to make a baby or something? I cringe at the thought. That sounds awful.

But fine, let's continue playing therapist mode. So why does that make you so angry, Lauren? Well, for one, because I'm sitting here talking to a damn teddy bear like it's my therapist, clearly proving that I'm insane.

Ugh, fine! I admit it. I feel guilty! I feel guilty for loving Romeo when Lorenzo is apparently being faithful to me and trying hard to get to know me. I'm a horrible person for loving someone else and being unfaithful to my fiancé when he's doing the opposite.

I cannot get Romeo out of my head. Everywhere I look, he's literally there. If he's not, then he's in my head. I want him so badly it hurts, and I don't understand why. We've done nothing but fight off these feelings for each other. Those few short months that led up to these feelings, is that really enough to show us we love each other? Yeah, we had some good conversations and got to know each other well. We have been forced together for so long, but do we think that might be the problem? Are these feelings because we're forced together in close spaces so much?

It's hard to believe that's true. Regardless, we're getting off topic here. So, fine. I'm angry at Lorenzo because he cares, and he shouldn't. I want to escape with Romeo and never look back. I want us both out of this dangerous world. Is that so bad?

A knock sounds on my door, and I shove my teddy bear under the covers as if I was caught with drugs. The door opens as I sit on the bear to further hide the evidence.

Romeo is standing in my doorway, staring at me with a grin on his face. "What are you hiding?" he asks, nodding his head toward the bulge under me.

"Nothing," I say too quickly.

His grin widens as he stalks toward me. "Then you won't mind if I lift your covers?"

I shake my head. "There's no need for that. There's nothing there."

He laughs this time. A full-on laugh and it makes those butterflies in my stomach appear. They quickly disappear as he tackles me and pushes me to the side so he can yank the teddy bear out from under the covers.

He inspects it, twisting it around, looking at it. "Why are you hiding a stuffed animal? Is it filled with drugs?"

This time I laugh. "No! I just... I don't know. I wasn't expecting anyone to come in!"

"What were you doing with it?" he asks.

I blush and say quietly, "Talking to it..."

He stares at me and then glances back at the bear. "What were you telling it?"

"What?"

"What were you saying to it?" he asks.

I shrug. "Nothing. It's not important."

Oddly, Romeo doesn't push it. He hands the bear back to me, and I embarrassingly give it a hug.

He smirks. "Seriously? It's a stuffed animal."

"Hey! It's Mr. Beary to you! He's been with me since the day I was born. He has helped me through plenty of crises in my life," I state, hitting him on the arm.

"Do you have one now that you were talking to him about?" Romeo asks seriously.

I look away from him and don't answer, but I don't need to. He knows the answer.

"It's time to go," he states.

I nod and lead the way out the door. Romeo is going to be present through this whole date with Lorenzo. Usually, he stays behind while we go alone, but Lorenzo insisted on having the extra backup, considering we'll be out in the open and in a crowded area.

Did I mention that we're heading to the fair? That's right, the fair. As in, cotton candy, games, and rides. Lorenzo is taking me to the fair. He thought it would be romantic and insisted that he wanted to go. I can't imagine him wanting to do such a thing, but who am I to disagree with the mafia boss?

So, now I'm awkwardly sitting in the car with Romeo, the man I love, to go to the fair with my fiancé, the man I don't love. Romeo is going to be watching our entire interaction, and I have to pretend not to notice him. I also have to pretend to be enjoying myself and into Lorenzo, at least a little. I'm just afraid that I'm going to give away my feelings for Romeo, and we're both going to end up killed. Or worse, Romeo will end up dead while I'm stuck living with knowing I'm the reason he's dead.

"Hey…" Romeo places his hand over mine as he drives the car.

Instinctively, I place my other hand on top of his.

"Lauren…" he starts, but I interrupt.

"Don't say anything. I can't right now," I state.

He nods and doesn't say anything more, but he keeps his hand between both of mine. We drive like that until we get off the exit for the fair and put on our faces, like we mean nothing to each other.

We park next to Lorenzo's car. Lorenzo gets out and opens my door, holding a hand out for me to take. I hesitate for a moment, but accept it. He helps me out, closes the door, and nods to Romeo.

I turn back to look at Romeo, who puts on a ball cap and wraps a scarf around his neck. Who wears a ball cap to the fair at night? I pull my eyes away from him and study Lorenzo, who is wearing a long black thick trench coat. It is cold tonight, so I'm glad I wore my fuzzy jacket with a pair of jeans and boots.

"You look beautiful, Lauren," he states smoothly.

"Thank you," I reply.

Am I supposed to compliment him back? I probably should, right? I mean, I did basically ask him to come inside my house to sleep with me the other night. Cringing at the thought, I'm thankful that he didn't take me up on that offer.

"You look handsome," I state while awkwardly placing my hand on his chest.

I see his lip twitch as he leads us to the entrance of the fair. He nods to the attendant who lets us go through without providing a ticket. Does he know everyone? Is everything just basically given to him because of who he is?

"What would you like to do first?" he asks, pulling me out of my thoughts.

"Uh... I don't know," I say.

He studies me for a moment. "Have you ever been to a fair before?"

I shake my head no.

"Seriously? You can't tell me they didn't have any in the south," he states.

I laugh. "No, they had plenty. We just never went. We aren't the fair going type of family."

He nods in understanding. I can imagine that his family was similar to mine. We don't spend much time together. Ever since I was little, my father was rarely around, and my mom kept busy around the house.

Lorenzo holds my hand and leads me up to a line for the Ferris Wheel. We stand there, waiting, and I can't help but laugh. The longer we wait, the harder I laugh.

"What is it?" he asks, and he looks amused.

"I'm sorry... I just... You're standing in line for a Ferris Wheel," I state.

He smirks. "I suppose I am."

We stare into each other's eyes for a moment, and both burst into laughter.

"Lorenzo, we really don't have to do this. We don't have to be here," I say.

"Do you not want to be?" he asks seriously.

"No, I mean... It's fine. It's just that I know this isn't your scene. Why are we here exactly?" I ask, studying him.

"I know all your friends were going to the fair. I figured you would want to as well. I didn't want to take the experience away from you when you've already missed so much because of me," he states seriously.

My heart squeezes. I want to be angry with Lorenzo, and I want to hate him. He's making both things difficult to do. He's really trying, and I don't know what to do about that. He's not supposed to be trying.

We finally get on the Ferris Wheel, and he sits close to me, placing his arm around my shoulders. It moves, and I look out into the night. It's cloudy, so I can't see the stars, but all the lights are beautiful. I can't help but think this is what Everly saw when she was here with James the other day. He proposed to her with a promise ring. I'm so happy for her, but jealousy sometimes creeps up when I think about them.

Lorenzo pulls me from my thoughts again as he leans closer and pushes the hair away from my face. I stare at him as he stares back, like he's debating something. I don't realize what that is until it's too late. His lips are on mine before I comprehend what's happening. The kiss is gentle and sweet. I don't pull back and he doesn't either.

Grabbing the back of his head, I pull him in to deepen the kiss. I try hard to get into it. I think about how sweet he's been today and the fact that he's my fiancé. We kiss for a few minutes until the ride stops at the bottom for us to get out. He steps off first, holding out his hand to help me off. I take it and walk with him as he leads me down the path with fair games on both sides.

I can't see where I'm going because all I can think about is that kiss. There was nothing there. There was no passion, no butterflies, nothing. I walk hand in hand with him through the fair, and I feel nothing for him. All I can think about is Romeo and how just a simple touch ignites a fire in me. I've officially made my decision. I won't be marrying Lorenzo, and I'll do whatever it takes.

Chapter Twenty-Six

ROMEO

It's official. I'm going to murder my brother, the don. The man that just kissed Lauren for at least five minutes straight on the Ferris Wheel. Watching them walk hand in hand through these stupid fairgrounds is one thing, but to watch them make out on a ride? During that ride, my hand found its way to my holstered gun. I wanted to shoot Lo. I wanted to kill him for touching what's mine.

Mine. She's mine. I've accepted it. Just now, at this moment, I've accepted it. There's no one else for me and there never will be. Watching this date has set me over the edge. If I can't handle watching them together now, how am I going to handle watching them get married?

How am I going to handle it when I know on their wedding night he's fucking her and taking her virginity? How am I going to handle it when she's carrying his fucking baby inside her? I want to vomit even thinking about that.

No, I can't do this. I can't watch them. Over time, I'm going to resent Lo. I love him too much for it to come to that, but at what cost? I clearly don't love him enough not to fall in love with his fiancé. Damn it, what are my options here?

As they sit at a table looking like a nauseating couple eating a funnel cake, I go over my options.

Option one. I can tell Lo how I'm feeling. I can tell him I betrayed him, lied to him, and fell in love with his fiancé. The most likely outcome, he kills me. He has killed for much less. There's no doubt that he would kill me. If he didn't, then he would send me away and pretend to have killed me. I'd lose everything in this option, including Lauren.

Option two. I continue this current path and fight my feelings for her. I distance myself as much as I can and never look at her once this babysitting duty is over. The most likely outcome, I slowly die on the inside. Just knowing that she's with Lo would destroy me. I might prefer option one so I can have a quick death. Lo would at least do that for me. He'd give me a quick death with our history.

Option three. Lauren and I plan an escape. We'd have to do it soon, so it would be sloppy, which isn't ideal. Running away from Lo is nearly impossible, but it is possible. I'd have to really think about this option if it's what I choose because if we're caught, it's certain that I'll be dead. Lauren would have to live with knowing I was killed. I can't even imagine how she would live with that because if it were the reverse, I wouldn't be able to.

Those are the only three I can think of right now, and none of them sound appealing. Maybe option three, but I have a nagging feeling that would lead exactly where I thought it would from the beginning, a tragedy. That option leads to both of our deaths. I know Lauren wouldn't live with herself after that, and I don't think I can choose an option that could lead to her death.

I'm snapped out of my debate by a man approaching their table. Silently cursing myself for being distracted, I make my way to Lo's side, reaching him right as the red-haired stranger does. I keep my hand on my gun as I watch his movements. He holds out his hand for Lo to shake, but he doesn't take it.

The stranger grins, and that alone makes me realize who would have the balls to approach Lo like this. Anthony.

Anthony places his hand in his pocket and says, "What a surprise it is to see you out enjoying the fair. I had to come say hello."

"Then you have done what you came to do," Lo responds shortly and places Lauren further behind his back.

I can't concentrate on her right now. I keep my eyes on Anthony and quickly scan the area for any other threats that he may have brought with him.

"Are you on a date with your fiancé? Lauren, right?" he asks while trying to peek around Lo to get a better look at her.

"What do you want, Anthony?" I ask, while taking a step closer to him.

He holds up his hands, and his grin widens. "I'm not an enemy. At least, I didn't think we were enemies, are we?"

Lo glares at him. "I didn't think so either, until you had a spy on the inside looking into what's mine. Is there a reason for this?"

His stupid grin falters before saying, "Nothing more than pure curiosity."

"Curiosity killed the cat. We killed his mole. The cat is next," I state.

Anthony looks at me and then back to Lo. "Is that a threat?"

"You tell me. Does it need to be?" Lo asks.

Anthony shakes his head and backs away. "As I said, I was merely curious. I see I'm intruding on a fun night, so I'll take my leave. I hope I'll be invited to the wedding."

We watch him walk away, and I scan the area again to make sure there's no other threat. When I turn back to Lo, he's looking between Lauren and me. I didn't even realize that I had grabbed her, holding her against me. For what? To keep her safe? To comfort her? Regardless, it was a mistake that I can't afford to make again. I let her go slowly, pretending it was all to make sure I was keeping her safe.

"It might be best to take Lauren home for the night," I state seriously.

"You're right," he says, grabbing Lauren's hand.

He pulls her close and says, "I'm sorry to cut this short, but we just want to make sure you're safe."

She nods and doesn't question anything as she lets Lo lead her toward his car. I guess he's driving her home tonight. I jump in my car and follow closely behind, trying to stay alert and not let my mind wander.

Nope. My mind wanders the entire time Lo is in Lauren's house. I know her parents are home, but I still can't help but think about what could happen there. I watch the cameras intently as they sit and talk in the living room. She gets him something to drink at one point, and I notice her looking up at the cameras too often. I hope he's not noticing because she's being pretty damn obvious right now.

Lo kisses her goodnight on the front porch again, and I quickly turn the screen off on my computer and pretend I'm watching Hockey on the tv when he walks in without knocking.

"How'd the rest of the date go?" I ask, turning the volume down.

He sits on the couch beside me, and I sit up from my lazy position to face him.

"Fine. Hanging out with her in her living room was less awkward than the fair," he states.

I laugh. "I was surprised when you told me you wanted to take her there. Did she enjoy it?"

He cocks his eyebrow. "You tell me."

"What do you mean?" I ask, keeping my voice even.

"You've been watching her for almost a year. You should know by now when she's enjoying something," he states.

I let out a silent sigh of relief. "Yeah, she's hard to read sometimes. I think she had fun. She looked like it was awkward, but I hadn't seen her laugh like she did tonight in a while."

Lo studies me for a moment before saying, "Yeah. She's gorgeous when she laughs. You're right, I needed to stop looking at her as a child because she's not. She's young, but she's smart, determined, and beautiful. I'm not sure how I'm going to keep her on a tight leash when we're married."

I don't say anything because I don't know how to respond to that.

Thankfully, he changes the topic. "Do you think Anthony is going to be a problem?"

I shake my head. "He's definitely going to be a problem. Have Matteo put someone to keep tabs on him."

Lo stands and pats me on the shoulder. "I can't wait until you're back as my underboss. I miss you."

I grin. "Of course you do. I'm the best you'll ever have."

"Yeah, don't tell Matteo that, but I hope you don't plan on going anywhere, anytime soon. I need you here with me. Don't do something stupid to get yourself killed," he says as he heads toward the door.

My insides twist at his words. There's no way he knows, right? But if he does, do his words have another meaning? Like, don't tell me you have feelings for her, or I'll have to kill you. Or don't try to run away because you know I'll have to kill you. Damn it, of course he doesn't know, but these thoughts aren't going anywhere. I'm going to constantly be looking over my shoulder if I don't figure out this thing with Lauren soon.

As soon as his car pulls out of her driveway, I pull all the cameras back up in her house. Lo doesn't expect me to be sitting around watching them. We have sensors on them to let us know when there's movement, specifically for people who aren't recognized by the camera. Yeah, Lo has some pretty amazing technology.

Movement on the outside camera at the back of the house catches my eye. The alert doesn't go off on my phone because I haven't set it to night mode yet, where it'll alert me of all movement, even if it's Lauren or her family members.

I watch as the figure descends from the second-floor window and makes a final leap to the ground. What is she doing sneaking out of her window? I widen the camera's view and stand to get ready to intercept her to wherever she's running off to, but I don't have to. I watch as she runs over to my house, looking over her shoulder a few times before heading to the backdoor.

I make it there before she does. Opening the door, I apparently scare the shit out of her because she jumps back and lets out a small scream before clapping a hand over her mouth. I can't help the large grin on my face at how cute she looks right now.

Pulling her inside, I close the door. "What are you doing here, Lauren?"

She takes a few quick breaths, like she's trying to catch her breath from being startled. "I needed to see you."

"For what?" I ask.

"This," she states as she pulls me in for a heated kiss.

My mouth crashes against hers, and I immediately lift her up by the ass as she wraps her legs around my waist. I carry her to my bedroom, forgetting everything else in the world right now. After watching her tonight with Lo, I need this moment, and I can tell she needs it too.

I lay her on my bed and crawl on top of her, never letting our lips part. She moans, which drives me insane, but I need to stop this before it goes too far. I know I do.

I reluctantly pull away. "What is it you want, Lauren? Tell me."

"I want you, Romeo. I need you. I can't be with Lorenzo when I love you, and I don't care what happens to us. Right now, I just need you. We'll worry about the rest later. That is, if you feel the same way…" Her words start off strong and slowly get weaker as she continues to speak.

Pressing a kiss to her forehead, I say, "Yes, Lauren. I feel the same way. I love you. God, you have no idea the amount of torture you put me through tonight watching you with Lo. I wanted to murder him for touching you, for kissing you."

She stares at me for a moment in the eyes before saying, "He can have those moments, but there's one I want with you and only ever you. Take my virginity. I want it to be yours. I don't know what after tonight looks like, but I need it to be yours."

Fuck. Her words are making me lose whatever little self-control I have left when I'm around her. I don't know how I'm going to resist her like this. She sounds so sure of herself, but I'm still battling with everything.

She grabs my face and places her forehead against mine. "Please Romeo. Please stop thinking about the future for just one night. I need this. We need this. Please."

Fuck! Whatever self-control I had left just snapped. I slam my lips against hers and pull at her hair as I roll us both over so she's on top of me. We part for a moment so I can stare at her and make sure this is truly what she wants. She's panting on top of me. One look into her determined eyes and I know this is happening tonight. There's no going back after this.

CHAPTER TWENTY-SEVEN

LAUREN

Romeo rolled me on top of him, and I know he did it because he wants me to know that I'm in control. He wants this just as badly as I do, but he's afraid to take it. I can tell that he's still battling with himself, but I'm determined to do this with him tonight.

I don't know what the future holds for us, but I don't care. If my future is to be with Lorenzo for the rest of my life, so be it. I want to have this one night to remember and always look back on. My virginity should be taken by someone I love. I want it to be taken by my first love.

Tossing aside thoughts of the future, I stay in the present moment. I need this. We need this. I pull my sweater and shirt over my head at the same time, throwing them to the floor. I'm wearing one of my sexy lingerie sets I bought at the mall, and I specifically put it on tonight thinking about Romeo.

He moans as he rubs his hands up my stomach to my breasts, squeezing them.

"Lauren... Did you wear this for me?"

I'm so turned on right now and his hands on me feel so good that it's difficult to respond. "Mmm hmm."

He chuckles and quickly unsnaps the bra, throwing it to the floor as well. "I would've preferred nothing."

I moan as he plays with my nipple with one hand and the other slides down into the waistband of my jeans.

I pull him to sit up for a moment. "It's only fair if your shirt comes off too," I state.

He grins. "Gladly."

He lifts the shirt over his head and throws it to lie with mine on the floor. He stays in his sitting position and grabs a nipple in his mouth, sucking. Geeze. If this feels so good already, how is having sex going to feel?

I grab the back of his head to pull him closer. He kisses up my neck and finds a sensitive spot to suck on. I feel embarrassed as I continue to moan with every touch and kiss on my body.

He pushes me down on the bed and unbuttons my jeans. Yanking them down, he takes the thong with them. I lay completely naked below him, and the way he's looking at me doesn't allow any time to feel insecure. He loves everything that he sees.

He kisses me again all the way from my mouth, down my neck, until he reaches just below my belly button. Parting my thighs, he kisses up my right leg all the way until he reaches the top of my upper thigh. He repeats the same thing to the other leg. My breathing becomes erratic, and I want nothing more than for him to be inside of me.

"Romeo..." I beg.

"Soon. Let me burn into memory every inch of your body," he growls.

Oh my God. Is it possible to have an orgasm from words alone? He finally makes his way to exactly where I need him. He's licking and moaning like he's enjoying it more than I am, and that's not possible.

As he pulls away for a moment, he rubs circles around my clit with his thumb. He then presses his finger to my entrance and slowly slides it in. I've never had anyone touch me like this before, and I've never done anything to myself. It feels weird at first, but as he eases his way in further and pulls back out slowly, I get into the rhythm, and it feels so good.

"Baby... You're so fucking tight," he says, as he continues sliding his finger in and out.

I grab the back of his head and pull on him, so he comes up to my level and kisses me. He slams his lips against mine and we both moan at the same time.

I pull away for a moment to say, "Romeo... I need you. I need to feel you inside of me."

"Fuck, Lauren..." he says while kneeling and unbuttoning his jeans.

It only takes a few seconds for his pants to come off and he's kneeling over me, completely naked. I stare at his long erection as he strokes it. Oh, yeah... I forgot how big he is. If his finger felt like that inside me... How...

Romeo smirks. "Don't think about it, baby. I'll take it slow, and you let me know what you need, okay?"

I gulp and nod. I guess I'm showing my concern on my face. That's embarrassing.

Leaning over the bed, he takes a condom from the nightstand. He tears open the foil, and I watch as he slowly rolls it on. He hovers over me again and kisses me gently. As we kiss, I can feel him lining himself up against my entrance. I stiffen for a moment, only because I don't know what to expect. Is it going to hurt? Don't they say the first time hurts?

"Are you sure you want to do this?" he asks.

I nod.

"I need to hear you say it," he says.

"Yes. Romeo, please. I need you," I say.

He kisses me again and starts pushing inside me. I can feel myself stretching and it burns a little, but he takes it so slowly that it subsides quickly. He groans like he's in pain but continues pushing inside.

As he gets a little further, I tense as I feel a sharp pain. He stops and watches me for a moment before pushing in deeper as I let out a groan.

"Just relax, baby," he says as he stops moving.

I nod and do as he says, relaxing my body.

"Good girl," he whispers in my ear, sending shivers through my body.

He pushes into me a little harder, which sends a zing of pain through my body. He notices because he praises me and apologizes with kisses on my forehead and down to my ear and neck.

I just realized he hasn't moved in a bit, waiting for me to adjust. "I'm okay."

He nods and rocks back and forth inside me again. He's slow at first, but as the time passes, he's picking up the pace, and I've gotten over the initial pain. I'm starting to feel that familiar rise of heat in my stomach that only he has made me feel before.

His thrusts become erratic, along with his breathing. He must be close and honestly, so am I. I pull him down on top of me as I slam my mouth to his. Our tongues collide as we frantically kiss, both so close to going over the edge.

"Lauren..." he pants. "I'm not going to last much longer."

His forehead leans against mine, and I can't say anything in return as I unexpectedly reach my own climax. I scream his name and feel myself tightening around him. He quickly follows and then slowly pulls out, removing the condom and tossing it in the trashcan beside his bed.

He lays down beside me and holds me. "Are you okay?"

I roll over to face him and look in his eyes. I feel my throat tighten and the telltale burn behind my eyes that I'm about to cry. Why the hell am I about to cry? I bury my face in his naked chest and hold my breath, trying to rein in my emotions.

He holds me tighter and kisses the top of my head. Ugh, of course he notices that I'm losing it. Why am I losing it?

"Shhh. It's okay, baby, I've got you. I'm so sorry," he says soothingly.

I shake my head and control my random sobs. "No, don't be sorry. I don't know why I'm crying..."

He lets out a small huff of a laugh.

He just holds me for a few minutes while I regain my composure. I don't really understand what all that was about, considering this was exactly what I asked for and needed. I love him so much that it hurts.

I look back up at him and kiss him. He kisses me back with the same passion as before. After a few moments, I pull away.

"I love you so much, Romeo," I whisper.

"I love you too, Lauren," he says back.

We lay completely naked in his bed, never wanting to let each other go. I try my best to pretend that this is exactly how it's supposed to be, and there's no alternative where I'm not with Romeo in the future. I close my eyes with my face against his chest as I drift off to sleep.

CHAPTER TWENTY-EIGHT

LAUREN

The morning after sleeping with Romeo, I finally got the courage to tell him my plan. Well, the beginning of my plan. My heart was racing the entire time I told him because I wasn't sure what he was going to say. I needed to make sure that he loved me and wanted to be with me. That night gave me the courage to tell him.

It didn't go as I hoped. When I saw my copy of Romeo and Juliet on my desk, the plan flashed before my eyes. It's simple, really, in theory. If I could pretend that I'm dead, then I can escape without Lorenzo coming to look for me. I would need to find a way to get that drug from my father, but I could do it.

As for Romeo, he would have to fake his death, too. I'm not sure how he would do it, but we can figure that out. I want to say we can do it the same way, but I don't want it to look suspicious. Stealing one dose of that drug might go unnoticed. I'm not sure about two doses.

Either way, Romeo didn't like the plan. He said there were too many variables and too short of a time to plan it perfectly. He said he would think about it. I haven't heard anything from him since. Maybe it is stupid. Or maybe I'm wrong about how he feels about me.

Now it's Halloween. I have less than two months until I'm supposed to marry Lorenzo. I already decided I can't do it, and I won't. I'm at the point that I'm going to do my plan with or without Romeo. The ultimatum is going to be given to him tonight. I just hope that he's not going to betray me at the last minute if he decides not to come with me.

"Ready?" Romeo asks as I meet him by the front door.

I basically melt as I look at his costume. He's wearing a long red regal coat that looks like a pirate king or something. He also has on knee-high black boots and a black masquerade mask. He hasn't touched me since the night we shared, and my body has been begging for him since.

"Romeo…" I breathe out.

He smirks, knowing exactly what I'm thinking. "You look amazing."

I smile, knowing that I look pretty good as I did it for him. I figured I'd dress as Harley Quinn, but it's a modest version of her. We're heading to Ashley's house, where her brother is home from college and throwing a Halloween party. It already started, but I told Romeo that I wanted to get there late. I thought about not going at all, but it would be miserable not having any fun until I do whatever it is I'm going to do.

I've still been keeping my friends at a distance, especially now that I know I'll be leaving them. The easiest excuse is claiming my parents don't want me to go out or I have something to do with Lorenzo. Keeping them at a distance is for the best if I'll never see them again. My heart hurts a little thinking about that. They've been amazing friends.

"What's wrong?" Romeo asks, always knowing when something is on my mind.

"It's nothing... I just..." I start, but stop, not wanting to get into it right now.

He looks around and then walks forward, pulling me into a hug. I lean into it because he always makes me feel better. I know my mother is still upstairs getting ready and my dad is always working in his office. They're supposed to leave in about an hour for a few days, even though Brandon is coming home to visit.

I step back and kiss Romeo on the lips. After only a few seconds, he pulls back and rubs his hand through his hair.

"Lauren, we can't do this here," he whispers.

I give a smirk. "You can erase the footage."

He shakes his head but grins and pulls me in for another kiss. He turns us around and pins me against the wall as he kisses me and rubs his hand up my shirt, over my stomach.

A man clears his throat behind us, and we part quickly. I mentally scold myself as I find my father staring at both of us, clearly seeing the whole thing. Oh my God, what did I just do? I want to instantly cry at my stupidity for doing this in the open with my parents at home. What was I thinking? It could cost us everything.

"Dad…" My voice cracks.

He puts up his hand to stop me from talking. "Lauren, can I talk to you for a moment?"

Romeo steps in front of me and says, "Sir…"

My father interrupts, "I just need a second with my daughter, and then we can talk."

I've never heard my father have so much confidence before. He must be really mad at us if he's willing to interrupt and talk to Romeo like that. Oh God… What have I done? I'm so freaking stupid.

"Now Lauren," he demands and turns around.

I follow him down the hall into his office with my head down. Tears are already falling, and I don't know what to do or say.

"Sit," he states.

I do as I'm told. What else am I supposed to do?

He sighs, places his glasses on his desk, and rubs his temples with his middle fingers.

"Dad, I…" I start, but I stop myself. I don't really know what to say.

"You are engaged to Lorenzo, the don of the Italian Mafia. Lauren, do you know what you've done?" he asks, looking like he's concerned for me.

I say nothing and just give a nod.

He sighs. "Why?"

"I... I didn't mean to. I'm sorry, I don't know how it happened, but I tried not to. We tried not to..." I say, and I know I'm not making any sense.

"You've fallen in love with him?" he asks.

"Yes..." I whisper.

"And him?" he asks.

"He says he loves me. He avoided me as much as he could and never meant to betray his brother. Dad, please. Please, can you forget this happened? He'll kill him, and I can't live without him," I beg and sob.

My father puts his glasses back on and stares at me for a moment. "So, you understand the severity of it, and you risked it anyway. Look, Lauren... I won't say anything, but you can't let this happen again."

I nod and thank him.

"Lauren, I love you, and I wish that I never made this deal with Lorenzo. There's nothing I can do now, though. It's done. All I've ever wanted since the day you were born was for you to be happy. For you to be taken care of. I love you," he states sincerely, which makes me cry even more.

I round the desk and hug him, not knowing why, but I do. I've been mad at him for so long because of this deal and feeling like he doesn't love me, but he does. He was just put into an impossible situation that he had no choice but to accept.

"Let me talk to Romeo for a few minutes," he states.

I nod and walk out the door, which Romeo is waiting right outside for me. He looks at me with concern and like he's sorry.

He's sorry he messed up, but it wasn't his fault. I started it, and he tried to stop it. I'm an idiot.

Why on earth did I kiss him out in the open like that? We were caught. What if it was Lorenzo that caught us? I shiver at the thought. I know my father said he won't tell him, but what if he has to? What if Lorenzo has his suspicions and asks my dad about it? Would my dad lie to him to keep me safe?

I watch Romeo walk into my father's office and close the door behind him. I lean against the wall and fall to the floor, wishing that I could go back in time and erase everything that had just happened.

Chapter Twenty-Nine

ROMEO

I'm a fucking idiot. What the hell was I thinking, making out with Lauren like that out in the open? I wasn't thinking, that's the problem. When it comes to Lauren, I don't think anymore. We can't continue like this. Someone's going to end up dead and most likely that's going to be me.

Or it's going to be her father. I've been thinking about ways I can kill him off without anyone knowing it was me the entire time Lauren was in the office with him. That would be stupid though, because the whole reason Lauren is engaged to Lo is because of him. He's important and we need him. See? Stupid. I'm fucking stupid when it comes to Lauren.

I sit in front of Lauren's father, the man who just caught us making out in his home. My survival instincts are kicking in, and I'm holding back the intimidating threats I would usually make in this situation. I need to be smart for once. I need to see where this man's head is at before I go throwing threats in his face.

We're both silent. He's waiting for me to speak, but I'm not going first. I study him. He looks tired and older than he really is. He's studying me as much as I'm studying him. I removed my mask, of course, which is currently in my pocket. The other has my blade.

"I don't need to state the obvious of what I caught you doing with my daughter. I just want to know why," he states.

Taking a deep breath, I think over my response before speaking. I have no idea what this man wants to hear, so maybe a toned-down version of the truth?

"She's an amazing woman, and I find it difficult to stay away from her," I state.

"Even though you're betraying Lorenzo?" he asks seriously.

I close my eyes for a moment and concentrate on my breathing. It's difficult not throwing out the threats to him that he needs to stay quiet. We both know what would happen if Lorenzo found out.

"We never meant for it to happen," I state, staring at him.

"Do you love her?" he asks.

I drag my hand through my hair and mutter under my breath as I debate how to answer his question. At this point, does it matter?

I go with the truth. "Yes."

He leans back in his chair and sighs. "I saw nothing. You picked up my daughter as usual to take her to her friend's Halloween party."

I stare at him like that can't be it. Is he just trying to save his daughter from having to deal with Lo's wrath?

I nod, stand up, and head to the door without saying a word.

Her father's words stop me before I open it. "You know… As a father, all I've wanted for Lauren is for her to be happy and taken care of. It's too bad she's engaged to another man because you seem like just the man that I've always wanted for her."

I stare at him, not knowing what to say or what he's getting at.

He continues, "I've made plenty of mistakes in my life when it comes to her. Forcing her into a marriage with someone is one of those. I fully expect her to never speak to me again once she's married. It's the price I signed up for. I've accepted never being part of my daughter's life and it has killed me knowing that she's not happy. I'd do anything to ensure her happiness, even if it means I pay the price."

I let those words sink in as I leave his office, and find Lauren curled up against the wall. I want nothing more than to sit there with her and let her cry into my arms, but I can't. Not after everything that just happened.

"It's going to be fine, Lauren. Let's go to the party," I state, holding out my hand to help her up.

She shakes her head. "I don't feel like going to the party."

I sigh. "You need to. Come on, we'll take the long way there so you can pull yourself together before getting there."

After a few moments of hesitation, she finally takes my hand and stands up. I walk out the front door first and let her slide inside the car before I round it, getting into the driver's seat. She doesn't say anything as I get in and stay quiet, too.

We are only a minute away from her friend's house and neither of us has spoken a word the entire drive. I've put everything that happened in the back of my mind so I can concentrate on my job, which is to keep her safe.

"Have you thought more about what we talked about the other day?" she asks, breaking the silence.

I knew this would come up again. Of course I've thought about what she talked about the other day. She wants to pretend to kill herself so we can leave everything behind and live happily ever after. Did today not show her that will never happen? Seriously, we were just caught by her father. How does she think we're going to pull that off in less than two months?

"I have," I state, not wanting to get into this right now.

We pull up to the house, and she quickly exits the car, slamming the door. She stomps off, and I grab her arm.

"Lauren..." I state, not wanting her to be angry the whole night.

"What?!" she yells.

I look around to make sure no one is watching us. "Be quiet. We already messed up. Let's not make a bigger mistake."

She angrily laughs. "Whatever, Romeo."

I can feel my blood beginning to boil. "If you want to talk, then let's do it elsewhere."

"Fine, follow me," she says as she walks into the house filled with teenagers dancing and drinking.

I keep my eyes trained on her but continue to scan the room as we push through the crowd. She leads me up the stairs and into a bedroom, locking the door behind us. I'm assuming this is Ashley's room by all the pictures of half-naked men on her wall.

"What do you want to talk about?" I ask her, folding my arms.

I'm not going to lie, I'm angry at her right now. The way she's acting is pissing me off, even though I know she's scared and confused. I don't think talking about anything right now is going to help our situation. We're both too emotional. Her more than me.

"So, you don't want to do it? You don't love me, right?" she asks.

Seriously? That's what she gets out of this?

"Lauren, I fucking love you. That's the problem. I don't want to make any huge decisions like this without really thinking it through. One minor mistake and we're both dead, for real. Don't you see that?" I plead with her.

She shakes her head. "I'm dead either way, Romeo."

I sigh and hug her, holding onto her longer than I probably should. Thankfully, I locked the door so no one could walk in on us.

"Are you at least willing? If we knew everything would work out, would you do it?" she asks in a whisper.

Is this what the problem is? Does she think that it's a matter of my not wanting to do this?

"I would give up everything to be with you, Lauren. The problem is there is no guarantee, and we really need to think this through, okay?"

She nods. "Then let's think this through."

"Later," I state.

I can see she's still upset as her voice rises a little. "We need to talk about this."

"We shouldn't talk about this here. We'll find time to talk later," I say, giving her a quick kiss on the forehead.

"We never have time," she argues.

I ignore her, head to the door, unlock and open it. She's following behind me, and I feel bad about ending the conversation, but it needs to end. We'll find time later to talk in private.

As I exit the room, I notice her friend Everly walking by. I avert my gaze and walk right by her, heading downstairs. Shit, was this mistake number two today? What the hell is my problem? I'm losing all common sense because of a girl.

If Everly heard any of that, it could be the end for us. There are so many risks we are taking with this relationship. If you can consider this a relationship, I don't even know what we are anymore. All I know is that it's forbidden to love her, but I've done it anyway.

Her plan may be the only option that we have left at this point. We're not willing to fight our feelings for each other anymore, so that's out. Telling Lo is definitely out. While her plan has way too many variables, it may be the only option we have left. Is it worth the risk, though?

Chapter Thirty

LAUREN

I walk out of Ashley's room behind Romeo and spot Everly immediately. Romeo continues walking, and I freeze in my spot trying to figure out how to explain this one away, if I need to.

"Who was that?" Everly asks as I walk closer to her.

I shake my head. "No one important."

I can tell that she wants to press me further, but I give her a look that indicates I don't want to talk about it. One good thing about Everly is that she never presses for more information. She can easily read the room and knows when I don't want to talk about something.

"We didn't think you would make it. You didn't respond to our texts," she says, changing the subject.

"Sorry, I had bad service. My parents also left late, so I was running behind," I say.

Honestly, I didn't even look at my phone all night, so I never saw the texts from them. I used the excuse of my parents because it always seems to work.

"Ashley is going to get a kick out of your costume," she says, looking me over.

That makes me smile because I just realized what Everly is wearing. "We probably should've coordinated. I didn't think you would dress as Harley Quinn too. You make a better one."

Everly laughs. "Well, I actually think Ashley makes the best one."

"No way! Ashley too?" I laugh this time as I walk toward the stairs.

"I'm hitting the bathroom, and I'll come find you. Just a warning, they left out the punch when making the alcohol spiked with punch," she offers her advice to me.

That doesn't sound like a bad thing right now. The punch at Dillon's parties is always laced with alcohol and not very much punch. I usually avoid it or only have a few sips, but tonight feels like I could use the liquid distraction.

When I walk down the stairs, I notice Ashley flirting with Declan in the living room. I was going to say hi to her, but I'll leave her be for now. I look over her sexy Harley Quinn outfit and smile. Everly was right. She's definitely the best one.

I head to the punch bowl and pour myself a cup. I take one sip and cough at the burn going down my throat. Yep, they forgot to add the punch. I don't think I can sit here and drink this leisurely, or I'll throw up from the taste. Holding my breath, I gulp it down. I'm more than halfway through the cup when I feel a hand on my shoulder.

"Trying to get drunk?" Ben asks as I turn around to look at him.

I smile at him. "Yep."

He plucks the cup from my hand and drinks the rest.

"Hey!" I yell, smacking his shoulder.

He pours water into the cup, handing it back to me. While I could've used more alcohol, it's probably best that I don't have anymore.

He puts his arm around my shoulders and leads me away from the punch bowl, back into the living room. I shake my head and stare at his handsome face, which looks normal because he doesn't have a costume or mask on.

"Where's your costume?" I ask.

He shrugs. "I didn't feel like dressing up tonight."

I don't push him to answer why he didn't feel like it. He didn't ask me why I wanted to get drunk.

"Have you been to the haunted house down the street?" Ben asks me.

I laugh. "No, have you?"

Ben shakes his head. "Nope. I've always wanted to. Do you want to go check it out and see if the rumors are real?"

I stare at him for a moment to see if he's joking. He's not joking.

"It's just a stupid story to keep kids out. It's not real," I say.

"What story?" Everly asks, sneaking up behind us.

"The abandoned house at the end of the street. It's haunted and they say if you are in the house at midnight the week of Halloween, you won't come out," Ben explains seriously.

I watch Everly look at her phone, probably to check the time.

"Let's do it," she says.

Ben looks excited. "Really?"

"I'm assuming you haven't been?" Everly asks him.

He shakes his head. "No one would ever do it with me. Jake refuses because he believes in all that ghost stuff."

Everly shrugs her shoulders. "Yeah, I'm down for it. Lauren, are you in?"

"No thanks, I'll stay here," I reply while taking a sip of my drink and glancing at Romeo.

Everly and Ben head out to the supposed haunted house, and I walk over toward Declan and Ashley. I'm surprised Everly didn't tell Declan she was leaving the house. He's not going to be happy. I don't particularly like snitching on my friends, but her safety comes first. Besides, she didn't ask me not to tell anyone.

"Everly and Ben are heading to the haunted house down the street," I say.

"Now?" Declan asks, looking over where Everly and Ben were just standing.

"Yeah, they already left."

Declan pushes off the wall and heads toward the door. I don't know why I want to do this, but I grab his arm to stop him.

Maybe it's the alcohol in my system, or maybe I just want to pretend I'm a normal teenager for one night.

"We should teach them a lesson by scaring them," I say.

Declan grins, and Ben's friend, Jake, who is standing beside us, speaks up. "Oh! Who are we scaring?"

I laugh. "Ben and Everly went to the haunted house down the street."

"Say no more, I'm on it," he says, walking out the front door.

Okay... He didn't even stop to discuss a plan with us. Whatever.

"Anyway, you should go inside the house and make some noise or something, scaring them. We'll jam the front door so they can't open it," I explain my plan as Ashley and Declan stare at me.

"What?" I ask.

Ashley laughs. "I didn't think you had it in you to do a prank."

I grin. "You have no idea the type of pranks I can play."

We leave the party and head down the street to the haunted house. Jake is probably already inside doing whatever it is he wants to do. Declan heads in quietly after he explained to us how we should jam the door with some rocks and lock it. It didn't take us long, and I'm hoping it works.

We hear a scream come from the inside, which sounds like Everly. We hold back our laughter as we race down the driveway a little way and hide in the trees. It takes a couple of minutes before we hear anything else coming from the house. It sounds like they are trying to open the front door and failing.

Ashley gives me a high five and whispers, "It worked. We jammed the door."

I grin as we both listen for more sounds. I think we hear a bang and more jiggling at the front door. We can hear some mumbling but can't make out what they are saying.

"Oh my God, we need to get out of here right now. NOW!" Everly yells inside the house.

Ashley and I are covering our mouths as we try our best not to laugh, but my chest hurts from holding it in. We hear banging on the front door as someone tries to body slam it open. There's a figure at the window trying to open it. I didn't even think about jamming the window.

We watch the window slide open as Everly yells, "The window!"

She's thrown out of the window by one of the boys and then Ben follows with Jake pushing him out. Jake falls on top of Ben, and we watch them scramble to their feet. Neither Ashley nor I can contain our laughter anymore as we lose it. They run past us but quickly stop when they finally hear our laughter as we come out of the trees to reveal ourselves. We all turn toward the house where we hear Declan laughing, walking out of the front door.

Everly starts laughing hysterically, looking like she's about to pee her pants, and Jake and Ben both begin laughing after letting out heavy breaths.

"Did you guys all plan this?!" Everly glares at Ashley, Declan, and me.

Declan smirks. "It was Lauren's idea."

Everyone looks at me, and I continue to laugh harder. I can't get the image out of my head of Everly being thrown out the window and Jake falling on top of Ben. They were all so scared and fumbling everywhere. I haven't laughed this hard in a long time.

"Seriously? Declan, you almost gave me a heart attack. I thought I was going to die!" Everly yells at him while pushing his shoulder.

Declan shrugs. "I figured it would teach you a lesson on leaving without telling me."

Everly shakes her head. I can tell she didn't even think about Declan as she left the party. I have to say that I have those moments too. Honestly, I didn't check to make sure that Romeo was following me. I just assume he is or completely forget he's there because he does a great job of keeping his distance. Taking a quick look around, I don't see him anywhere. I hope he noticed I left the party...

We all walk back to the party together, laughing about everything that happened. I slow my pace and look at everyone around me. My throat tightens with a knot in it as my stomach sinks, watching them. They are all so happy, and we had a great time tonight. It was just a stupid prank, but it felt like so much more with my friends.

It's been a while since I've been this happy, and it kills me to think that I'm going to lose all this soon. I'm going to lose all of them. One way or another, this is all going to disappear. If I leave, then I'll never see them again or know what's happening in their lives. If I stay here with Lorenzo, then I still lose them because I won't be allowed back to school or out of the house. It hurts thinking that this is going to be the last Halloween I have with them.

I decide to end the night on a high note and sneak out when they are all distracted back in the house. Heading toward Romeo's car, he opens my door for me before I get there. I get in and don't say anything to him as he rounds the car and drives off.

"Everything okay?" he asks, glancing over at me.

"Yeah," I state unconvincingly.

"Talk to me, Lauren," he says.

I look over at him, studying his costume. As depressed as I felt moments ago, I'm now feeling a completely different emotion. I was angry with Romeo earlier, but all of that is forgotten as I stare at his tight black pants showing his leg muscles and that sexy pirate king jacket.

"Lauren..." he says again, pulling me from my thoughts.

"Hmm?"

He smirks. "You looked upset a moment ago, but now you look like you want to jump me."

I laugh because he's spot on. "Would it be so bad if I did?"

"I wouldn't object," he growls.

Those familiar flutters begin inside my stomach. I want nothing more than to do exactly that, but I know that's not going to solve anything.

"I think we should talk first," I say.

"Agreed."

"Should we pull over somewhere? Or should I sneak into your room again tonight?" I ask, hoping he'll say the latter.

"I'll pull over at this restaurant. It'll look like you wanted to stop and grab something to eat," he says.

I nod because I don't want to voice my disappointment. He pulls the car over, away from all the others. It's a secluded spot and with the windows tinted, no one would know if we were doing something in the back seat.

I glance to the back to see if that's something workable. Scanning the amount of space there, I decide that while he is a large man, he would fit. I'm small, so I could easily fit back there with him, especially if I was on top of him.

"We're not having sex in the back seat," he groans.

My head snaps to look at him, and I can feel myself blushing. How did he know what I was thinking? Was it that obvious?

"Okay," I say.

He shakes his head. "It's not that I don't want to... Fuck, Lauren. I want you, but we need to figure this out."

"Yeah, you're right," I try to say professionally.

We both stare at each other for a moment, and I know he's waiting for me to begin the conversation, but I decide to be impulsive instead. I throw myself across the seat, wrap my hand around the back of his head, and pull him in for a kiss. He doesn't protest and grabs me, pulling me onto his lap, deepening the kiss.

The steering wheel digs into my back and my leg is caught on the middle console. It's the most uncomfortable position I've ever been in, but I don't care. I can't stop kissing him. Our tongues collide and he lifts my shirt, running his hand underneath it to cup my breast. I lean back just an inch, trying to get a little more comfortable when we're both startled apart as the car horn honks as my elbow hits it.

"Oops," I say with a grin on my face.

Romeo sighs and pushes me off, back into my own seat.

"Lauren, I need you to stay over there," he demands.

"Yes, sir," I state.

He groans.

I knew that would get him. He's right though, I need to stay over here. We really need to talk about this, but that was an amazing mini make-out session. I really needed that.

He adjusts himself in his pants, and I know he wants more as much as I do.

"I was thinking at the party about your plan. Are you one hundred percent sure that's what you want to do?" he asks.

"Yes," I say without hesitating.

He leans forward a little, looking me in the eye. "If we did this, then we both would have to disappear forever. We couldn't ever return here or even to any neighboring states. You could never contact your friends or family. Everyone would have to think you're dead. That includes your brother."

When I was coming up with this plan, that was my main hesitation. I would hate to make my family and friends believe that I've died. I know how much it would destroy them, but it would only be for a moment, right? Time always heals, and they all have so much to live for. I've kept my distance as much as I could from Ashley and Everly. My brother is my main concern, but he has his best friend, Olivia, that will keep him going.

"I know what I'll be giving up, but I've really thought about it, Romeo. I can't marry Lorenzo. I don't want to be part of his world. I'd basically be a prisoner, and I'd always have a target on my back. At any moment, I could be kidnapped or murdered. With that, I also can't imagine a life without being with you. I need you, Romeo. I love you, and I want to spend the rest of my life with you," I state while holding onto his hand.

His eyes soften as he listens to me. "If you are sure... But Lauren, you have to know this is all a gamble. There's only a small percentage that this will work. You have to be willing to accept the consequences of failure. Are you?"

Without hesitation I answer, "Yes."

"I'm going to go through them with you and ask you again. There's a chance the drug fails, and the entire plan is out the window. You will be on suicide watch and still stuck in your current situation. Are you willing to accept that and accept defeat if that happens? It'll be too late for a backup plan," he explains.

"Yes," I state.

He nods. "There's a chance that Lo finds out about this. I don't know the exact consequences, but I can assure you that he will kill me. You will be punished and most likely a prisoner for the rest of your life. Are you willing to accept those consequences?"

"If you are willing to put your life on the line for me, then yes. I will never live in a world that you're not a part of. I'll follow you to the afterlife," I state seriously.

He doesn't say anything for a moment before he continues, "Then there is a chance that whoever helps us doesn't administer the drug to counteract it in time or the drug fails. You will die. Are you willing to die?"

"Yes. I'd rather be dead than live like this for the rest of my life. Especially if there's a chance that we can have our own happily ever after. I don't care if it's only one percent of a chance. It's worth the risk," I say, pulling him in for another kiss.

We part and he continues staring at me like he's debating if he's willing to accept these consequences. My heart races as he takes his time to consider everything. I'm doubting that he will want to go through with it. He's going to think the risks are too great. He would be right, though. They are high-stake risks, but I'm willing to take it for a chance of forever with him.

He lifts my hand to his mouth and kisses it. "Alright, we'll do this. I'll make the arrangements and tell you the plans. The only thing you need to do now is convince your friends how depressed you are. Write your suicide note and be prepared to leave everything behind. Once this is in motion, there's no going back. So, I'm going to ask you one more time. You're one hundred percent sure?"

I nod, lean forward to kiss him, and say, "One hundred per-cent."

Chapter Thirty-One

ROMEO

Making the arrangements to fake a death is a near impossible task. I'm starting to believe that making the arrangements to fake two deaths is actually impossible.

Lo and I have run in the same circle for most of our lives. We have the same friends and family. We have the same contacts. Everyone who knows me knows Lo. Finding someone that I can trust not to tell him and to actually do the job is difficult. After spending all night going through every single person I have ever met in my life, I've finally found who I want to ask.

He's the perfect person for the job. He owes me a favor, and he likes to stay anonymous. He's dealt with Lo once or twice, but he's never met him in person. Lo has no idea who he is. In fact, I may be the only one who knows his real name.

I sit in my car in a large, empty parking lot. He chooses the meetup place and time, while I follow his directions exactly. In thirty seconds, he should be hopping into the passenger seat.

Right on time, he opens the car door and plops in. He's wearing a full navy suit that complements his dark skin and sunglasses. His black hair is slicked back, and his short beard and mustache are perfectly trimmed. He stares straight ahead without looking my way.

"How can I help you, Romeo?" he asks in his thick accent.

I have no idea where he is originally from or what that accent is, but I don't care to ask. He doesn't like questions.

"I need to make two people disappear and start a new life. One to suicide and the other to murder or accident. It doesn't matter. The drug will already be acquired for the suicide. The EMTs will have to be prompt taking out the body, the 911 call dealt with, and the counteracting drug given within a certain timeframe," I state and allow him time to process the information.

He pulls out his phone and looks through it. He has a privacy screen, so there's no way I can see what he's doing.

It feels like an eternity before he speaks. "Date for the suicide and timeframe."

"December 23, 2017. The 911 call will come shortly after 9 a.m. and the counteracting drug must be given by 7 p.m. at the latest. Preferably much sooner." I spit out the facts and let him enter the information into his phone.

"Timeframe for the murder," he continues.

"At least a month after the suicide," I state.

I've been doing a lot of thinking while planning this. I don't have second thoughts, but I do feel bad for Lo. I don't want to leave him immediately after Lauren's death because he's going to be a mess, but I don't want to leave Lauren alone for too long. Also, if it's too close together, it may look suspicious.

"New identities and a place to live is needed? Jobs? Money?" he asks.

"Yes, new identities and a place to live needs to be ready to go. The suicide will be brought there immediately. I'll hand off money to have there and for the new bank account. No job is needed."

"Alright, all I need are the names," he states.

I hesitate for a moment, hoping that I can really trust him. "Lauren Rae Faucett for the suicide."

For the first time since he entered my car, he pulls off his sunglasses and looks over at me. "Lorenzo's fiancé?"

I nod. "Is that a problem?"

He smirks. "No problem. For the murder?"

I stare him straight in the eyes and say, "Me."

He grins. "You fell in love with your brother's fiancé."

It wasn't a question. I don't respond to him, and I don't need to. It's obvious what's going on, but also, I'm not about to be giving up unnecessary information. He takes a while, looking through his phone and typing in information.

"The best I can do for the murder is six months after the suicide, on June 24, 2018."

My heart sinks. Six months after Lauren fakes her death? I'll have to go six months without having contact with her and trusting that she's alive and well? What if something happens within those six months?

"That's too long," I argue.

He shakes his head. "With who you are, that's the best I can do."

I take a deep breath and let it out. "Alright, tell me the details."

I walk into my house to find Matteo, Nico, and Lo sitting in the living room. I had asked Matteo to watch Lauren so I could meet with my contact, but I didn't give him any information on what I was doing. My heart races as I worry they found out what's going on. There's really no way they could have, but they could at least be suspicious.

"That was quick," Matteo states.

"Yeah, thanks. Just had something to take care of," I say while sitting in the chair across from Lo.

"Where'd you go?" Nico asks with a grin on his face.

I shrug my shoulders and don't answer.

"Why don't you want to tell us?" Matteo narrows his eyes at me and my heart stops.

Shit. Should I just make something up? I don't even know what to say at this point that's believable. I'm going to have to just keep avoiding the question at this rate and hope that they eventually drop it.

"What is everyone doing here?" I ask, looking over toward Nico and Lo.

"It's been a while since we've all hung out, so we thought it would be nice to have a family dinner," Nico states with his friendly face.

Nico is one scary dude. He acts like a perfect gentleman and has the face of an angel. He will fool the shit out of you that he's a good guy, when in reality, he will skin you alive. Literally. I've watched him skin someone before, and it's scary. His good boy demeanor can completely change to the devil in an instant.

"Yeah, sounds nice considering I've been kicked out of the group to babysit Lo's fiancé," I say.

"It won't be much longer, brother," Lo replies.

"So, are you going to tell us where you were?" Matteo pushes again.

"There's no need for you to know," I say it like it's no big deal.

Nico laughs. "I knew it. It was to hook up with a girl, right? I told these idiots there's no way you could survive this long without having a hookup."

I shrug my shoulders again and grin. I don't answer the question, but I don't deny it. Apparently, they buy it because Lo and Matteo pull out their wallets and hand Nico some cash. Usually, I'd be mad if they made a bet on me, but in this case, it works in my favor.

"I hear Lauren is having her bachelorette party two weekends before the wedding. Since you need to be watching her, we'll do Lo's the weekend of the wedding on the night of the 22nd. Lauren will be instructed not to leave the house that weekend. Zane will be on duty to watch her," Matteo explains.

I push down a mini panic attack. This changes some things if we're going to do this. I want to argue about leaving Lauren here alone with Zane watching her, but I know Lo wants me at his bachelor party. I need a minute to process this.

"Sounds fun. Let me know what you guys have planned. I'll be back in a second," I state as I stand up and walk toward my room.

I lock the door behind me and rub my hands down my face. Fuck, fuck, fuck. I just made these plans, and they are already getting screwed up not even an hour later. Is this a sign that this was doomed from the beginning?

I take a couple of deep breaths to calm myself and ease the panic surfacing. Alright, the current plan involved me being here, but maybe this could work. Zane won't be watching the cameras consistently and even if he was, there aren't any cameras in Lauren's bedroom and bathroom. I'll have to make sure she stays in there the whole time Zane is watching.

He'll be made aware the next morning once the EMTs arrive at her house, but even if he goes in there to see what's going on, he won't be able to do anything. They will take her away. Zane is loyal, but somewhat of a coward. He might even take flight once he finds out she killed herself while he was on watch. He'll believe Lo will kill him for it, even though it's not his fault. I'm not sure if Lo will or not. It wouldn't be a huge loss if he did. Why the fuck are they entrusting her with Zane?

Alright, that's fine. I'll have to let Samuel, my contact, know the change of plans. He's good with stuff like this, that's why he's the best. Something could backfire or change two minutes before, and he'd have it figured out. It's going to be fine.

I change my clothes quickly to make it seem like I did something in my room other than have a mini freakout with the information they just provided me. When I emerge from the room, everyone is sitting at the table with Chinese takeout. We haven't had that in so many years. Nostalgia hits, and I force my feelings back down. I can't be thinking about this stuff right now, or ever.

I sit with my brothers at the table and enjoy the dinner and company. It's great having us all together again on a normal night. My heart sinks, thinking that this may be the last time we're all together like this. Just a normal night hanging out with my brothers. Something I'll be missing out on for the rest of my life once we go through with this.

I watch them joking and laughing with each other. I plant a fake smile on my face as I watch them. Am I being stupid? Am I really going to give all this up for a girl? I've thought about getting out of this world plenty of times before, but it wasn't in the cards for someone like me.

I sigh and shake my head. No, I'm doing this. Lauren isn't just some girl. She's mine. If I sit here and think too long about what I'm going to be missing out on with my brothers, it's going to make it more difficult. I was never meant for their world, anyway. I've made my decision, and I need to stick to it. Any hesitation on either of our parts will be the death of us. I'm in too deep to back out now.

Chapter Thirty-Two

LAUREN

I want to say I slept well last night knowing that we are going to disappear together, but I didn't. Romeo listed scenarios in which this may not work. I think he wanted me to back out, but I didn't. I'm surprised he didn't either. I thought them through in detail last night and the outcomes all ended the same. If this fails, then my life is over. I've never thought about taking my own life before, but the thought of living with Romeo dead because of me is unthinkable. With that said, I'm going to do whatever it takes to make this work. Failure isn't an option.

"Morning, sis," Brandon startles me out of my thoughts.

"Morning," I reply.

I take a deep breath and a sip of my orange juice to calm my racing heart. I'm way too jumpy because of everything going on, and I can't be that way around Brandon. He notices everything.

"Did you have a good night at the party?" he asks, sitting in the chair next to me at the table.

"Yeah, it was fun," I say, but don't elaborate.

"Sad that I missed it," he says.

Brandon has been planning to come home this weekend for a few months now, which is why I was surprised my parents went out of town. Usually if my dad has a business trip, my mother will stay home so she can spend time with her son. Works in my favor, though. The less they're around, the better the chances of our success. Especially since my dad already knows Romeo and I have feelings for each other.

"Any plans today?" he asks.

"Nope. Never do," I respond.

"Good. Liv came up with me, so I was thinking the three of us could hang out today," he says, stealing one of the sausages off my plate.

My mood instantly shifts to excitement. "I didn't know she was coming. Did she stay in the guest room last night?"

"Yeah, I heard her in the shower half an hour ago, so she should be down soon."

Liv, her real name Olivia, has been best friends with Brandon since they were in middle school. I know she has a crush on him, even though she has never admitted it. Brandon seems to look at her only as a friend, though, which makes my heart hurt. I've been hoping that one day he'll see how amazing she is and finally get together with her, but I'm not sure that will ever happen. He has had a couple of girlfriends through the years, but I never liked them. None of them come even close to comparing to Liv.

"So, why did she come with you this time?" I ask.

"We're skipping classes for a couple of days to check out a college near here. We've both applied and plan to transfer for the next semester," he says nonchalantly.

"What?" I ask like I didn't hear what he said.

"We're transferring to a school up here. Dad said he can pull some strings. He makes enough now that he'll pay for both Liv and me to go to school here."

"What about all your friends and hers?" I ask with my heart racing.

He shrugs his shoulders. "We'll make new friends. Liv is the only friend I need."

"Aww, so sweet," Liv says as she comes around the corner.

I stand up and give her a quick hug. I love Liv. She has always been like a big sister to me, probably because of Brandon.

"Are you seriously transferring schools to come here? Why?" I ask her.

She shrugs her shoulders and sits down at the table. "Your brother will never admit it, but he wants to be close to you. As for me, I can't deny my tuition being paid for, and it's a better school. Plus, Brandon would be lost without me."

Brandon rolls his eyes but doesn't say anything. She's probably right. He would be lost without her. I know she says all those things, but they are all lies. What she really wants to say is that she can't imagine not being near Brandon. I also know she took a while to come to terms with someone else paying for her schooling. She's so self-sufficient, she never asks for help. My parents love her, though. Actually, I'm positive my mother loves her more than me.

Liv changes the topic. "So where are you at with the wedding plans?"

I groan. "Not involved."

Brandon puts his hand on mine. "I'm doing everything I can, Lauren."

I give him a small smile and look back toward Liv, who looks a little disappointed. I know she loves weddings and has always tried to be positive about me marrying Lorenzo, but at this point, nothing is going to help. Especially since I'm not going to be marrying him.

"Oh, come on. If you can't control who you're going to marry, then do what you can control," she says with a gleam in her eye.

Oh no. "What do you mean?"

She chuckles. "Shopping, of course! He's obviously rich, so let's go spend his money."

I laugh because I know that's the furthest thing she would do. Like I said, she's self-sufficient and hates taking things from others. This is her way of lashing out at the marriage, and it's honestly not a bad idea. It felt really good buying that lingerie with his credit card. I do still have it, as he told me to keep it.

Brandon groans, "I don't think that's a good idea."

"Sure, it is. She needs stuff for the wedding and after, right? You can buy me a dress for it, too. Really work that card of his," she grins.

I can't help but smile and think she may be right. I haven't been shopping in a while and that sounds fun. Especially buying things for her. Though I do feel a little guilty. Lorenzo has been really trying with me, and I'm over here screwing his brother and planning to run away forever. This would be nice to do, though. A nice parting gift for Liv and one last fun day with my brother and her.

"Let's do it," I say while standing.

Liv jumps to her feet. Her blond wavy hair bounces as she gets up. Her blue eyes gleam with excitement. I can't help but stare at her and at how beautiful she is. It makes me angry Brandon doesn't see what he has right in front of him. I've brought it up to him multiple times before, but he shoots me down every time. He says that she is his best friend, and he doesn't see her more than like he sees me, his sister. He loves her, but it'll never be that way.

"Lauren…" Brandon says, giving me a concerned look.

"It'll be fun, Brandon. I'll get you something to wear too," I reply while walking off toward my room to get ready.

He doesn't say anything, so I take that as acceptance he lost this battle. I think he's concerned about what Lorenzo will do to me if he finds out I'm spending his money. Brandon knows exactly the type of man that Lorenzo is, but Liv doesn't. He's been trying to keep her out of this world as much as possible, and I don't blame him. I wish I wasn't part of it. I won't be soon.

I shake my head and start feeling a little nervous. Alright, as much as I want to spend a bunch of Lorenzo's money, I just don't feel right about it anymore. A few months ago, I probably would without hesitation. Knowing that Lorenzo is really trying with me and I'm feeling more guilty about a lot of things, I can't.

I grab my phone and take a deep breath as I hover my finger over his name in my contacts. I urge myself to push the button, but my finger doesn't move. Ugh. I get mad at myself for always being so nervous and scared to do anything. Just do it! I push his name and the phone rings.

"Lauren?" he answers on the first ring.

"Hey," I say, taking another deep breath.

"Is everything okay?" he asks.

Ugh, yeah, I don't usually just call him, but I thought that a text message would be too long and impersonal. I didn't really think this through.

"Uh, yeah. I just had a quick question. Is now a good time?" I ask.

"Of course," he says.

I take another deep breath. "My brother and his best friend are here for the weekend. We're going out today and she was talking about the wedding. Well, I was wondering if you wouldn't mind me using your card to get a few things. And maybe something for her and him to wear to the wedding? I know it's a lot to ask. If not, that's okay. I just thought..."

Lorenzo interrupts my ridiculous rambling. "Lauren. I gave you that card to use whenever you want. Use it. You don't have to ask me whenever you want to buy something."

I let out a breath. "I know, but it could be a lot..."

He interrupts again. "Unless you plan to spend half a million dollars in one purchase, just use it. Even then, just send me a text so I know it's you."

"Half a million?" I whisper out.

He chuckles. "Yes."

I'm silent for a moment, thinking about what he just said. He would be cool with me spending half a million dollars? I knew he was rich, but that's ridiculously rich. No wonder Romeo said there's no way we could succeed at running away. He probably has the money to pay every single person on this planet to look for us.

"Lauren?" He breaks me out of my thoughts.

"Yeah?" I ask.

"Go have fun with your brother and friend," he says sincerely.

"Okay... Thank you Lorenzo," I continue whispering.

"Goodbye, Lauren."

"Goodbye," I say as he hangs up the phone.

Well, I just got permission to buy whatever I want with Lorenzo's money. Feeling better about spending it, not about the fact I didn't know how rich he is, I quickly throw some clothes on and text Romeo about the plans for today.

I leave my room to find my brother in the hall, waiting for me.

"We don't have to go shopping. We can find something more fun to do," he says, looking concerned.

I give him a smile. "Is it you don't want to go shopping with two girls, or you don't want to spend Lorenzo's money?"

"Lauren..." he says seriously.

I laugh. "It's fine Brandon. I called him, and he insisted I spend his money today on myself, you and Liv. Just don't tell her that."

He sighs and nods. "Alright, if that's what you want to do."

"Yes. I want to spend my fiancé's money on my brother and his best friend. What's the use of being engaged to someone so rich if I can't use his money for some good?" I ask, winking at him.

This time he laughs. "Alright, let's get out of here before I change my mind."

I nudge him as I walk by him with my shoulder and head toward the door while we wait for Liv. This will be good. This is a good way to say goodbye to Liv and my brother. I'm going to have a fun day with them and buy them everything they want. Or mostly Liv, because I know my brother isn't going to accept more than something to wear for the wedding.

Chapter Thirty-Three

LAUREN

A month has gone by quickly, and I'm getting nervous. In exactly one month, I'll be faking my death. I still need to figure out a way to get the vial from my father's lab. A lot has been going on, preventing me from figuring that part out.

Romeo explained to me he has someone who will help us disappear. I know exactly what I need to do to fake my death, so that's not an issue. My issue is that I will have to go six months without Romeo. I understand the need to ensure that his murder looks real, but half a year without him is too long for my liking.

Anything can happen in six months. In his line of work, he could die within that time and be murdered for real. I won't have any contact at all with him, so there's no way that I would know. I just have to trust that he'll come to me after six months, just like he's going to have to trust his contact got me out safely. I also have no idea where I'm going to be living for the rest of my life, but I don't care as long as it's with Romeo and out of this world.

I've been using this time wisely, pretending to be more depressed than usual with my friends. I've been mostly staying in, but they convinced me to go to the Friendsgiving gathering that Ashley's father held. Now that was a disaster.

It was beautiful and well put together with around three hundred people attending. We got dressed up and enjoyed the night until dinner was served, when Everly's plate was filled with dead frogs and a note threatening her and her friends. The commotion stirred everyone up, and the night ended sooner than it should have.

Romeo wanted to investigate this threat further since it technically was a threat against me as well, but I begged him not to. Everly has a great security team, and I know they will figure it out. She was thinking it was her ex-boyfriend that did it. I don't know exactly what went on between them, but I know whatever it was isn't good. Either way, we have too much to do in the next month to get involved with that.

So, between that, the increasing dates with Lorenzo, and wedding planning, there hasn't been time to do much else. I plan to sit down tonight after Thanksgiving and really think through a plan to get that vial. My primary concern is that my father now knows about Romeo and me, so I don't know what that means. He hasn't brought it up at all and we've been careful not to show affection when we're not in private.

"Lauren?" my mother asks, breaking me out of my thoughts.

"Hmm?" I look up from my plate of food to find her glaring at me.

"Your fiancé asked you a question," she states.

I look over at Lorenzo to find his eyebrows drawn together, looking at me with concern. Crap, what were they all talking about? What did he ask me? I glance around the table and see everyone staring at me. I feel the heat rising to my cheeks as embarrassment sets in. Everyone is here. It's Thanksgiving after all.

Lorenzo's uncle, Nico, Romeo, and Matteo all sit at this table with us, along with my mother, father, and Brandon. It's awkward, and I can only imagine that this is how it would be if I were to marry Lorenzo. Eventually, the amount of people would grow as everyone else finds women to spend the rest of their lives with. I shiver, thinking about how that would eventually be Romeo. Thankfully, we're going to be taking care of that, so thinking about it is pointless.

"Are you alright?" Lorenzo places his hand on my leg and rubs it.

I look up at him and give him a small smile. "Yeah, I'm sorry. I just have a headache. What was your question?"

He removes his hand and asks, "Have you gotten your wedding dress?"

I nod. "Yes, it's beautiful. Thank you."

I didn't feel like going wedding dress shopping, so he sent an assistant to bring me a bunch to try on. I didn't even try them on and just picked a random one on the hanger. The lady wasn't impressed by me, but she knew better than to argue with Lorenzo's fiancé. While Ashley and Everly tried to get me to do it the right way, I refused. It's bad enough they are forcing me to have a bachelorette party. I didn't need to do some stupid tradition with friends and wedding dress shopping when none of this was real. My heart sinks a little, thinking about how I will never have a real wedding.

"You don't look well, Lauren. Do you need to lie down?" my father asks with a concerned look on his face.

"Of course she isn't well. She's being forced to get married," my brother mutters under his breath.

I can't help but smile at his attempts to make it known how he feels about this whole thing. He's been on my side since the beginning and trying to get me out of it. Obviously, that hasn't worked, but I appreciate his support.

I watch my mom smack his arm, and I shake my head. "I do have a really bad headache, but I don't want to be rude."

Lorenzo places his napkin down and scoots his chair back. "Nonsense. I'll take you home."

He stands and holds his hand out to me. I take it and stand with him, not wanting to argue. I've been here long enough, anyway. It's funny, I'm supposed to be acting like I'm depressed to convince everyone I killed myself, but I really don't need to act.

"Lorenzo," his uncle stops him. Lorenzo looks over toward him as his uncle continues. "We need to discuss that issue."

Before Lorenzo can say anything, Romeo speaks up. "I'll take her back, Lo."

Lorenzo looks me over, places his hands cupping my face, asking, "You'll be alright?"

I nod. "Yeah, I'm fine. I'm just going to lie in bed until the headache subsides." I look over toward the table and continue, "Thank you everyone for a nice Thanksgiving."

Romeo walks me out, and I get in his car. When he turns it on, I realize it's only two in the afternoon. I can't believe I didn't make it more than an hour at a holiday lunch with my fiancé and family.

"Are you okay?" Romeo asks before driving off.

"Yeah, I'm supposed to be depressed. Remember?"

He shakes his head. "You're supposed to be pretending, not really depressed. What's wrong?"

"Nothing," I say too quickly.

"Lauren…"

"I said nothing! Drop it Romeo," I snap at him.

He doesn't say anything else as he drives down the driveway. I stare out the window and feel something wet hit the back of my hand. I look down, confused, and swipe it to notice another drop hits my other hand. Huh?

I swipe at my cheek, and it's wet. I'm crying? Am I going insane? I don't even feel like I'm crying. Honestly, I'm not really feeling much of anything at this moment. How am I crying? Why?

"Lauren…" Romeo starts, and I continue looking out the window.

He pulls the car over into an empty church parking lot and shifts in his seat to face me. He pulls my face toward him and kisses me on the forehead.

"Talk to me, baby."

Okay, what the heck? That just broke the dam and now the tears are flooding down my face. I let out a little sob as I bury my face in his chest. I don't even know why I'm crying. He lets me cry in his chest until the tears subside.

Pulling away, I look at him. "I'm sorry. I really don't know why I'm crying."

He nods and kisses me again on the top of my head. "There's a lot going on, and we only have a month left. I've felt it too, especially when being around my family. It's hard knowing that we're going to be leaving them forever and never doing this again. Once it's done, it'll be worth it, though. We'll have each other and we'll create our own family. We'll be safe and out of this world."

Romeo always knows what to say. He's right, it'll be worth it. I don't have second thoughts about doing it, but it doesn't make it any easier. I sometimes question if I'm doing the right thing or if I was acting on impulse and emotions when I decided to do this. Probably, but Romeo agreed to it too. So, it must be right, right?

"Romeo, I'm sorry. I didn't mean to take you away from your family on the last Thanksgiving you'll have with them. Let's go back. I can't take this away from you," I say.

"No. Honestly, it's better this way," he says, and doesn't elaborate.

"You're sure this is what you want to do? I find it hard to believe that you are willing to leave them and your whole life for me..." I state.

He groans. "Lauren, I already told you this. I love you. You are worth it. I'll give up everything for you, and I'll do it fifty times over if it means being with you and making you happy. Don't ever question it again."

I nod and say nothing back. I still don't understand how he's so willing to give up everything for me when he has everything here. I, on the other hand, have nothing to lose. Yeah, I have my friends, but I've only known them for a short time. I've never been close to my parents and my brother has his own life. So, I have nothing to lose, especially since I'm supposed to be a prisoner once I'm married to Lorenzo. He's right. It's worth it.

CHAPTER THIRTY-FOUR

ROMEO

It was hard dropping Lauren off at her house and not following her inside. I know she needs me right now, but we can't risk it. In just a short amount of time, we'll be together forever. What she was saying earlier has been weighing on me, though.

I didn't think about this being the last Thanksgiving with my family. When Lo was going to take her home, I was panicking. I hate him being alone with her. Hell, I hate seeing him with her at all. I wanted to punch him every time he touched her. She's mine.

Those feelings are exactly why I know I'm making the right decision about running away with her. I've already betrayed my brother, and there's no going back. Eventually, he would find out about the betrayal and kill me. At least, that's what I keep telling myself. What Lauren was saying is making me go down a stupid rabbit hole of guilt, which I don't have the luxury of feeling.

She gets out of here in exactly a month. I have a full seven months left living here with my family. I'm going to be the one picking up the damn pieces when Lo finds out that Lauren killed herself. Is six months going to be enough time to do that?

Then I'm going to be breaking him into pieces again by my death. My brother is going to go fucking postal when he finds out I was murdered. Is he going to recover from that? Fuck this damn rabbit hole of guilt that Lauren just put me in. I've been doing good keeping these thoughts under control, but not anymore. One fucking month away from beginning this plan and I'm feeling fucking guilty. How the hell am I supposed to do this for another seven months?

A knock on my front door pulls me out of my guilt fest. I pull up the camera on my phone quickly to see who it is. Nico's grinning like an idiot into the camera. I unlock and swing the front door open, but don't move from the entrance.

"What? Not going to let your favorite cousin in?" he asks, taking a step forward even though I'm blocking him.

"What do you want?"

"Ouch. What's with you?" he asks with his grin faltering for only a second.

I sigh and open the door wider, stepping out of the way so he can come in. He shoves past me and heads straight to the fridge, pulling out a beer.

"Help yourself..." I mutter.

He pops the top and chugs half of it, sitting down on the stool at the island. I follow suit and grab one of my own. I don't drink beer often, as I enjoy the hard stuff more, but this will do for now.

We stare at each other in silence, and I'm confused why he's here. He's acting as if I should be saying something to him, but he's the one that showed up uninvited to my house.

"Spit it out, Nico," I state.

He chuckles and places his beer on the island. "Never with the small talk… Let's trade places. I'll watch Lauren for this last month, so you can get back to what you do best."

I sit up straighter, my body tensing on high alert. "Why?"

He takes another sip of his beer and continues to smile at me. He gives nothing away with his body language.

He shrugs his shoulders. "Lorenzo needs his underboss back, and I'm bored."

That's bullshit. There's something more going on. "It's just one more month. I'm good."

Nico swirls his beer around. I knew there was something more. He's staring at me, not giving anything up. Is something going on with Lo? I wish he'd just spit it out already.

Nico sighs. "I think giving you a break from watching Lauren will do everyone some good."

My heart rate picks up, and I'm on the defense within seconds. "Why?"

"Do I really have to say it?" His face turns serious.

"Clearly you do," I state.

"I see the way you look at her. I had my suspicions, but tonight you proved me right with how you were staring at Lorenzo every time he touched her," he states.

The way he moves his body back shows he's ready for a fight. Does he think I would kill him for knowing this information? Whatever, I can't think about that right now. I need to diffuse this situation which is going to be hard. Fuck Nico and being able to read people so easily. That is why I never play poker with the guy.

"That's a serious accusation you're throwing out, Nico," I bite out.

He puts his hands up in surrender. "It will never be spoken about outside of this conversation."

I shake my head. "I would hope not because it's not true. Lauren is Lo's fiancé. I am ensuring her safety and nothing more."

"Either way, you've been out of the game long enough. Lo needs you back, and I plan to stay in town permanently," he states.

Well, that's news to me. Nico takes care of things out of state with his family, and he's a great connection piece between us. I wonder what changed. I'll have to get that information later because right now, I still need to convince him that there's nothing going on between Lauren and me.

"It's only another month. Thanks for the offer, but I can handle it. Once they're married, everything will go back to normal," I state evenly.

I will my body not to betray my words. He can't know what we're planning. We have gotten this far. I don't know what I'd do if I ruined it for us now. We just have one more month. One month. How have we been fucking this up so badly that now one person knows about us and another suspects something?

Nico studies me a little too long before nodding. "Alright, if you say so. The offer stands at any point if you change your mind."

I lift my beer and tilt it to him. "Thanks, but don't ever fucking accuse me of that shit again. Lo would have my head if he even heard your suspicions."

Nico watches me for a moment again before saying, "I'm not sure that's true, but it wouldn't be good. He loves you like a brother. Blood or not, you are his brother."

I shake my head and stop myself from digging into his deeper meaning with all that. This conversation needs to end. There's nothing good that'll come out of it.

"Is that all you wanted? You left Thanksgiving dinner early to come here for that?" I ask.

Nico laughs. "Nah, there's no way I could stand another minute with my father. Lorenzo and Matteo are talking business with him, and Lauren's family left. I figured if I snuck out, no one would really care."

I shake my head. "I doubt that, but we've been used to not having you around. I'm glad to have you back for good. I'll deny that I said it, but I've missed having you around."

Nico grins, and we move on to lighter conversation. I am actually happy that Nico is back. That means Lo will have one more person at his side when Lauren and I disappear. He's going to need all the help he can get, and I'll feel better leaving him if he has both Nico and Matteo. They will take care of him and make sure he's alright.

I get up to pull out the scotch and offer some to Nico. With the way this holiday is going, I need something much stronger.

Chapter Thirty-Five

LAUREN

I stare in the mirror, watching myself as my heart races and the nausea grows. My face looks pale, and I look guilty. How do people lie and do sneaky things and get away with it? Romeo would be able to do this. Maybe I should've asked him to. I still can…

No. I need to do this. This was my plan, and there's no reason I can't do it. I'm going to have to live six months by myself without Romeo or anyone that I know. If I can't do this, then there's no way I'm going to be able to do that. I groan, trying to push the thoughts away about being alone for six months. I haven't even thought about that yet, and I don't plan to.

I take a deep breath and place a baseball cap on my head. I don't wear hats often, but they are great when I'm having a bad hair day or I'm trying to hide my intentions with something. In this case, I'm hiding my intentions. I'm about to go steal from my father's lab. I've thought of all the consequences of this, and if I make one wrong move, everything is ruined.

If I'm caught, I'll get in trouble for stealing and possibly giving up our plan. There would be no way I could continue with my plan to fake my suicide. Not only that, but my father would most likely get reprimanded as well. For the fact that he brought me in there and that the vial was stolen under his watch. Who knows what Lorenzo would do to him or me if he found out?

So, here I am, making myself sick, thinking about everything that could go wrong. I made sure that I had pockets in my pants, on my shirt, and even in my boots. I need to make sure that I have some place safe and discreet to stash what I'm stealing.

I shiver and take a deep breath. Needing to get this done with, I leave my room and head downstairs to my father's office. Before I can knock on his door, he walks out.

"Are you ready?" he asks.

I nod and say, "Yeah, let's go."

I follow behind him as he leads us out of the house and into his car. Romeo will follow behind us, as usual. As my father drives away, there's an unbearable silence. I know he wants to ask about Romeo and me, but he doesn't. He hasn't brought up anything about Romeo since the day in his office after he found us making out.

I turn on a radio station to drown out the silence in the car, and my father doesn't object. I look out the window and don't pay attention to anything I'm seeing. All I can think about is what I'm about to do, which is steal the necessary component for our plan to work.

"I'm glad you're coming with me today. I miss spending time with you," my father states.

"Me too," I say, not knowing what else to say.

I'm supposed to meet Lorenzo later at a bakery to do some cake testing. Of course, I told him I don't care what our wedding cake is, but he insisted. My father said that today would be a quick day at work. He just has to enter some counts into the system and then we could head over there afterward. He hasn't been part of the wedding planning and wanted to be part of this because cake was always our thing when I was a little girl.

If this was a real wedding, then I would be overjoyed that my father wants to be part of this. He might not be present much in my life, but he used to love baking cakes with me. Half the time, they turned out looking horrible. It didn't matter though, they always tasted good, and I enjoyed the one-on-one time with him.

We pull up to the warehouse where my father works. After getting out of the car, I glance back and watch Romeo get out of his car. I know he will follow us in, but won't come to our floor. This place is heavily guarded, so I doubt that anything would happen.

When I look back toward my father, I notice him watching me closely and then he glances back toward Romeo. Crap. I'm so freaking obvious, it's not even funny. This would be the perfect opportunity for him to bring up the topic of us again, but he doesn't. I have no idea what he's thinking.

We enter the drug room, as I like to call it, and once again, there's no one here. Thank God.

"Do you want my help with anything?" I ask.

He grabs a clipboard and pen from the wall and hands it to me. Grabbing it, I look it over to find a chart written on the paper with a bunch of numbers on the left-hand side.

"I'll tell you which number the count belongs to, and then I need you to write exactly the number I say, okay?" he asks, looking at me seriously.

I nod. "Yeah dad. I think I can handle that."

He acts like I'm five and might not be able to write the correct number. I try not to take offense, but concentrating on that frustration is better than concentrating on my nerves for figuring out how to get this stupid drug I need.

We walk to each cubicle as he enters the passcode in to enter. We both go in, he counts them, I write the number, and he enters it into the computer inside the cubicle. We walk out of the cubicle, close the door tightly, and make sure it's locked. I don't really understand why I have to write the number on this paper when he's entering it into the computer system, but I guess maybe it's used as a backup in case the system fails.

We repeat this process more times than I can count until we get to the cubicle with the drug that I need. My heart pounds even harder against my chest than it was before. I can feel my hands trembling, and I take a deep breath to calm myself. How am I supposed to get this? He's been in each cubicle with me the entire time. I want to so badly just give up right now, but I know I can't. If I do, then my life is doomed to be married to Lorenzo for the rest of my life. I can't do that to Romeo. He's counting on me.

I steady my breaths as my father unlocks the cubicle and we enter. He looks over each vial and does a quick count as he heads toward his computer.

"For this one, it's the next two on the list. Number 7852 and number 7853, which is the antidote. There's seven for both," he states casually as he types on the computer.

I swear my heart stops as my breath catches. "Seven?" I ask.

"Yes, seven," he states without looking back at me.

I quickly count each vial, and there's clearly eight. I count three more times, and I know that I'm not miscounting. There's for sure eight of them. He's only entering seven. This is my chance. No one will know the difference because the count won't be off. Did he really just miscount them? I shake my head to clear it because I can't think about this right now. I need to figure out a way to grab both the drug and the antidote without him seeing.

"Alright, we have two more to do. Let's finish up," he states as he turns around.

He's about to walk away from the computer when a crash sounds behind him. He turns to see that he knocked off the little caddy filled with paper, pens, and little tools. They're scattered all over the floor.

He looks down at the mess and sighs. "Mind cleaning that up? I'll head to the next. Make sure the door is locked as you leave."

I watch him exit the cubicle and head toward the next. What? Seriously? I force myself to act instead of standing here like an idiot thinking about what just happened. As I begin to pick up the tools, I watch my father enter the next cubicle and have his back facing me.

I can't waste any more time. I quickly lift the lid to the drug, grab the blue vial and do the same to grab the green one with the antidote in it. The safest place to put them is in my boots. I bend over to place one in each and then continue cleaning up the mess on the floor.

After I finish, I take one last glance at the drugs and antidotes, counting them again. Seven. There are seven of each there now. Just as my father had counted earlier. Was this planned? Does he somehow know what I'm planning to do? If so, is this his way of giving me his permission to do it?

I push back all the thoughts before I get too emotional to finish the job. After completing the last two, we head back to the lobby. I'm walking carefully to ensure they don't somehow slip out or break inside my boots. They aren't exactly small, but thankfully they can't be seen.

"Hey! Patrick! I've been meaning to talk to you," my father states to a man as we exit the elevator.

The guy smiles at my father and heads our way.

"Sorry, Lauren. This is going to take a bit. I don't want you to be late to the cake testing with Lorenzo, so have Romeo take you. I'll catch up shortly. Okay?" he asks, and I just nod in response.

I catch up to Romeo and tell him what my father said. He leads me to his car, and I jump in faster than I ever have before. As we pull away from the warehouse, I let out a breath and start laughing. All that tension of getting caught dissipates, and I can't be happier to have completed the task successfully. I hold up both vials, showing Romeo.

He grins and says, "Fucking yes! You did it Lauren."

"We did it…" I breathe out happily.

He opens the little secret compartment in his car where he keeps his gun, and he places both vials in there. I'm glad that I'm no longer responsible for them. I try not to think about having to actually use them because that's going to give me a whole new set of anxieties. We need to take this win for now.

"What about the cameras?" I ask, thinking about the one thing that could hurt our chances.

"I already took care of it. The only issue now is the count," he states.

I grin. "Nope. My father miscounted. There were eight, but he said seven. So, the count is accurate."

Romeo is silent for a moment, like he's contemplating something. "And I saw he conveniently dumped materials on the floor, leaving you in there alone to clean up. He knew you were going to take it."

I thought the same thing. It was all too convenient. My father planned all of this from the beginning. He took me when he was doing the counts and asked me to help write it down. He wanted me to take them. Then he let me ride with Romeo to go to the cake testing so I could pass off the vials.

I spend the rest of the drive thinking about this and not knowing how to feel. I have been so angry with my father for setting up this arranged marriage and forcing me to follow through with it. He found out about Romeo and me and hasn't brought it up again after the initial talk. It's a little scary having someone else know about our plan, but at this point, there's nothing we can do about it. He let me have the drugs. He's willing to let me fake my death so I can be happy.

I close my eyes and take a labored deep breath in. Tears prick at the back of my eyes, but I hold them in. I need to concentrate on getting through the next hour with Lorenzo, then I can race to my room and cry in the shower.

Chapter Thirty-Six

ROMEO

Next weekend. Next weekend, Lauren will kill herself while we have Lo's bachelor party. Fuck. How did we get here so fast? It's not that I don't want to do it, but everything is going to change. Everything.

I can't stand watching Lo with Lauren, and I just want to be with her fully. I want to be able to touch her whenever I want to, hold her hand in public, and make her my wife. I can't wait to do all that, but damn it, why did it have to be this way?

I want to do all that and get married to her with my brothers by my side. Leaving them forever isn't something I want to do, but I have to. I feel like a fucking pussy today as I'm sitting here depressed and feeling sorry for myself. In less than two hours, I have to watch out for Lauren at her bachelorette party, so I need to get my shit together.

I slam the notebook closed that I've been writing in for the past couple of months. I've written everything I can think of that my brothers are going to need when I'm gone. Every password, every contact, and every piece of knowledge I possess is written in that book. I hope it helps them.

Then I have another little notebook beside it. I've been writing sentimental shit in that for each of them to read. I want to make sure they know how much each of them means to me. How much they changed my life and how they need to keep going and forget about me. It fucking sucks writing this shit, but I have to. I'm trying to write it like it's just in case I die, versus I know I'm going to die.

Sighing, I lean back on the couch, contemplating my life choices again. I can't believe that I'm leaving my life for a girl. I shake my head. Fuck. She's not just any girl. She's mine, and she's worth me giving up everything. I just wish I didn't have to, but with the world we live in, it would be impossible for me to have her. It would make Lo look weak. It could cost him his position or worse, his life.

I groan and force myself off the couch. Alright, this pity party is over. I pull up the cameras and watch as Everly and Ashley are at her house getting ready for the bachelorette party.

They got fake IDs and are hitting a club tonight. Apparently, Lauren's mother thinks they are going to a movie and then spending the night at Everly's house. How she thinks they are going to a movie dressed like that, I have no clue.

I checked out the club, and it's one of the best around. I don't know much about the owner, Asher Terion, but I know of him. He stays out of trouble and doesn't run in our world. The amount of money he has and businesses he owns is astronomical. For the fact he isn't involved in anything illegal that anyone knows of, he's doing well for himself.

Of course, Lo wanted them to come to one of our clubs so we could all watch out for them. Lauren begged him to let her go to this one because it's where Everly really wanted to go, and she just wanted a weekend away from our world before marrying into it. To my surprise, he agreed.

So here I am now, sitting at a bar watching three girls get drunk. Everly has Declan and Barry from her security team with her. They drove the girls and entered together with them. At least I only have to worry about monitoring Lauren.

There's only one seat between me and the girls. I told Lauren I would stay close tonight because if someone wanted to make a move on Lo's fiancé, tonight would be the perfect night to do so. If Everly and Ashley hadn't figured out I'm watching Lauren yet, they never will.

Lauren keeps sneaking glances over at me, and I raise my eyebrows at her. Does she want them to find out about me? She's being too obvious. I take a sip of my water as I listen in on their conversation. I'm not usually close enough to hear them. They just ordered a round of shots.

Everly asks Ashley, "So how are you and Shawn doing?"

Ashley cringes and says, "I guess we're okay. He took me to play Dungeons and Dragons with his friends the other night."

Geeze. Dungeons and Dragons? That still exists? These teenagers are really boring and nerdy these days. I shake my head and continue listening to their girly conversation.

"So, you didn't have a good time?" Lauren asks, while downing her shot and shaking her head from the burn.

Ashley shrugs her shoulders. "I thought it might be fun, but that's definitely not my thing. We're also not going to talk about the kiss we shared."

I can't help but grin at this conversation and how Lauren takes another peek at me after Ashley says that. She blushes, and I know she's thinking about the many kisses we've been sharing lately.

"What happened?" Everly asks.

Ashley downs a second shot and says, "I just said we're not going to talk about it!"

The girls laugh, and Lauren demands, "Well, you can't bring it up and not share the details, so spill it."

Ashley groans. "Fine… It was the worst kiss I've ever had. It was sloppy and so inexperienced. I was hoping it would get better with time, but it's getting worse."

"That sounds awful. So did you break up with him?" Everly asks.

I don't hear her response because I'm too focused on the man in a ridiculously colorful suit, walking out from around the corner. His eyes are on the girls as he stands leaning against the wall. I'm about to confront him until I recognize him, Asher. The owner of the club. I'm not going to let my guard down, though. I don't trust anyone.

The girls did another round of shots and are now dancing on the dance floor. I'm finding it difficult to drag my gaze away from Lauren. This isn't the time or place to be sporting a hard on for her. Regardless, my dick doesn't get that memo.

I watch two men approach them. One places his hands on Ashley as she dances while the other stands behind Lauren, wanting a dance. Fuck no. She looks uncomfortable, but the guy isn't getting the hint. I growl and try to keep myself planted in my seat a little longer to see how this plays out. When the fucker doesn't get the hint, I stand and stalk toward them, not caring about keeping myself unknown.

Before I make it to the group, Asher is already there, looking like he's going to kill the guy behind Ashley.

He clears his throat. "Ladies, come join me at my table."

He pushes between both men and places his hands on Lauren and Ashley's lower backs. Both girls pause for a moment, but Everly gives them a reassuring look. They all sit at the table that Asher leads them to, and I stand close by, but keep myself hidden. Asher leaves them there, and I lean in a little to listen to their conversation.

"Who is that?" Ashley asks.

"That's Asher. He works here. He's really nice and helped me out last time I was here," Everly says, reassuring them.

"Why did he bring us over here?" Lauren asks.

I can tell she's uncomfortable about everything that just happened. I mean, what did she expect? Dancing like that in the tight-fitting dress she has on. She's not showing much skin, but damn, it doesn't leave much to the imagination on what's underneath. She is gorgeous, young, and in a club with a bunch of drunks.

Everly shrugs. "Not sure, but he didn't seem too happy with the guy behind Ashley. Maybe he knows him and wanted to get us away because he's no good."

Asher walks back to their table with three waters, handing one to each of them. They take a drink, and my eyes are trained on Asher, trying to figure out his intentions. Clearly, he knows Everly, but his eyes have been on Ashley since he came out of the back-office area. He's obviously into her. Damn, is that how obvious I am when it comes to Lauren? If so, no wonder Nico caught on.

Asher tells them to order whatever they want because it's on him tonight. He then gestures for Everly to follow him to the back. As much as I want to listen in on their conversation, I stay close to Lauren.

When Everly returns to the table, they order a bunch of food and more drinks. They get up a few times to dance and thankfully, no other men try to dance with them. I've done so good staying undetected by her friends that I would hate to ruin it by having to punch someone who touches Lauren. I said I would hate to, not that I wouldn't.

Lauren excuses herself from her friends to head toward the bathroom. I follow behind her and watch her slip inside the women's room. No one's gone in there in a while, so I take my chances and slip in behind her. I was right, no one else is here.

Locking the door behind me, I lean against it, waiting for Lauren to come out of the stall. When she does, she nearly falls over at the sight of me. I grin and stalk toward her.

"Romeo! What are you doing in here?" she asks, looking around to make sure no one else is here.

"We're alone," I state and push her up against the wall.

"What are you doing?" she asks with her eyes wide and pupils dilated.

I growl as I kiss up her neck and reach her ear. "You've been torturing me all night, shaking that ass while dancing, knowing that I can't touch you. Were you doing it on purpose?"

Her breath hitches as she whispers, "I was wishing you could dance with me."

I groan at her words and slam my mouth against hers. Our kiss is hard, sloppy, and passionate. Our tongues clash, and I bite her lower lip, drawing blood.

She gasps. "Romeo... We can't..."

I chuckle. "I locked the door. We can and we will."

I pull her toward the little lounge area in the bathroom. I push her down on the chair and lift her dress above her hips. Fuck, she's wearing a lacy thong. Was she hoping for this? I don't waste any more time as I pull it off and pocket her thong.

She's about to say something, but I press my tongue against her center, silencing any protests she has. I spread her legs further apart as she groans, and I devour her like I haven't eaten in months.

She tugs on my hair and pants out, "Romeo... I'm..."

I grin and say against her, "Don't hold back. Come for me. Come on my face like a good girl."

She immediately comes undone after my words, and I slow my rhythm against her. She's panting, and I lift myself off the floor to plant a kiss against her soft lips, which taste like alcohol. Mine taste like her, and I can tell she's surprised at that fact as she pulls back.

"Romeo..." she pants.

"What do you want now, Lauren?" I ask, hoping she says she wants me inside her.

She looks back and forth between my eyes before she pushes me off. I groan in protest, not wanting that reaction.

"Sit," she demands.

I grin and do as she says. I'm not usually one to take orders, but fuck if that isn't hot. She kneels in front of me and unzips my pants. My cock springs free a moment later, ready for whatever she wants to do next.

She looks at me like she's uncertain about what she's about to do. "Baby, you don't have to do anything you don't want to."

I try to keep my voice even because damn if I haven't pictured that pretty mouth on my cock for the past nine months. Burying myself inside her was fantastic, but I know her mouth will be amazing too.

She doesn't hesitate any longer as she licks down my length and wraps her lips around my tip, swirling her tongue. Fuck.

I grab her hair, and she pulls me in deeper. I try to stay still as she gets used to taking me in her mouth. After a couple of minutes, she takes me further, almost all the way. Shit, she doesn't even gag as she's basically deep throating me. I'm not going to last.

I pull her head back, so she looks up at me. "Shit, Lauren. I'm not going to last."

She nods and asks, "What do you want me to do?"

"Whatever you want," I say, just wanting her to do something to finish me off.

She lifts her dress and straddles me. "I want you to come inside me."

I groan. "I don't have a condom."

She shakes her head. "I'm on the pill. It's fine."

That's all the encouragement I need as I position her on top of me and she lowers down on my aching cock. She rides me for no more than a minute before we're both finding our release and I spill inside her. As fucked up as it is, I can't help but imagine filling her with my baby. It's not a thought that belongs in this moment, but one day, I plan to do exactly that.

She stands off me and heads to the sink to clean herself up. I tuck myself back in and zip up my pants before joining her at the sink. Kissing the back of her neck, we stare at each other in the mirror with our eyes locked.

"I love you so fucking much Lauren," I say, continuing to kiss down her neck and back up again.

She turns around and grabs my face with her hands. "I love you, Romeo."

We kiss for less than a minute because I'm already getting hard again. If we're gone any longer, her friends are going to come looking for her. I unlock the door and leave her in the bathroom. She exits shortly after me and rejoins her friends to finish out the night. I lean against the wall, watching her and scanning the room. I find Everly's guard, Declan, staring at me. Fuck. Is he another that knows about us? What the hell is wrong with me?

He heads my way while keeping an eye on the girls. He leans against the wall beside me, and I wait for the accusation to come.

"I assume you'll be following us back and staying the night outside the house?" he asks.

I let out the breath I was holding. "Yeah."

He nods. "We have a room for you to stay in, if you want. I'll let you in after the girls are upstairs, so they don't know you're there."

I watch him for a moment before saying anything. That's an interestingly nice offer, and I'm not sure why he's making it. At first, I'm suspicious, but they have no reason to off me. They know who Lo is and that would put Everly in danger, along with everyone else they know.

Declan chuckles. "I'm not going to murder you in your sleep. It's just an offer you can take it or leave it. I know how fun sleeping in the car is. At least this way you can get some solid sleep and have access to Lauren."

"Yeah, alright. Thanks," I state, taking up his offer.

I won't be letting Lauren know that I'm staying inside the house, or she might try to sneak into my room. As fun as that seems, we can't risk it. We're so close to getting out of here and being together forever. We just need to be patient, though patience has never been my strong suit.

CHAPTER THIRTY-SEVEN

LAUREN

Today is the last day I will ever see my friends and family. It's finally here. This will be the last time that I wake up in my bedroom. It'll be the last time that I get ready for school. It'll be my last day at school, which it would've been anyway if I were to marry Lorenzo. My friends still didn't know that part. I figured they didn't need to since I'll be dead soon, at least, in their eyes.

My heart races, I feel sick, and I just want to cry. This is what needs to be done. I want to do this. I need to, but it doesn't make it any easier. Pulling the large leather-bound book out from under the covers, I flip through the pages. It's a ridiculously huge journal that looks like something from a movie about witches, but it's really cool, and my brother gave it to me for Christmas one year. Since I decided to go this route with pretending to kill myself, I started writing in it like a diary. I needed to make this seem like I've been increasingly getting depressed through the months and this suicide is real.

I also used these pages to write notes to each of my friends, my brother, Lorenzo, and my parents. One specifically to my father, thanking him for everything he's done for me and how much I love him. He is the only one that knows the truth, but he'll never be able to tell anyone or know where I am. I hope he can live with that.

I have each of their notes in envelopes with their names on them, inside this book. The suicide note that I'm going to place on the bathroom counter when I do it is also in here. The note will tell them where to find this journal and the envelopes for everyone. I open my closet and bury the journal so no one sees it before it's supposed to be found.

A couple of months ago, Romeo helped me get a will ready and make it known that I have one. I made it clear to Lorenzo as well that I wanted one because of how unsafe his world is. He tried to reassure me I would be safe, but ultimately, he used his lawyer to help me. I was adamant that I didn't want anyone seeing my dead body. Obviously, that is necessary since I won't really be in the casket. Romeo said he's got it taken care of, so I trust him. When having this conversation with Lorenzo, I also made him promise me he would always take care of my family, along with Ashley and Everly. He had no problems making that promise, and I believe he will be true to his word. They'll be okay, I know they will.

I get ready for school for the last time ever and sling my backpack over my shoulders. Looking at myself in the mirror, I look miserable. What did I expect? I barely slept last night and

I'm about to leave my entire life behind. I'm making my friends and family think that I've killed myself. It's screwed up. It's all a mess, and at this moment, I hate everyone who put me in this position.

I'm just thankful that Romeo is going to be coming with me. It makes it all worth it to know that we're going to live our lives together and be happy. It may not be the way we wanted, but at least we will have each other.

We will build a new life with new friends far away from here. Romeo got us new identities, and we'll already be married. The hardest part about all of this is going to be the six months that I have to wait to see him again. I just hope it all goes according to plan. If it doesn't, then I hope I don't get the antidote in time and die. I can't live without him.

I shake off my thoughts, and Romeo drives me to school. I snuck over to his house last night and we spent one last night together in each other's arms, making love. It felt like it was the last time we'd ever be able to do that, and I kept pushing that thought away. It's going to be fine. This is all going to work as planned, and we're going to get our happily ever after. We have to.

He pulls over just before we reach the school and grabs my face, kissing me hard. I feel the tears streaming down my face.

"Do you remember the plan for everything?" he asks me.

I nod.

"Tell me it," he says in his work voice.

"Everly's guards are going to drive me home from school with her, and we'll spend the night in my room. I'll say I'm not allowed out. I will stay in my room and not come out. Once Everly is asleep, I'll set her alarm to nine a.m. to ensure she wakes up to find me. At seven a.m. I'll take the drug, which you put in that disposable container that I'll flush down the toilet. The fake pill bottle and suicide note will be on the counter. From there, I'll pass out on the floor and hopefully wake up far away from here."

He shakes his head. "You will wake up Lauren. You're going to be alone for six months, but you're going to have everything you need, okay? Just stay put and wait for me to get there. I know we won't be able to talk, but we'll know that each other is okay."

"How?" I whisper.

He grabs my hand, places it over his heart as he places his hand over mine. "We'll be able to feel it. I love you so fucking much, Lauren. This is going to work. We're meant to be together."

I'm sobbing now. "What am I going to do when I'm missing you? I don't know how I'm going to make it the whole six months without you."

He leans his forehead against mine. "You will. Make a plan for everything you want to do with me when I get there, okay? Think about everything you want to do in life, and we're going to do it together. Wake up every morning for the sunrise and watch it, knowing that I'm right there watching it every day with you."

He wipes my tears, and I nod. "I will. Every day."

"This isn't goodbye, Lauren. I'm going to see you in six months. It'll be here before we know it, okay?"

I nod as he kisses me for longer than we should. We're far enough away we shouldn't get caught, but there's always the chance. I'm finding it hard to care at this moment, knowing this is the last time I'm going to see him for half a year.

We finally pull apart and I say, "I love you, Romeo. I love you so much. Please be safe and come find me when it's time."

He kisses me one more time. "I love you too, Lauren. I'll find my way to you, I promise. Go, now. This is the beginning of our forever."

I finally force myself out of his car and hesitate before closing the door. We're both staring at each other, and I can see the pain in his eyes as well. I close my eyes, take a deep breath, and slam the car door shut as I walk away without looking back.

Everly and I drop our backpacks in my bedroom as we get home from school. I rode home with her and her security guards. Ashley said she couldn't join us because of a family thing, which Romeo ensured was the case. It's easier to do this with just one person. I hate the fact that I had to choose, but I chose Everly to be the one to find me.

I feel like crap for doing it. It's going to destroy her, but I feel like she will get over it better than Ashley would. As much as I've tried not to become close to anyone, it was difficult not to with these two. We all got pretty close, no matter how much distance I tried to put between us. They are too loyal.

I figured Everly has so many people that love her. She'll be okay. The boys who are basically her brothers and James will surround her. She has a great relationship with Declan, and her father will be there for her. She has Mr. and Mrs. Crawford as well, who she lives with. Not that Ashley doesn't have people, but Everly just has an amazing support system that I know she'll be okay.

I was extra clingy with Ashley today, which I know she noticed. Hopefully she just thought it was because I'm getting married in a few days. I gave her a long hug, which she didn't question. It took everything in me not to cry. I wanted to say goodbye to her, but not make her suspicious that I'm going to be taking my life before she gets here tomorrow.

"So, what do you want to do tonight?" Everly asks me.

I shrug my shoulders and plop myself on the bed. I want to say I'm pretending to be depressed, but I really don't have to pretend at this moment.

"Come on Lauren, we only have a few days left. Unless you decide to take me up on the offer to get you out of here. I know we can hide you," she says, really hoping I'll take her up on it.

"I promise they will find me Everly," I state seriously.

She sighs. "Fine, then we need to make these last few days before your marriage fun. What do you want to do? We can do anything you want."

I sit up in bed and look at her seriously. "You mean anything that I want in the house? I'm not allowed to leave until after the wedding. Which I'll be leaving with Lorenzo and into his bed."

I shiver at that thought, and I'm thankful I have a plan out of that.

Everly looks angry before saying, "I'm going to go get us some snacks."

I nod, and she walks out the door. Sitting in silence, I stare at my phone. I'm so tempted to call Romeo, but I know I can't. We said our goodbyes, and I'm just going to be patient and trust that everything is going to work out as planned. It hurts so much thinking about all the time we are going to be apart.

My phone buzzes with a text, and I get my hopes up that it's Romeo, but I know it's not. It's Lorenzo.

Lorenzo

I hope you had a good last day of school. Have fun with your friends this weekend. I can't wait to marry you on Monday.

My heart skips a beat, and I read his message three more times. Did he really just say that? Was he saying that just to be nice and make me feel better about it? My heart sinks at the thought that

I won't ever be seeing him again. I groan as I lay back on my bed. What is wrong with me? Now I'm feeling guilty about leaving Lorenzo, the whole reason I have to fake my suicide in the first place!

But it isn't really his fault. He was forced into this marriage as much as I was, and he's been trying hard to make me happy. As much as I hate to admit it, he's been sweet. It's more than I ever thought would happen from a mafia boss. I wrote him a note for after my suicide, but I owe it to him to talk to him one last time before I leave.

I text him back.

> Can I facetime you?

Not even two seconds after I send the message, my phone is ringing with a FaceTime call. I hold it out in front of me to position it at a decent angle and hit the answer button.

"Hey," I say as I answer the phone.

Lorenzo is on the screen with a concerned look on his face. "Is everything okay?"

"Yeah, it is... I just... I just thought I'd call and say that I hope you have fun tonight at your bachelor party," I state, trying to figure out what to say.

I know he's getting ready to head out for his bachelor party with Romeo, Nico, and Matteo. I'm not entirely sure where they are going, but it works out that it's tonight. They have some guy named Zane in Romeo's house watching over me tonight, which is why I'm staying in and staying inside my bedroom. Thankfully, there are no cameras in my bedroom or bathroom.

He smirks. "Thank you. I hope you have fun with Everly tonight. Have any plans?"

I smile because it really is easy to talk to Lorenzo now. I used to be so afraid of him, and I don't even remember why. At first he was pretty strict with me, but I understand why.

"Not really. We're just going to hang out and watch some movies and eat tons of junk food," I say.

"Sounds better than what these guys have planned for me," he says, turning the camera to face the three guys sitting on the couch.

Romeo sits in the middle, and my heart catches in my throat at seeing him. I wasn't expecting to see him again, and the tears want to fall. I close my eyes and take a deep breath, trying to control my emotions.

Lorenzo brings the camera back to his face, and I say, "I'm sure you guys are going to have a great night. I won't keep you. I just wanted to say good night."

He smiles, and before I hang up, he says, "Lauren."

"Yeah?" I ask.

"Have a good night... I... I love you," he states seriously.

I gasp, and I know my mouth is wide open. He has never said that before. He doesn't mean it, right? He's just saying that because we're about to get married. It's something you should say to the person you're about to marry. That's all that is. Right, that's it. At least, that's what I'm going to tell myself to keep from having a panic attack.

With my voice low, I say, "Good night. I love you too."

He gives a genuine smile and hangs up the phone. No... No, no, no, no, no... He didn't mean it. There's no way he meant it. I take a deep breath and concentrate on my breathing. In and out, in and out. I feel sick. That wasn't supposed to happen. And crap... Romeo heard all of that. He heard me say I love you to him. Does he know that I said it just to say it? What if he doesn't? What if he has second thoughts because he heard Lorenzo say it? I can't text him or talk to him to make sure we're still on the same page. What if he changes his mind?

No. No, I'm not going there. We made a promise to each other. We came up with this plan and we both agreed to go through with it, no matter what. This is that no matter what situation. When he sees I did it, he's going to know that I love him and only him. He'll come to me. I have to trust that he'll come to me.

Everly walks back into the room with a giant roll of cookie dough. My favorite and exactly what I need right now. We sit on the bed eating it and binge-watch anime. We've been obsessed with *Marmalade Boy* lately, so that's what we chose to watch tonight. It has some depressing moments, which is good because I can let out a few tears here and there without being questioned.

It gets late, and I lay down to pretend I'm falling asleep. I'm hoping she'll go to sleep soon so I can set the alarm on her phone for the morning to find me. She takes out her phone and begins texting someone. I'm pretty sure I know who. I take this opportunity to say some things that I want to say to her.

I stare at her and ask, "Were you texting James?"

She nods but doesn't say anything. She probably thinks that I'm jealous, which maybe in a few ways I am.

I sigh. "You're lucky Everly. Never take him for granted."

"You're right. Thank you for reminding me. I won't," she says.

Sitting up in bed, I turn the volume down on the tv. "You know, I always wanted to be a therapist. I wanted to help people with their problems and make them feel better. To make them not feel so alone in this world."

She looks at me like she pities me. "Lauren, you're not alone. Ashley and I will always be here. You have your brother, too."

I give her a sad smile. "After high school, you guys are going off to college. You won't be around, and that's not your fault. I want you to have fun and a good life. I want you both to be with your true loves and concentrate on them. My life with Lorenzo is supposed to be me at home, being a wife and eventually a mother."

I say all this really meaning it. I mean, I'm literally pretending to fake my suicide so I can be with my true love and concentrate on him. I'm being selfish and giving up everyone in my life to be with him. They deserve to be happy too and have that true love.

Everly and James are meant to be together. I can see their love, and it'll last forever.

"That's not so terrible, though, is it? And I can go to college anywhere. Heck, if you want, I can take courses online in your living room while he's working. I'm here for you Lauren. I'm not going anywhere," she says, and it sounds like she means every word.

I feel like crap with what she's saying. She would really give up having a college experience for me? Of course she would, and I bet Ashley would too. They are both so selfless, and I'm so selfish. What did I ever do to deserve them? And now I'm throwing their friendship away.

I laugh, only because I don't know what else to do. "I could never ask you to stop living your life, Everly. You need to live it and enjoy every moment. Life is too short..." I pause for a moment, thinking about what to say next. "Can I tell you a secret?"

She nods.

I say seriously, "I've never wanted to be a mother. In fact, I hate children. Do you know he wants at least five kids? What would I do with five kids that I hate?"

I need to keep this going about why I can't stay in this life. She needs to know that it has nothing to do with her. She's offering me everything, and I don't want her thinking she didn't do enough to keep me from killing myself.

"Lauren... you will not hate your kids. No one likes kids, especially at our age. They are sticky and annoying. But you will be a great mother and love your kids. I know you will," she says sincerely.

"Thank you for being here, Everly. You're such a good friend," I whisper, not knowing what else I can say to end this last night with her.

Laying back down, I roll over on the bed. I want to cry, but I keep it in for now. She curls up against me and holds me. I pretend to fall asleep, and I wait until her breaths even out, knowing she's fallen asleep. I sneak out from under her and set her alarm for nine a.m. It's well after midnight now, and I know I'm not going to sleep tonight.

I lay awake for the next few hours, staring at the ceiling and feeling guilty for what I'm about to do. I think about everyone in my life and how they are going to react. Not wanting to back out of this, I tried not to think about all this before. Shaking my thoughts away, I concentrate on what I'm going to do. I can feel guilty and wallow when I'm out of here and waiting for Romeo to join me. I deserve to feel guilty for everything, and I will, but not right now.

I look at the clock to see it's 6:45 a.m. Fifteen minutes before I'm to take the drug. I roll off the bed and stare at Everly sleeping peacefully. The tears flow freely from my eyes now, and I know it's time I head into the bathroom. I grab my suicide note, the pill bottle, and the suicide drug from my closet. I head into the bathroom and take one last look at Everly as I close the door behind me and lock it.

I place the pill bottle on the counter along with the suicide note. I take one last look around my bathroom and all my belongings, knowing that I'll never see any of this again. Glancing at the time, I find it's now seven a.m. It's time. I open the container and drink the vile tasting drug. It's bitter on my tongue and burns my throat going down.

Once every drop is gone, I throw it in the toilet and flush. I flush a second time to ensure that it went completely down and there's no way they will find it. Staring at myself in the mirror, I feel strangely calm and numb. I wonder if it's the drug or if I've finally come to terms with my decision.

A wave of dizziness hits, and I know it's working. I slowly lower myself to the floor and lay down, so I don't fall. Everything is fuzzy, and I feel funny. I could feel and hear my heartbeat in my chest earlier, but now it's slowing and getting slower, and slower. Taking one last deep breath, I picture Romeo standing in front of me, waiting for me. I close my eyes as my breathing becomes more difficult, and I'm pulled under into the darkness.

CHAPTER THIRTY-EIGHT

ROMEO

It's seven a.m. It's time for Lauren to take the drug. My mind has been racing all night as I haven't slept a wink. We didn't get back until almost four a.m. from Lo's bachelor party. Everyone is currently passed out, but not me. I can't stop thinking about what's about to happen.

I tried my best to have a good night with my brothers. I had my moments where I let loose a little and laughed with them, but everything that's about to happen has been sitting in the back of my mind. Not only that, but the conversation I overheard with Lauren and Lo has played on repeat in my head all night.

The way Lauren said I love you back to Lo isn't my concern. I know how she says it when she means it, and that wasn't it. She said it just to say it back and probably to ease some of the guilt. I know she was shocked hearing him say it because fuck, I was shocked.

Lo doesn't say shit to just say it. They've been spending a lot of time together these past few months, and he's been trying really hard to make her happy. He never wanted this marriage in the first place, but I think he got used to the idea of it and with Lauren. God, it's so easy to fall in love with Lauren. Why didn't I see it before? He fucking fell in love with her, even if he didn't want to show it.

That guilt sits like a fifty-pound weight in my chest. It physically fucking hurts. Lo is going to wake up to a call that Lauren is dead. That the girl he fucking loves killed herself. I was fully prepared to pick up the pieces and help him get back on his feet, but now I'm not so sure I'll be able to. I'm an idiot for not seeing it sooner. I was so fucking blind because I've been so concerned about us that I didn't pay attention to Lo.

Had I paid attention, I could've tried to stop him from falling in love. I could've done something. I could've ensured they went on fewer dates or poisoned his mind about her and what she was doing, showing she didn't love him. I don't know what I could've done, but I could've fucking done something. I'm so damn selfish that I'm letting my brother, my best friend, have a broken heart for the rest of his life. And I'm the cause of it.

I look back over at the clock taunting me as it now says 7:50 a.m. At this point, Lauren is laying on the floor unconscious as her body is slowing down. Soon it'll look like she's dead. I'm glad that I'm not going to be around for that. I don't know what I'd do if I saw her lifeless, even though I know it's not real. It would be an image burned into my brain forever. My stomach rolls as I think about Everly, who is going to find her in about an hour. Fuck.

Did we even think any of this through? No, we didn't. I know we didn't. The thoughts popped into our heads, and we just pushed them aside like they were nothing. We didn't think about any of this because we knew we would back out. There's no going back now, but damn it, I hope we made the right decision. I just feel so damn selfish. It's going to eat at me for the next six months, and probably for the rest of my life.

It's now a few minutes past nine. I get out of the bed that I didn't even fall asleep in and head to the little kitchen. Grabbing a glass of water, I chug it to counteract the hangover that's occurring. I drank a little too much last night to numb the pain while they drank too much to have fun.

Lo's phone rings, and the bile is crawling up the back of my throat. I'm going to throw up. He answers the phone and shouts, but I can't make out what he's saying. I rush to his doorway, wanting to be there for him for this. I know I look like a mess, so I'm thankful that I drank so much to hide my guilt.

"This better be a fucking joke..." Lo shouts.

There's a long pause, and he closes his eyes, taking a deep breath.

"Where?" he asks.

There's another long pause before Lo says, "Got it."

Lo sits carefully on the edge of his bed and stares at the wall. He doesn't say a word. He doesn't move.

"What happened, Lo?" I ask and swallow the knot in my throat.

I fucking know what happened. Lo turns his head slowly toward me and opens his mouth to speak, but nothing comes out. I can see it in his eyes. He's processing. He's going through the stages of grief right in this moment. The look on his face is denial. It's not true yet. He can't fathom it being true.

"She's dead," he finally states in a monotone voice.

"Who?" I ask, knowing my voice is breaking.

He shakes his head. "Lauren. She killed herself."

I'm frozen. I don't know what to do. Hearing him like this... Seeing him like this... I was supposed to pick up the pieces, but I can't even fucking move.

What snaps me out of my trance is Lo shooting up from the bed, screaming, and throwing his phone against the wall as it smashes into a hundred tiny pieces. The next stage, anger.

Matteo and Nico come running to the room to see what the commotion is. They both stop in the doorway as we watch Lo pick up the lamp on the nightstand and throw it across the room next. He grabs the alarm clock, and that goes too.

Nico and Matteo try to calm him, but he lashes out at them, so they back off. After a couple of minutes of destroying the room, he finally yells out to them too that she's dead. He stomps past me and heads out through the doorway.

"Lo!" I yell after him, and surprisingly, he stops to look back at me.

Maybe it's because I haven't said a word since he told me she was dead or because I'm his brother. Either way, he waits for me to say what I need to say.

"Let me come with you," I say, knowing that he wants to go see her body for himself.

He nods, and we head out the door. I drive because I'm in a better mental state than he is, or at least, I should be. At this point, I'm numb. I knew Lo would be angry and upset, but this... The look in his eyes... I've never seen him like this before.

I pull up to the hospital where Lo was told they took her body. Obviously, she's not actually here. The records state she is, but she's not. I have to find some way to convince him not to go in.

"Lo... Remember in her will, she didn't want anyone to see her body," I state.

He glares at me. "You're fucking kidding me, right? I need to see for myself that she's dead."

He goes to open the door, but I grab his arm. He looks like he's about to rip my head off.

"Let me. Let me do it. You don't need to see her like that. She wouldn't have wanted you to see her like this," I state, pleading with him.

He's contemplating for a moment, but he doesn't look like he cares. "She killed herself. She doesn't get a say in what happens now."

He steps out of the car and slams the door shut. Shit. I quickly follow him and try one more time to stop him.

"Do you trust me?" I yell after him and wait for him to answer, but he doesn't. "Lo... Do you trust me?"

"Of course I fucking trust you," he spits.

"Then please stay here and let me. Just trust me," I plead with him.

He finally nods and takes a few steps back to lean against the car. I turn around and head inside. Instead of heading to the morgue, I walk into the bathroom. She's not down there, and I don't need to bring attention to that fact to the workers.

Samuel keeps the amount of people touching a job like this at a minimum. I have no idea who took Lauren's body, but they picked her up from her house and put her in a body bag immediately, bringing her to the ambulance and away. At least, that's what I was told would happen. Obviously, they are not real EMTs. He hijacked the 911 call, too. It's in the system, but the information went to his guys versus actual EMTs. The police, on the other hand, are real. It's suicide, so not much of an investigation is to be had with that.

When enough time has passed, I walk out of the building back toward my car, where Lo hasn't moved an inch. He's still leaning on it, but his gaze travels to me the moment I exit the building. My heart literally stops beating as I see the look in his eyes. He's hopeful that I'm about to tell him it's not her. That she's alive and kidnapped. That we'll get her back. I know that's exactly what he's hoping for, and I want to throw up thinking about breaking this news to him.

I stop in front of him, shake my head, and wrap him in a fucking hug because I'm too much of a coward to say the damn words. He leans into the hug for maybe ten seconds before pushing me off.

"Say it Romeo," he growls.

I give him a pitying look while trying to get the words out.

"Say it!" he yells in my face.

"She's gone, Lo," I state.

It's not a lie. I can't bring myself to say the words she's dead because she's not, but she is gone. I can say that. I don't want to lie to my brother any more than I have to. He turns around and punches the roof of his car, putting a giant dent in it. He whips open the door and gets inside without another word.

As I round the car, I watch him and see the tears running down his face. Fuck, Lo. Fuck me. What have I done? Before reaching for the car door handle, I lean over into a small bush and throw up the contents of my stomach. I fucking torture men for a living and don't get queasy. Here I am getting sick over the guilt of what I've done to my brother?

After expelling every last drop in my stomach, I get in the driver's seat and start the car. "Where to?"

"Fucking anywhere but here," he says.

I nod and drive off, knowing exactly where to go.

Chapter Thirty-Nine

ROMEO

The day of Lauren's funeral has finally arrived. It's been less than two weeks, and it feels like an eternity. Lo wanted to have the funeral sooner. We could have with his influence, but he wanted to be hands off and let her family do what they needed to grieve. They wanted to take care of all the arrangements.

So, it took longer than it needed to because of the fucking holidays. These funeral homes act as if people don't die during the holidays. We had to sit through Christmas and New Years before getting to this point. Happy fucking new year.

Lo has basically been drunk since the day he found out about her death. He sobered up yesterday and hasn't had a sip of alcohol since. I, on the other hand, feel like an alcoholic as I started drinking at seven this morning. I've never felt like this before. With how depressed I am, you would think she's really dead.

Speaking of, I'm hoping she's not. The problem with this plan is that I'm placing my complete trust in Samuel. We're keeping our contact to a minimum, so the only thing I heard from him was the next day he sent me a thumbs up emoji indicating that she's alive and hopefully where she's supposed to be.

He has no idea where she is, as he passed that off to a guy that I don't know. I don't like not knowing, but it's a good process to ensure that the secret doesn't get out. Even if he was found out and tortured for information, he wouldn't be able to tell them where she is. I trust him, as he has never let me down before. That's all I have going for me.

I've been staying at Lo's place since that day. He took the week off work while Matteo and Nico took over. He and I have been drinking ourselves to the point of passing out and just going through the motions of surviving. I wanted to be stronger for him, but this damn guilt is weighing me down.

I've never seen Lo like this before. He hasn't said much, but I know he blames himself. He's burying himself in his office, and I'm not entirely sure what he's doing in there. Maybe catching up on work or trying to figure out how to make it up to Lauren's family. Maybe he's concerned that Lauren's dad will no longer be working for us. I'm not sure what that plan is, but Lauren and I are pretty sure her dad knows exactly what we were planning.

Pounding begins on my door, or head, and I watch Nico stride in. He stops at the end of my bed, where I'm sitting up against the headboard.

I lift the bottle of scotch, saluting him with it and take a sip. "Hey! What's up?"

Nico looks angry and snatches the bottle from my hand, placing it on the desk in the far corner. "Get yourself together, man. It's been almost two weeks. Lo needs you today."

I cock my eyebrow at him. "Hey, I've been there for Lo every day. I'm here now and ready to go whenever he is."

Nico closes his eyes and mutters something in Italian. I've picked up words and phrases through them, but I never fully learned the language. Just enough to get by.

"Alright, geeze. I'm coming," I say as I try to stand up.

I trip over my own feet and sway to the side, falling into the wall. Nico curses and grabs my arm to steady me.

"Romeo... *Cazzo*, sit down for a moment and drink some water," he says while pushing me back on the bed and throwing a water bottle at me.

I unscrew the lid and chug half of it. He's right, I need to pull myself together. Today is a big day, and I need to be there for Lo. I've been drowning and taking him with me. I promised I would be here for him to pick up the pieces, not be depressed because I'm the worst fucking brother alive. Who knew that I could feel so much guilt? I have no problem torturing and killing people, and yet one betrayal to my brother and I'm a fucking mess.

Nico sits beside me and places his hand on my shoulder. "I know you loved her Romeo, but you need to be there for Lo. No one saw it coming, but he fell for her. He needs you right now. This whole thing fucking sucks, but we need to suit up and move on."

Well, damn. Is that what all this looks like? Like I'm grieving for her too? If Nico did really see that I fell for her, I suppose it looks like that. That's not necessarily a bad thing. I've been worried about my guilt being apparent and somehow our plan coming out.

I don't know if it's my drunken state or if it really is a good idea, but I have sudden clarity of how I can ensure our plan stays secret from everyone. This is exactly how I do that.

I laugh and pat his shoulder. "You fucking see through everything, don't you? I'm not surprised Lo fell in love with her. She's so easy to fall in love with. Fuck, man. What do we do now?"

Nico gives me a pitying look and pulls me into a hug. I hate hugs, but somehow, this one is exactly what I needed. This works well. I can use this. Nico knows I loved her, so when I go off making stupid decisions, it makes sense. Then when I get myself murdered, it'll be unfortunate, but it'll make sense. Perfect.

"What we do now is move on. I'm not going to tell you to forget about her, but let's focus elsewhere. After the funeral, you're back in the game, underboss. There are some trying to take advantage of Lo's current state. Let's show them they can't do that."

I nod. "Yeah, alright. Let me know who, when, and where, and I'll be there."

Nico grins and pats me on the shoulder before standing up. "See you in ten minutes. We're all driving together."

Lo wanted to be discreet about being at the funeral, so the four of us sit in the back during Lauren's service. We don't say a word to anyone. Lo didn't think that anyone would want us there, considering the circumstances.

Lauren's brother is a mess. I'm going to have to figure out what to do about him because, according to Matteo, he's getting into drugs and going to get himself killed. Lauren's mother looks like nothing but a shell of a person and her father just looks sad. I suppose he's not horrible because he knows that she's not really dead, or at least he hopes she's not. He still lost her though, as he'll never see her again.

I was hoping that Ashley and Everly would be sitting together, but they are on opposite sides of the room. It looks like they aren't even on speaking terms. Fuck, what happened? They were supposed to have each other to get through this.

There are hundreds of people here, and it pisses me off. There are a lot of students from her school attending, and I don't think half of them even knew she existed. I hate funerals. It's not about the person who died but all the people still alive. This is why I don't want a funeral and Lo knows that. They'll get together and drink themselves until they pass out, remembering the good times with me. That's better than whatever is happening here right now.

So many are going up to tell stories about Lauren and what an amazing person she was. So many have said she was such a kind soul, and she died too young. I suppose that all would be true. It's funny though because they are all so sad for her now, but where was that when she was alive and not having a choice about how her life would turn out? To her, that marriage arrangement was a death sentence.

After the service ends, we're the first to walk out. We find a spot in the trees to keep our presence unknown but are able to watch as everyone places flowers on the casket and says their goodbyes. The casket is lowered, some dirt is thrown on it, and people trickle out one by one.

Nico, Matteo, and I stand beside Lo, allowing him the time he needs. We don't dare move until he's ready. As pretty much everyone has left, we walk a little closer and stand, staring at her gravesite. The only person left is Everly. Her boyfriend and guards are a distance away, giving her space.

We watch as Everly looks up in our direction. I suppose it's hard to miss four big guys dressed in expensive black suits standing in the middle of a graveyard. Her eyes stay trained on us, as it looks like she's contemplating something. I can see when recognition hits her as her body grows tense and her face shows her anger. Great.

She stomps toward us, showing no fear. I glance over toward her guards, who are on alert and start approaching as well. She's about to start a fight. This is not what we need today.

She marches right up to Lorenzo and, without a word, slaps him in the face. Nico, Matteo, and I each take a couple of steps forward at the same time, but Lo just holds up his hand to stop us. We take a step back to let him deal with it.

"You must be Everly," Lo says with no emotion.

Good on him for taking a slap like that to the face and not getting angry. He has always been the most levelheaded of all four of us.

"And you must be Lorenzo," Everly says, trying to match his tone, but her voice breaks halfway through the sentence.

Lo nods. "I'm sorry for your loss."

Everly laughs, and it's not a good laugh. "You're sorry? You don't look very sorry and you're the one that drove her to kill herself!"

I watch Lo as his eyes shift to guilt. Fuck. She hit him exactly where he's hurting right now. I know Everly is hurting, but I want nothing more than to throw her over my shoulder and pass her off to Declan to take home. Lo doesn't need this.

I can see the moment Everly just breaks. She cries and starts pounding on Lo's chest, who doesn't do a thing to stop her. He feels responsible for Lauren's death. He'll let Everly use him like a punching bag. Hell, he would probably let Everly stab him in the fucking chest if she had a knife and wanted to.

"She didn't want to marry you! You took everything from her!" She pounds two more times on his chest. "She had dreams and a full life planned for herself!" She pounds three more times. "You made her kill herself! She was so fucking scared to live the life you were forcing on her!" Two more times. "Then you made me become the bad guy! I'm the one who was a few feet from where she killed herself! I'm the one that found her dead and couldn't save her! I'm the one to blame for letting this happen, but you're the one to blame for it happening in the first place!" She continues to pound on his chest until, finally, Declan wraps his arms around her, pinning her arms to her side. She continues to yell anyway, "If only you at least pretended to love her! She just wanted to be loved!"

I watch her sink to the ground, crying, as Declan holds her steady to ensure she doesn't attack again and to comfort her.

Lo mutters, "I'm sorry."

He turns to walk away, so we all turn with him. Matteo and Nico each have a hand on his back, comforting him. I should be the one doing that, but he needs them. I'm about to be the next one to tear out his fucking heart by pretending to be murdered.

I glance back to see Everly's boyfriend kneeling beside her. He holds out his hand to her, but she doesn't take it. She gets up and walks away from him, with Declan following behind her. I look away and close my eyes for a second, taking a deep breath. We knew this would be hard on everyone but fuck if we ever could've guessed it would be this hard. I'm thankful Lauren isn't here to see any of this.

"They're gone, Lo. Did you want some time alone with her?" Nico asks as we're already halfway through the cemetery, back to the car.

"No," Lo replies and keeps walking, with Matteo by his side.

Nico grabs my arm to stop me and waits until they are out of eyesight before saying, "You should take a minute with her. Say goodbye."

I stare at him for a moment and contemplate what I should do. I just nod, and Nico heads off toward the car as well. What will it look like to Nico if I don't? What will it look like to Lo if I'm not in the car yet? Regardless, I walk back toward her grave and figure I can give it a few minutes.

I stop behind a tree as I see someone standing above her grave, looking down. His hands are in his pockets, and he looks up toward the sky for a moment. My heart sinks as I recognize him. Benjamin Crawford. I look around and don't see anyone else around, except Jacob Hale, leaning against a tree in the distance, watching him.

Benjamin crouches down and he's speaking. I'm not close enough to hear what he's saying, but watching this makes me feel even more sick. The people we considered the most were her close friends and Lo. People like him never crossed my mind.

I thought for a while that he had a crush on her, but she insisted he was just being nice. She was having a crappy first day of school, and he took it upon himself to do what he could to make her feel better. He saved her from the "mean girls" at school, as she said, even though he didn't know her well.

What is this like for someone like him? Does he feel guilty for not being able to see she was going to commit suicide? He was always there for her at school to ensure that she was okay. Fuck. I stop those thoughts and jog away toward the car. I rip open the back door and shove myself inside with the three of them waiting.

Nico is driving and doesn't ask if we're ready before pulling away. Lo is sitting in the passenger seat up front and Matteo is in the back, staring at me. Stop fucking staring at me. I know I'm a damn mess. This is ridiculous. I'm a grown ass man who is a killer, and I'm acting like an emotional thirteen-year-old girl.

Matteo won't stop staring at me, and I want to yell at him, but don't. My heart is racing, and I take a few deep breaths to calm myself. It's a thirty-minute drive back to Lo's house, and I don't know if I can sit here like this for that long.

Nico's gaze meets mine in the rearview mirror and fuck, I just lose it. I'm buried in so much guilt that I don't even know how I'm still breathing.

"Fuck. Pull over and let me out here," I curse at Nico.

"What are you going to do?" he asks me and doesn't even slow the car down.

I unbuckle my seatbelt and pull my suit jacket off, tossing it on Matteo's head to give me five seconds without him staring at me. I roll up my sleeves and rub my hands through my hair.

"I'm going to run the rest of the way back. Fucking pull over or I'll jump out of this moving car," I say, fully ready to do a tuck and roll out of here.

Nico curses in Italian and slows the car, pulling off on the side of the road. I fling the door open and take off without closing it. Lo yells something at me, but I completely ignore him. I need to run off some of this steam. My dress shoes are annoying the hell out of me as I try to run. It's freezing outside and there's snow on the ground. I couldn't care less because the burn from the cold and the pain from my shoes allows me to forget about my guilt for the time being.

CHAPTER FORTY

ROMEO

My white dress shirt is now a crimson shade from the blood that covers the front of it. I go to wipe my blade clean, but there's not a single spot on my shirt not covered in this asshole's blood. Sighing, I head to the sink and clean my blade with water. I suppose it's time to give it a good clean, anyway.

The door opens and slams closed a second later. Heavy footsteps walk toward the middle of the room, where the lifeless body sags in the chair. I told Nico he'd get a few moments with the guy this time, but I lied. The fucker pissed me off.

"Damn it, Romeo! I needed to talk to this one," Nico says, and I know he's shaking his head in disappointment behind me.

I turn off the water and dry my knife with the towel as I turn around to look at him. "He didn't have any information. Trust me, he would've talked."

I walk back toward him and study the bloody mess on the floor, the chair, and on his body. Yeah, I probably should've tortured him a little slower, but it wouldn't have changed the outcome.

"What did he say?" Nico asks.

I shrug. "Not much. Sounds like we'll be at war with the Irish in the near future."

"*Merda*," Nico curses.

Yeah, shit. The damn Irish are somehow getting stronger. They took advantage of the month Lo and I were distracted with Lauren's death. I've been trying to make up for it by taking out some of their foot soldiers and getting information out of them, but it hasn't helped much. We've been debating taking out the head, but I'm not sure his son is much better than he is.

"Oh, and get this. Apparently, they have some sort of arrangement with the Crawfords. They were trying to arrange a marriage between Anthony and Everly over the summer. That was short-lived when Thomas told him to fuck off. I knew I liked the guy," I state.

"Wait, really? Why do they need a tie like that?" Nico asks, looking concerned.

"Apparently, the Crawfords are trying to stay clean. Since the current CEO took over, he has a conscious. He doesn't want to work with the mafia or have any illegal dealings. They're trying to get out of everything they're tied into," I explain.

"Interesting... That explains why our offers have been declined immediately from them. If they cut ties completely, what does that mean for the Irish?" Nico asks.

I shrug my shoulders. "Not sure. I don't know what their agreement is or what they get from them, but clearly, it's something important if they were willing to offer an arranged marriage with Thomas's daughter."

"Well, that's information we need to find out," he says as he types something into his phone.

Yeah, it is, and it's probably going to take a while to get that information. I have just under four months left with them, and I don't think I'll be able to get all the information needed to be helpful in this situation. I've been having fun and distracting myself with killing idiots and writing every necessary piece of information in my notebook for them.

"Come on, let's get home. I texted the cleanup crew to deal with this," he says, gesturing toward the mess I've made with this Irish guy.

"Yeah, alright. Let me get cleaned up real fast," I say and head toward the bathroom off the room.

I take my clothes off and toss them in the bin to be burned. I jump in the shower and start scrubbing off the blood on my arms. My mind drifts to Lo and everything I'm leaving them behind with. These past couple of months have been pure torture for me. Sometimes I wish someone would put me out of my misery like I did with that unfortunate soul out there.

I wonder daily how Lauren is doing. I hope she's okay and getting everything ready for our lives. It's hard to picture what my life is going to be like in four months. How am I going to go from extracting information from people, killing people, and trying to pick up the pieces of Lo's broken heart to literally doing nothing?

I know that I'll be with Lauren, and we can finally be together, but this guilt is never ending. No matter how much I do to ensure Lo, Nico, and Matteo are set for a life without me, it's not making it any easier.

When we get back to the house, Lo is out, so Nico waits in the living room as I go grab my giant notebook in my room that I'm keeping all the information in for these guys. After Lauren's funeral, I stayed living at Lo's house. He offered, and I accepted. I moved all my stuff out of the house beside Lauren's and brought it directly here. I actually got rid of most of it because it's not like I'll be bringing it with me when I go live with Lauren. That way, there won't be much that they have to go through when I'm gone.

I decide to bring the notebook out into the living room and write in it there. It's time for Nico to know about it. I want to make sure they know where the information is.

"What's that?" Nico asks as I jot down a few notes from today.

"It's just a bunch of important information, like my passcodes, contacts, and information I've extracted from people. You know, in case anyone ever offs me, and you need it," I state like it's just a normal conversation.

Nico is silent as he stares at me with a concerned face. What the fuck is that look for?

"Romeo..." he begins, but he doesn't finish.

"What?" I ask, placing the notebook down on the coffee table.

He shakes his head. "You're not going to kill yourself... Are you?"

His voice actually sounds hurt, as if he believes that. What have I done to show that I'm going to do that?

"What?" I ask, surprised, not even needing to act.

"Answer the question," he demands.

"Of course fucking not. Why would I do that?" I state and ask as seriously as I can.

Nico sighs. "You're depressed. You're spiraling, torturing people, and murdering them quicker than we can even say the word murder. You jump into situations quickly without thinking and could get shot. You got rid of pretty much all your belongings when you moved in here with Lorenzo, and now you're writing everything in a notebook in case you die... Those are some major signs of someone that plans to take their own life."

Fuck, he's right. I'm being too obvious. I should've known that Nico would put something together with all that. Thankfully, he hasn't figured out the entire truth. I can't have him thinking that I'm suicidal though, because that would make it difficult to pull off our plans.

"You should be a fucking therapist. No, I'm not planning on committing suicide. I could never do that to Lo. The guy hasn't recovered from Lauren's death yet. You think I'd do that to my brother?" I ask, but the guilt hits full force.

That's exactly what I'm fucking doing to my brother. Damn it, I need to find someone else to torture. I've been doing decently keeping this guilt at bay, but Nico has a tendency to bring out my emotions within seconds. I need to stay away from the guy.

Nico takes a moment before responding. "I think that someone with heightened emotions can do anything. Losing someone you love can do that to you. You don't think clearly and sometimes just want the pain to end…"

With the way Nico is saying this, I have a feeling he's talking from experience. I want to ask, but I need to take this conversation down a notch.

"She was never fucking mine to begin with, Nico. I'm not going to kill myself over someone who was never mine," I state angrily.

We both turn toward a sound behind us to find Lo standing in the doorway. Fuck! How the hell did we not notice him enter? For two guys who stay alive in our world, we can't even recognize when someone is entering a room?

"So, you did love her," Lo states.

Fuck, fuck, fuck. How many times can I say fuck? FUCK!

The guilt has been piling so high, and I'm fucking everything up. I can't control myself anymore, and I just lash out.

"Fuck you both. You're my brother, Lo. You really think I could do that to you?" I ask, but the guilt just increases. Yeah, that's exactly what I did and am doing. I continue anyway. "I watched her for almost a full year and kept her safe for you. I did my job… for you! I'm sorry I fucked up and let her die. That's my fault. I'll forever live with knowing that I failed you… I failed her."

I turn to walk out the door as tears are now fucking falling from my eyes. What the hell is wrong with me? Oh, that's right, I'm a bastard. I'm betraying my brother, lying to him, and now throwing shit at him to make him feel guilty. I'm supposed to be easing his pain, not adding to it. What have I done?

Lo grabs my arm to stop me from leaving. I don't look at him. I can't.

"*Cazzo!* Romeo, look at me," he says.

I don't, but I don't pull away either.

"That's a command for my underboss," he demands.

Damn it. I angrily look at Lo, straight in the eyes. His face softens when he sees mine. When he sees my weakness. He pulls me in for a hug and pats me on the back.

He pulls away after a few seconds. "You didn't fail her, and you certainly didn't fail me. I never thanked you for taking on the job to watch out for her. It's not your fault. It's time we both move on. Blaming ourselves isn't going to bring her back, it's just going to destroy us. So, let's get drunk and erase this part of our lives. Yeah?"

Nico stands, grabbing us some alcohol, and I just nod. Yeah, he's right. We need to have one good night where we just let it all out and move on. If he can do that, so can I. I can bury this guilt and just be the best brother I can to him until I'm gone.

CHAPTER FORTY-ONE

ROMEO

There's less than a month until I get to join Lauren. The more time that passes, the more I know we made the right decision. I was afraid that being away from her for so long would show me that maybe I didn't feel as strongly for her as I thought I did, but it's the opposite. I'm going crazy being apart from her for so long.

Things between Lo and me have gone back to normal. We haven't brought up anything about Lauren since the night we all got drunk together and just let it all go. I've been working closer with Matteo and Nico as well, involving one of them in everything I'm doing. I want to make sure they know how to take care of things the way I do. I hate to say it, but they're going to be fine without me. I'm glad they will because that was my plan, but it hurts a little knowing they will move on and not need me.

Matteo has been working hard, running his club and expanding it. Which is great for money laundering. He will most likely become Lo's underboss after I'm gone, so hopefully he won't have too much on his plate. I think he's grooming Lauren's brother, Brandon, though.

That was a shock to me. Brandon wasn't taking Lauren's death well. He ended up quitting college, and Matteo offered him a job, starting out from the bottom as a basic drug dealer. He sees something in him though, and he's pushing him harder and involving him in more of the business.

I was a little worried that he might kill Lo, but I think they've worked out their issues or are at least working on it. Brandon's scared of him, so that'll keep him in his place. I've been trying to keep tabs on him, along with Lauren's other two friends, Ashley and Everly.

Ashley seems okay, other than being depressed and upping her drug usage. She'll be heading to college in Georgia when she graduates. Her daily routine seems to consist of going to school and heading straight home. At least she's staying out of trouble and is talking to Everly again.

Everly, on the other hand, is not taking Lauren's suicide well. I don't think either of us could have predicted how she would take it. She seemed okay at first, until she started making stupid decisions. She started hanging out with Brandon, which he easily became her drug dealer. Apparently, she even had a run in with Matteo and Lo at Matteo's club. With the way she was talking, they thought she might be depressed, but they didn't get a chance to dig into that. Declan barged in, aiming his gun at Lo's head.

They told her to stay away from Brandon and their world. I think she listened. Not long after, she tried to commit suicide herself. Thankfully, she was saved and sent to a rehab facility. She seems to be doing better now, and I don't think she'll try it again. She's thinking about attending college in Georgia with Ashley. I felt so sick when I found out she tried to kill herself, though. I don't think Lauren would've been able to get past that had she succeeded.

Lo is doing his best to keep tabs on them as well because he promised Lauren he'd take care of them. Just like he promised to take care of her brother, and he is. I don't know that Lauren will like the fact Brandon has gotten mixed up with our world, but at least we have his back. Or at least they do. I have to remember I won't be here forever.

Tying up every loose end is impossible. I'm doing my best to tie up as many as I can, but I'm getting more and more antsy as the date nears. The issue with the Irish is going to take a lot longer than the amount of time I have left. The good news is my death is going to do some good. So far, the plan is still a go.

I have a meeting set up that day, and Samuel is sending one of the Irish's men to "murder" me. He made a deal with him to get him out of this world, which we all know is impossible unless you die or disappear. This will all be on camera, so Lo will know exactly who did it. Murdering the underboss is an act of war. It'll start things in motion, especially because they won't be able to hand over the guy to Lo because he'll be long gone. Lo is going to go postal and demand retribution.

So, with all this planned out, I need to ensure that Matteo understands everything that's going on, especially in the next few months. I head to his office at the club and plan to go over the schedule with him. He did a great job taking over for me for the year I was watching Lauren, so I know he'll be fine. It's just going to be the initial shock with Lo going off the deep end. We can't let the Irish or anyone else get the upper hand like they did after Lauren's death.

I walk into the club and it's empty, minus a couple of workers cleaning up and getting ready for a busy night. Walking to the back where the offices are, I follow the hallway down to Matteo's. I knock on his door and wait for his response.

"Come in," he answers.

I open the door and close it behind me, locking it. Locking doors is a habit. We don't need the enemy to barge right in, catching us off guard. At least if it's locked, we'll have the upper hand of knowing they're here until they break it down or start shooting bullets through the door, which they shouldn't be able to with these doors.

"Ready to go over everything?" I ask, pulling the chair from in front of his desk to behind it near him.

"Yeah, let me finish this real fast," he says while typing something on his computer.

I look around the room and my eyes settle on his desk. He has a picture of the four of us from when we were younger, much younger. Lo and I can't be more than twelve years old, which means Nico and Matteo are even younger. I pick it up and inspect it.

"*Stai zitto*," Matteo mutters as he continues working without looking at me.

I laugh. "I wasn't going to say anything. Though, is this the last picture we've all taken together?"

This time, he stops working to look at me. He glances at the picture and contemplates for a moment. "I suppose it is."

I place it back down on his desk and shake my head. "That's sad. We should probably remedy that."

He leans back in his chair and studies me. "Are you planning on going somewhere?"

My heart literally stops in my chest at his question. "What?"

He stares at me and crosses his arms. "You wanted to come in to tell me about the meetings we have going on for the next couple months and then you talk about getting a picture of the four of us. Why are you being so sentimental?"

I force another laugh. "Damn, who are you, Nico? Sorry I brought it up. Just think you need a better picture than the one from before we hit puberty. As for the meetings, I want to make sure we know where we all are at any given time, with the Irish getting stronger. If you don't want to do this, we don't have to."

Matteo shakes his head. "Yeah, okay. I'll pull up the calendar."

We go through the two meetings I have this week and then skip to the 24th of June. I explain what the meeting is for and who it's with, but he stops me.

"Who's going with you?" he asks.

"I'll handle this one alone. I think it's better to go in alone than intimidate him with backup," I state.

"Are you sure? I feel you should have someone at least on the outside with you on this one," he suggests.

"I'll be fine, as always," I lie.

I've always been a good liar, when it comes to others, not my brothers. It sickens me to think how easily lying to them has become. The guilt creeps in sometimes, but mostly, I'm over it. I push it aside and don't think about it. It's just like before Lauren's fake suicide. We couldn't feel guilty if we didn't think about the damage it would do to those around us. I'll apply the same principle here.

"Alright, well, let me know if you change your mind," he says.

We go through the rest of the calendar, which thankfully isn't much. After finishing up, I gather my stuff up to leave.

"Let's all grab some drinks tonight, here at the bar. I'll get one of the bartenders to take that picture," Matteo suggests.

I grin. "Yeah, that sounds good. I'll shoot a text to Lo and Nico to meet us here tonight."

As I walk out the door, an unfamiliar sensation prickles at my insides. I've dealt with so much guilt recently that I don't even know my own emotions anymore. What is this? Am I just being sentimental? Whatever it is, I push it back down inside, deep down. I don't need to be feeling anything else right now. I need to enjoy tonight because it might be the last time all four of us are together like this.

Chapter Forty-Two

ROMEO

Here we are. Today's the day. I've been waiting for this day for what feels like forever, but I've also been dreading it. As much as I don't want to leave my family, I'm ready. I'm ready to be with Lauren and start our lives together. I'm ready to be out of this fucked up world of ours and taking care of what's mine. I'm ready to be married and start a family with her. I'm ready.

I sit at the kitchen island eating breakfast as Lo walks in. I watch him head to the coffeepot and pour himself some coffee. That familiar nagging feeling nips at my insides again. I try to push it down, but this time it stays put. Fuck, I'm not ready.

"What's on your agenda today?" I ask, trying to make small talk to ease this pain in my chest.

"I have a few meetings with Matteo and some clients. What about you?" he asks as he sips his coffee.

Oh, not much. Just making sure that I tie up all my loose ends before I pretend to be murdered tonight and go live happily ever after with your supposed to be dead fiancé. You know, having a happily ever after while you're miserable and stuck here for the rest of your life not knowing of the betrayal from your fiancé and brother. It's fine. It's just another normal day, no big deal.

"Just catching up on some paperwork, and then I have a meeting with one of our Chinese buddies," I say, like it's nothing.

"Who's going with you?" Lo asks.

I laugh. "Matteo asked the same. There's no need. It's just a check in, and I don't want to ruin our relationship by intimidating them. You know how easily they scare."

Thankfully, Lo nods. "Alright, be careful."

"Always am," I lie again.

The extra benefit to being murdered during this meeting is that the Chinese won't be happy with the Irish for murdering me during our meeting. Tension is already high between them, like it is with everyone and the Irish. I don't know how the Irish is getting so strong, but they are. I try not to think too much about it because I'm not going to be here to give Lo advice on how to deal with all this. Matteo and Nico are smart. They've got this.

"Alright, I'll see you tonight when you get back," he states as he grabs his keys and heads toward the door.

My heart sinks at his words. I stand up and want to give my brother a hug and say goodbye, but obviously that's not something I can do without raising red flags.

"Oh, hey. This weekend is that charity gala. It's been a while. I need you there, so clean up and buy a new suit," he smirks as he opens the door and leaves without a response.

I rub my hand over my mouth and will the nausea to subside. I feel sick. Hearing Lo make plans for us this weekend, knowing that I won't be around, kills me. And he had to fucking add in that he needs me there.

I pace around the room, pulling at my hair. Letting out a growl, I scream angrily. I want to break something or kill someone. I want to do anything but think about how I'm leaving Lo, Nico, and Matteo. How I'm betraying them.

I've had moments where I considered scratching this whole thing for five seconds. Just to ease my conscience, I went through the scenario of what would happen if I stayed. What if I didn't go through with it? If I stayed here, then we could continue like it was before Lauren came into our lives. Lauren would be upset for a while, but she'd eventually get over it. She would be set for life, and she would move on and eventually find someone else.

That's why it ended in five seconds. Knowing that she would be hurting and not happy for even a minute longer than necessary destroys me. Then thinking about her with someone else? No. I would want to kill whoever touches her. She's mine.

So, there's no choice. I'm committed to doing this, and I will, tonight. It fucking sucks, and I'm sure I'm going to feel like shit for a while. We both will, but we'll have each other, and we'll be safe. In this world, there's no guarantee there'll be a tomorrow. You're constantly looking over your shoulder to make sure someone's not coming after you. You're constantly worried about everyone you love. I never wanted that, and neither did she.

I walk back to my room to make the final preparations for not coming back. I set up my desk with the new picture we took at the club the other night. Matteo gave it to me in a picture frame and slapped me on the shoulder, laughing about how sentimental I am. Oddly, I laughed with him instead of getting angry because he's right; I am being sentimental.

I place the notebook with all the information for them on top of the desk, open to the last page. It has the notes of this meeting that I'm going to attend and not return from. Also, in the back are three envelopes addressed to Lo, Matteo, and Nico. They'll find them in there when they pick them up. Each one has a sappy, sentimental message for them disguised as a "just in case I die" letter. I don't know if it'll help with the grieving, but I need them to hear what I have to say and what they each meant to me. I was the little orphan boy taken in by Lo and Matteo's father and they treated me like family from the start. I'll never forget that.

Once I suck it up and ignore my feelings, I take one last look around the room to make sure everything is left where I need it to be. I walk out the door and slowly close it behind me until I hear the click. I take a deep breath and walk through the house and out the front door, knowing this will be the last time I ever step foot here again.

Here we go. It's time. My heart races as I walk through the warehouse and pinpoint exactly where all the cameras are. I do it discreetly, so it doesn't look like I'm looking for them. I had my guy, Hank, send me some footage from these cameras, so I could see exactly what the best angles are and where the blind spots are.

I'm not taking any chances of making a mistake and being in a blind spot. Lo needs to get the footage of these cameras and see that I'm dead. There can't be any question that I'm alive and being held captive.

I'm wearing a loose T-shirt and jeans, which thankfully is usual to wear to this type of meeting. I needed to wear something baggy to hide the bullet-proof vest underneath. This vest is also special, as when a bullet is shot into it, it will leak out a liquid that looks exactly like blood.

I pace the room like I normally would while waiting for my appointment to arrive. I try not to think about how many ways this could go wrong because there are so many. The main one is that I could be shot in the head, really being killed. While I might deserve it with my betrayal, it would fucking suck to have gone through all this for nothing. Let's just hope the guy is a good shot. The amount of trust I have had to put in people I don't know is concerning. So far Samuel hasn't let me down, so let's hope he doesn't start here.

Another issue is that it depends on this Chinese guy I'm meeting with. Typically, they don't like to get involved and scare easily, so we're banking on him running the moment the first shot rings out. If he stays and fights, then we have a different problem. The odds of that are slim though, but I'm hoping Samuel has a backup plan. He always has a backup plan.

Somehow, everything has gone smoothly so far. The fact that Lauren was able to easily get the drug to fake her own suicide made me start believing in fate. Maybe this was all meant to happen, and we were meant to be together, so that's why everything has been going according to plan and falling into place. Okay, a lot of work has gone into all of this, but still. Usually, the best laid out plans have hiccups. I shake my head and stop thinking about it. I don't need to be jinxing it now. Damn, why am I acting all superstitious suddenly?

My heart rate picks up again as my appointment arrives. I walk to meet him halfway across the room and shake his hand.

"It's a pleasure to finally meet the famous Romeo," Chen says with his Chinese accent.

"The pleasure is mine," I say.

I take a few steps back to ensure there's a good shot at me without having him in the way. Chen continues to speak, and I try to concentrate on what he's saying, but I'm panicking on the inside. With the plan, I shouldn't have had the opportunity to make it up to shake Chen's hand. It was supposed to go down immediately when he walked into the room to ensure his safety and his quick disappearance after being scared off.

Chen asks a few questions about the deal we made with them, and I respond with my typical answers while discreetly scanning the room for the guy that's supposed to kill me. After about ten minutes, my heart sinks, knowing this isn't going to happen. That the guy never shows, and I have to walk back into that house to see Lo and create another plan with Samuel, prolonging the amount of time before getting to see Lauren.

What would she think if I don't show up tomorrow as planned? She might think that I backed out, and I'm not coming for her. She might assume the worst, that I died for real. I push all those thoughts down and finish the meeting with Chen. We shake hands and part ways. I watch him walk toward the front of the warehouse when I hear the gunshot ring out.

I'm knocked back on my feet by the force and pain in my stomach. Thankfully, the vest is doing its job, but it doesn't stop all the pain. That's going to bruise. I know I have shock written all over my face because I was so sure this plan was going to backfire.

I look at Chen, who watches me for a split second before he bolts. I knew it. Coward. I'm holding the "wound" and bending over like I would if I was really shot. Another shot rings out and hits me just above where my hand is. Fuck, that would've hurt if he hit my hands. I stumble forward as the liquid oozes out, and I try to reach for my own gun. The shooter rushes up to me and knocks my gun to the ground, kicking it away. He punches me in the face, and I stumble back, falling to the hard concrete ground.

I fumble to stand up, and he grabs a handful of my t-shirt to help steady me on my feet. I know this is about to be it. The moment where I blackout, and I wake up somewhere on the way to see Lauren again. The plan is to have him shoot me a couple of times, knock me out, and then shoot me about four more times to ensure I couldn't survive.

He pulls me close and whispers in my ear, "Enjoy your slice of heaven. I'll see you in hell later."

The searing pain of the back of the gun hitting my head lasts for only a split second before the darkness takes me under.

Chapter Forty-Three

LAUREN

The past six months were nothing like I thought they would be. There were days I didn't think I would survive, and then there were days filled with hope. There were tears, so many tears, and there were broken items thrown across the room. I've lived in fifty different worlds, as I've read over fifty books to keep my dark thoughts locked away.

After I faked my death, I woke up in a dark room on a soft bed. I panicked and tripped over the nightstand to turn on a light. The room was basic and looked like a guest room with everything someone would need. It took me a few moments to remember what had happened.

When I left the room, a large living room and kitchen immediately greeted me in an open concept house. As I continued to walk through the house, I found the dining room off to the left of the kitchen and to the right was a little mudroom. Two other bedrooms sat on the other side of the kitchen, each with their own bathroom. There was also an office off the foyer that was filled with bookshelves overflowing with books. It's a beautiful house, but I felt out of place.

I found a note sitting on the island and a gift-wrapped box. I lifted the note to read it.

Lauren,

Welcome home, love. I hope you take the time to make this home yours and everything you've dreamed it to be before I get here. I know the next six months are going to be hard, but just keep thinking about what it's going to be like once I arrive. Our story doesn't end as a tragedy after all. It ends with a happily ever after. I love you, and I can't wait to start our forever.

Love,

Romeo

I read that note at least a hundred times over the last six months whenever I was feeling down. Along with reading the note, I was hugging on and sleeping with the present he sent with me. Mr. Beary. I'm pretty sure I cried for three days straight when I first got here, but eventually I stopped.

Then the guilt set in thinking about my friends and family having to bury me. Thinking about how they must have felt guilty for not being able to save me. Especially for Everly. The nightmares kept me awake every night for months. I honestly don't know how I got through it all, but I did. Just knowing that Romeo would be here one day with me to spend the rest of my life with kept me going.

I tried really hard to stay off the internet, but my boredom, curiosity, and need to torture myself won out. I have been spending way too much time looking up every and any information that I can find about all of them. Right now, there hasn't been much information other than public appearances for things.

My death made it into the paper and on the school's website. There were so many comments about me from people who I didn't even know. There were no comments from anyone that I did know, which hurt even more because I knew they were hurting.

I saved a special kind of torture for nights that I was feeling really horrible, which was looking at pictures of all my friends on the school's website. They update the page frequently with random pictures around the school. For the first few months, any picture that had Everly or Ashley in it made me cry. They both looked so lost and sad. Then there was Ben. I know there weren't any goodbyes, but I feel like I got closure with pretty much everyone in my life, but I didn't with Ben. He was always there for me when I needed him, and I hate to think that he's hurting and blaming himself too.

I've toned down the number of times that I look for information about them all, but I don't think I'll ever be able to stop. I want to know that they are doing well, and I can't wait until I get to read about when they all get married. I just want them to be happy, even though that's without me in their lives. Especially Lorenzo. I cried over that last phone call we had almost every night. If he really loved me... No, I'm not thinking about it again.

After a couple of weeks of staying in, I finally left the house for the first time. I was running out of food that was stocked in the house before I got there, so I needed to get some groceries. I was left with a debit card, a new ID, and a ton of cash. The house was stocked with everything else that I needed, including clothes, makeup, and kitchen supplies. I didn't want to leave the house until Romeo got there, but obviously I needed food to survive.

There was a car in the driveway for me. I rarely drove in New York, so it was an adventure, especially with snow everywhere. I used the GPS in the car to get to the nearest small town grocery store ten minutes away. Oh, did I mention I found myself living in the middle of nowhere in the mountains? I figured we would be living somewhere off the grid, but I never expected to find myself in Colorado. The only reason that I knew it was Colorado was from my license.

My license also states that my name is Lisa Brown. Romeo's license says Robert Brown. They aren't very original names, but I suppose it's probably best to have a common name. Robert isn't bad either. It will be easy to remember, and I can get used to it. Lisa isn't too different from Lauren. It'll take some time to get used to, but it'll work.

Anyway, I didn't leave the house much unless I had to. I did make a friend at a local coffee shop. The barista was really sweet, and I think she could tell I needed a friend. I stop by there sometimes, and we have gone to dinner a couple of times. I have been avoiding telling her much about my life because I want to make sure that my story matches whatever stories Romeo wants us to tell. I did tell her that I'm married, but that my husband was gone to work for a few months.

Oh, speaking of being married... I also found a gorgeous wedding ring set sitting on my nightstand. I assumed those rings were for me to wear from Romeo to ensure everyone I run into knows that I'm married. They're gorgeous, and I love that he thought of literally everything.

So here I am, sitting on the couch in the living room, trying to read one of the new books I bought yesterday. I say trying because I haven't been able to concentrate on it as I keep thinking about Romeo coming today.

I have no idea what time he's supposed to be here, but I was told it would be today. My mind keeps wandering to fifty different places. I keep thinking about what if he doesn't show up? What if he changed his mind and decided not to come or what if he was killed? To push those thoughts to the side, I try to think about how our life is going to be when he gets here.

I've spent a lot of time thinking about what I want from life with him, and I want everything. Since we're already technically married, I want to eventually have kids with him. First, I want us to go out and make some couple friends to hang out with. I want us to live a safe and boring life. I want to stay in on most weekends, cuddle on the couch, and watch a movie. I want to be near him at all times, and I don't know if that's just because he hasn't been here or if I'll always feel that way, but it's what I want.

I'm fully prepared for the first few months to be hard for him and us. Every day I would think about how he was doing and feeling. I can't even imagine the aftermath of my death and the pieces he had to put back together. Then knowing that he was going to be leaving his family and hurting them again by faking his death... I can't even imagine how guilty he was feeling.

I felt so guilty and still do about hurting my friends and family. I am prepared for him to not be in the best mental state, and I want to be there for him through it all. We'll get through all of it together, just like we planned.

Finally giving up reading, I lay staring at the ceiling. I'm so nervous and excited at the same time that it's impossible to do anything else. I've already cleaned the entire house to perfection.

I hear a car engine as it pulls up to the house, and I shoot up off the couch. I race to the front door, and I'm barefoot, but I don't care. Whipping the front door open, I find Romeo walking up the front steps, and I just want to cry. I race out the door and throw myself at him. He catches me as I wrap my legs around him and hang onto him like a koala.

He lets out a deep laugh that I feel all the way to my soul. I'm balling like an idiot and he's laughing.

"Romeo..." I cry out into his shoulder.

"Shhh. I'm here now, baby," he says, whispering in my ear.

After what feels like an eternity, he lowers me onto the top step, and I cup his face with my hands to really look at him. He's really here. He has some bruises on his face, but it's him.

He cups my face. "We did it, Lauren. We did it."

This time, I laugh through my tears and kiss him. "We did. We actually did it."

We spend a few minutes holding onto each other and kissing like we never want to let go of this moment.

He pulls away and smiles down at me. "Let's go inside. Show me our home and let's start our forever."

I take his hand, lead him inside, and close the door as we leave behind the past to begin our happily ever after.

Want to know more about Lauren's friends and see this story play out through Everly's POV? Read the fALLINg series now!

fALLINg into Summer

I'm used to spending every summer in New York at the Crawford's house while my father is away on business, so I expected this to be another lazy summer reading by the pool. The two boys I'm living with, and their two best friends next door, have different ideas. We're all single for the first summer in a while, so we decided to create a bucket list to complete together before the three of us head into our senior year of high school and the other two go back to college. After a difficult year in school last year, I plan to make the most of it. Let's see how spending a summer filled with four hot boys who came up with the bucket list items including skinny dipping, playing an epic prank, and getting fake IDs turns out.

If you'd like the inside scoop of upcoming books and releases, join my Facebook group:

www.facebook.com/groups/snchristensenreaders/

Follow me on TikTok
@authorsnchristensen

ACKNOWLEDGMENTS

There are so many who I want to thank for the success of writing and getting my books out into the world. First, and foremost, to my Lord and Savior Jesus Christ who died for my sins so I may have eternal life.

To my biggest supporter since I was little, Aunt Karen. Not only have you always been supportive of my writing and every dream I've had, but you also spend countless hours editing my books and listening to my story ideas. These books would hardly be readable without you.

To my husband, who read my stories as I wrote them, listened to every crazy idea that I had, and bounced back ideas. For taking care of the kids and allowing me to dedicate time to writing. For being understanding and taking on whatever role was needed when I was exhausted and stressed.

To Jordin, who read this book in less than a day. You have been so excited and listened to every idea I've had for each and every character. You encouraged me to write what I wanted to even when I second guessed if I should. You continue to be invested in my stories and characters, which means more to me than you will ever know.

To Kelli, who was my first reader and for being invested in my stories and characters. For understanding me and my anxiety by being there for me and texting as many times as I needed to support me.

To all my friends including Kim, Ashley, Wes, Sydney, Wendi, and Kelly for believing in me and being excited for me to write these books. For continuing to support me through my writing journey and allowing me to share my excitement with you.

To my children, who have been patient with me and never once making me feel bad for spending time writing instead of time with you. To Amara, who constantly asked me how my book was coming along and being proud of me for being a writer. To Aiden, who graciously allowed me to go write and made me smile every time I finished for the day by being excited to see me again.

To my mother and father, who both believed in me from day one when I said I wanted to write a book. For always encouraging me to write the moment I said I wanted to be an author when I was little. For being excited and proud of me for my accomplishments.

To my ARC readers, for taking the time to read, review, and be honest about my book before it was released. For all the kind words and excitement for upcoming books and loving my characters the way I do.

And finally, to all my readers. I wrote these books because it was something that I'm passionate about. When I put them out there, I never expected anyone to actually read them. So, thank you for taking the time to read my stories and for getting invested in my characters. I can't wait to continue the stories of the characters and see where they take us.

S. N. Christensen

ABOUT THE AUTHOR

S. N. Christensen lives in a town outside of Atlanta, Georgia. She holds a BA in English and MA in Secondary Education. From a young age, she has dreamed of being a writer. She loves writing in the fantasy, thriller, and romance genres.

When she is not writing or reading, she can be found teaching at her church preschool and serving at her church. When she is at home, she loves to spend time with her husband and two children playing games and crafting.